Two men consumed by death...

THE KILLER
spins a web of perverse obsession...

suspending his victims in a perfect moment of beauty and peace. The moment of death.

THE INVESTIGATOR
spins a web of fractured mirrors...

reflecting the killer's obsession. And making it his own.

When two spiders feed from the same web, pray for the living... and the dead.

"A CAT-AND-MOUSE TALE OF WIDE-EYED TERROR."
—*Mystery & Detective News*

Prayer for the Dead

The shocking novel of two men who shared a terrible obsession. . . .

JOHN BECKER

left the FBI because he was too good at his job. He could think like a killer. And he enjoyed the thrill of the hunt . . . too much.

ROGER DYCE

was the serial killer whose twisted crimes would lure Becker back to his old profession. But this time, Becker is closer to his prey than ever before. . . .

Close enough to kill.

Also by David Wiltse

HOME AGAIN
THE FIFTH ANGEL
THE SERPENT
THE WEDDING GUEST

PLAYS

TEMPORARY HELP
HATCHETMAN
DANCE LESSON
A GRAND ROMANCE
DOUBLES
SUGGS

PRAYER FOR THE DEAD

DAVID WILTSE

B

BERKLEY BOOKS, NEW YORK

PRAYER FOR THE DEAD

A Berkley Book/published by arrangement with
the author

PRINTING HISTORY
G. P. Putnam's Sons edition/July 1991
Published simultaneously in Canada
Berkley edition/October 1992

ISBN: 0-425-13398-2

A BERKLEY BOOK® TM 757,375
Berkley Books are published by The Berkley Publishing Group,
200 Madison Avenue, New York, New York 10016.
The name "Berkley" and the "B" logo
are trademarks belonging to Berkley Publishing Corporation.

PRINTED IN THE UNITED STATES OF AMERICA

10 9 8 7 6 5 4 3 2 1

I wish to express my gratitude to: Jack Rosenthal and Maureen Lipman of the Muswell Hill Laboratories for their extensive investigations into paraphilia; to Denis King and Astrid Ronning King of the Dubrey Foundation for their innovations in the area; and finally, and most gratefully, to Annie Keefe, D.S.M., who was indispensable to my own personal research.

CHAPTER 1

UNEARTHLY cries rose from the group in black in Section Ten. The women were keening in shrill, high-pitched tones alien to a land accustomed to stifled sobs and low moans. There was something counterfeit about this grief, something entirely too public and overdone, like a Mediterranean funeral packed with hired mourners. Dyce knew the real sound of sorrow, and it was no banshee cry for general display. True grief was something to be borne, not vented. It froze the heart and stilled the soul, transforming everything within to a heavy, leaden state that never truly lifted. It weighed like pennies on the eyes and dragged the body to a torpor that matched the spirit's. One did not have the energy to wail or pound fists so theatrically for the benefit of others. A real sufferer withdrew to a dark place like a wounded animal and conserved himself.

Dyce knew the sounds of grief, the slow measured tones of sorrow, the drained, pale, dolorous look of sadness. This black-clad band of shriekers were indulging themselves and seemed as foreign to the graveyard of New England as a desert dweller's tent. He looked at them with contempt, willing them gone. One of them caught his eye: a little girl with dark hair and enormous eyes who had drifted from the group. She seemed as offended by this overly demonstrative expression of grief as Dyce was. One of the adults in the group, perhaps her father, turned once and summoned her to return with a quick motion of his hand, then turned back to the open grave, adjusting his hat.

Instead of obeying the paternal command, the girl moved toward Dyce like a mote in sunlight. Her progress slowed as her attention drifted first to a bouquet of flowers on a grave, then to twigs on the walkway, and finally to the cawing of a distant crow.

Dyce liked children because, although they questioned everything, they did so out of pure curiosity. What they discovered, they accepted without censure. They never questioned the fact of *him*. He fit neatly enough into the wide category, adults; children, unlike their elders, did not distinguish certain members of that category as "odd," "different," or "peculiar."

Dyce knew she was still approaching even after he'd turned his back to her. He heard her stop a pace behind him where he squatted on the grass. He knew without looking that she was wondering what he had found to study so intently. Using a blade of grass, he gently touched one of the threads of the spider's web that was strung between the headstone and the plastic flowers in the funerary urn. The spider raced forward, then stopped. Sensing trickery, it quickly withdrew to the edge of the web. Dyce knew he would not be able to fool it again.

"I got lucky," Dyce said, as if he had been speaking to the girl all along. "Usually the spider will react only to the movement of its real prey. They make very specific movements when they're caught, and if I happen to duplicate them, it's just luck."

The girl squatted beside him on the grass. Dyce did not look at her. Now using the blade of grass as a baton, he pointed to the web. "It's like a tightrope act in the circus. There are some threads he has to walk on to keep from getting stuck himself. The other threads are very sticky, and even he can't go on them. But he never makes a mistake. Or at least I've never seen one caught in his own web."

The girl reached forward and Dyce caught her hand at the wrist. He was careful not to squeeze or frighten her. "You'll break it. It's very strong on its own scale. The main threads are stronger than steel for their size. But it's not meant for humans." He released his grip but did not remove his hand, letting her do that, wanting her to feel she was still in control.

"You can blow on it," he said. The girl hesitated. Dyce blew softly and the web swayed, the spider riding the bucking threads with unruffled ease.

The girl leaned forward and blew, softly at first, then harder. Dyce allowed himself to look at her. Her dress, a pale blue party frock with the ribbons removed in concession to the occasion, had been ripped in several places at the hem. Dyce felt a surge of anger at the ritual being imposed upon the child.

"Who died?" he asked.

"Sydney's bubbe."

Dyce looked at the group of mourners. They were chanting now, the shrieks of grief easily and conveniently converted into the sonorous, false comfort of religious rhythm. No one in the group seemed to miss the child's presence.

"They made you look at her, didn't they?"

"Yes." The girl blew at the web again, trying to dislodge the patient spider with her wind.

"Did you want to?"

"I told them I didn't want to," she said.

Dyce nodded. "But they said you should, they said you had to."

Dyce could picture the event, adults pushing the child toward the open coffin, telling her to show a love and respect she neither felt nor understood. He imagined the faces of the adults bent over her, serious but urgent with their own needs, leaning too close to her, breaths fragrant with smoke and garlic. One of them would have picked her up, held her over the deceased, prodded her to kiss the waxen skin, fuller and less wrinkled now than in life. She would have been lowered toward the mask of death, protesting, powerless, frightened, as voices murmured their notions of duty to her and the odor of preservative and heavy cosmetics filled her nostrils. Dyce quivered with a deep pang of sympathy.

"Did they make you kiss her?"

The girl made a face of distaste. "She was Sydney's bubbe," she said.

"Did you look closely?"

The girl stood, losing interest. Dyce resisted the urge to restrain her.

"Did you look closely?" he repeated.

The girl took a hesitant step away from Dyce. She did not want to stay with the man and his spider but neither did she want to return to the moans and foreign chants.

"Wasn't she beautiful?" he asked.

THE others wandered past him in their informal procession, adrift and purposeless now that the ceremony was over. The little girl was in the middle of them, each hand held by an adult, like a prisoner shackled to warders. She looked toward Dyce through the shifting bodies. There was no particular meaning in her expression; he was just a momentary diversion to her, and he accepted that but nonetheless could not suppress a desire, a longing really, to have a child of his own.

Dyce reflected on the women he might marry, the kinds of mothers they would make, and the kinds of children he might have. There was Gisella in accounting, a shy, serious young woman who did not shave her legs. Dyce felt a certain warmth in her presence, but her intensity made him uneasy. He suspected her of strong convictions about things like macrobiotics and holistic medicine. There was a blonde who tended the cash register where Dyce shopped for groceries. She was plump and sweet and always acted as if Dyce's arrival were the event she had been awaiting all day long. In the few minutes it took for her to price and pack his few supplies, the blonde always managed to have a conversation with him. Thinking about it, Dyce realized he actually knew quite a bit about her. Over the past few years she had volunteered information about her birthday—which Dyce had forgotten—her mother's failing health, her own weight problems. She had a habit of commenting on his groceries, declaring whether or not she was allowed to eat each item—a minor smash with her car, which cost her more than she could afford, her feelings about the melodramatics of the royal family as reported in the tabloids by her counter. She had spoken to him of airline crashes, her new hairdo, a rash of racial incidents in Boston. Once, Dyce recalled, she had been uncharacteristically quiet and her eyes were red from weeping. Surprising himself, he had asked her if anything was wrong. When she told him she had had a fight with her boyfriend, Dyce had felt a surge of jealousy that puzzled him.

He speculated on life with the blonde checkout girl. He could not decide what kind of mother she would be. Nor could he remember her name, although the tag on her uniform seemed to dance before his eyes.

Dyce rose from the graveside and swept the spider web away with a swipe of his hand. He rolled the threads into a tiny ball and flicked them away, then walked to where the workmen were shoveling fresh gravel on the paths. A tall, weary-looking worker raked the stones level, reforming the edges with an almost geometrical sharpness. The man watched Dyce pick up a few of the stones and examine them.

"For my grandfather," Dyce explained.

The man shrugged and returned to his raking.

Dyce selected one of the more symmetrical of the stones, one that was nearly round and as wide as a quarter. The dust of the rock crusher was still on the pebbles, and he felt it both grainy and slick between his fingers. Dyce placed the stone on the gravestone and walked away, feeling the other two stones in his palm, rolling them as if they were dice.

When he reached his car he tossed one of the stones aside and dropped the other in his pocket. It was only then that he remembered what he had waiting for him at home.

THE man dreamed he was dreaming. The inner nightmare had him wrapped in the coils of a humanheaded serpent that bobbed its face close to his own, staring at him with oddly benevolent eyes. His limbs were wrapped and immobile, but somehow the familiar face of the serpent kept him from feeling great fear. There was a certain comfort in the bondage, just as there was a degree of reassurance in the mildly bobbing face. Even when the human head detached itself from the serpent and drifted off on its own, he was more interested than frightened.

In his dream he watched himself within the nightmare and wondered at his lack of concern. Within the dream as in the dreamer's dream he felt only a sort of somnolent unconcern. Perhaps I am drugged, he thought, meaning within the serpent's coils. Perhaps I feel so relaxed and torpid because I am drugged, or there is magic in the serpent's scales, a soothing poison that has lulled me into serenity.

The detached human head opened its mouth as if to speak and more serpents slithered out. The dreamer told himself not to be alarmed: It was only a dream, and even when the little serpents attached themselves to his eyes and cheeks and ears he was more curious than upset.

The dreamer watching the inner dream analyzed it

detachedly. They are not true serpents but eels, he
thought, and they are there only to suck your blood.
And that is why the man caught in the nightmare was
so calm—he was losing blood. He was weak from the
loss, but the blood was being siphoned out for medi-
cal reasons. There seemed no cause to be agitated.
There was nothing to be done about it in any event.
He could not move and did not have the strength to
try.

The detached head opened its mouth again and
issued a scraping sound. That is something else,
thought the man in the nightmare, which then dis-
solved and left only the dreamer within the dream.
And then another sound, and the dream evaporated
and the man dreaming opened his eyes.

He came to consciousness as if stepping out of a set
of Russian dolls. Even once he was finally awake, he
did not at first believe it. With the same calm as in the
dreams, he beheld the scene before him. Clumps of
black lace, like moss from a Mississippi oak, hung
down in a series, moving from left to right. The older
ones to the left were black as soot but they grew
lighter, lifting through shades of gray, as they pro-
gressed toward the right. In the far right corner of the
ceiling were threads of nearly translucent white, not
clumped in a mass but spread with geometric precision. He realized the sooty clumps were cobwebs,
spun and abandoned and left to gather dust and
decay, while another new one was built by the spider
that moved now on the latest web in the corner.

An insect had flown into the web and was still
struggling violently as the spider pounced. With speed
and dexterity it wrapped the insect, paused, wrapped

it again. The insect continued to struggle within the cocoon as the spider retired to the edge of the web to wait. Several other packages hung down on single threads, moving in delicate sympathy with the one still-living prey.

He observed with the serenity of a Buddha as the struggle of life played itself out before him. Spiders must live, too, he thought. There was a place for all things in creation and nothing they did could disturb him. He was vaguely aware that he could not move, but this did not trouble him, either. There seemed no need for motion; the spectacle before him was enough for anyone and he had never felt more comfortable. His body seemed to collapse into the padding with the complete surrender of a man into the arms of his lover. The straps were as reassuring as swaddling to a babe. They did not restrain him so much as hold him together.

He slowly became conscious that something was in his mouth, but it did not matter either since he had no need to speak. He did not want to think about it in any event; he wanted merely to drift, perhaps sleep some more.

And then the cobwebs moved in a breeze created when a door was opened, and the man felt a sudden wave of terror. His skin lurched to life, then tingled. He tried to scream, but the obstruction in his mouth kept his tongue down. Forcing air from his lungs, he could feel the tape across his lips tug against his skin. Only a muffled sound emerged, more a moan than a cry.

He heard the sounds of someone approaching and strained his gaze to the side. He hoped desperately that he would awake yet again, but his body knew this was not a dream. This nightmare was real and coming toward him.

As Dyce approached, the man squeezed his eyes closed, hoping to feign sleep.

"I've been to see my grandfather," Dyce said. "I go to see him about once a month. Some people might find that a bit—I don't know, sentimental, morbid, something—going that often, but I don't. It comforts me. I hope it comforts him. I haven't really decided about that, life after death, that whole thing. Maybe. What do you think?"

Dyce checked the needle leading from the femoral artery in the man's groin. The connection was secure, the tape undisturbed. The bottle between the man's feet was nearly full of blood. Dyce squatted to determine the precise level in the container.

"That's good, you're doing well. I mean, it would be nice to believe the spirit lives on. It would be great, but can you really believe it, that's the thing. It makes people feel better. I guess that's the point. I know you're awake, you know. You breathe differently. There's no way you can fake that."

A syringe was taped to the inside of the man's upper arm. Dyce carefully read the amount of the drug still in the cylinder and made a note of it.

"My boss is such an asshole. He passed me over again today. I mean, it's not official yet or anything, but he gave the Steinkraus job to Chaney, and it's obvious whoever handles Steinkraus is on the way up. He doesn't like me, he just doesn't like me. No flash, you see. I'm not one of the flashy ones. I just do my job better than anyone else in the office, that's all. But

I don't tell jokes, I don't suck up to him, I don't
charm him. Chaney practically oozes oil he's so pa-
thetically slick. I mean, it is pathetic. To have to get
by that way. He'll run out of grease some day, and
suddenly everyone will look at him and say, wait a
minute, what does he actually know? Is he a good
actuary or is he a fake? Does he really do the work or
is he living off of Roger Dyce's figures? There's got to
be some justice sometime, don't you think? What the
hell kind of world is it, otherwise? . . . How long have
you been awake?"

The man kept his eyes closed and tried to breathe
in what he felt was a sleeper's rhythm.

"How long have you been awake? I need to know
so I can adjust your dosage. Open your eyes . . . Open
your eyes."

Dyce touched the man's eyeballs gently. The lids
shot up.

"There you go," said Dyce. "Now I want you to
close your right eye if you've been awake more than
an hour. You would know because you would have
heard the clock chime at five o'clock. Did you hear it?
Close your right eye if you heard it."

The man's eyes stayed open, wide and frightened.

"It's for your own comfort, so you'd be smart to
cooperate. You'll feel better if you're asleep, don't
you think? Yes? Did you hear the chime? No? All
right, now I want you to estimate for me just how
long you've been awake. Close your right eye if you
think it was more than half an hour. No? More than
fifteen minutes? No? Did you wake up just a minute
or two before I got home?"

The man closed his right eye and kept it closed.

"Good, good," said Dyce. "So five point five cc's is just about right. It varies a lot, you'd be surprised. It's not just body size. Personal tolerance seems to have a lot to do with it, too. Some men just seem to want to be awake more. I don't know. Some like to sleep. You're sort of a sleeper yourself. This is your third day—did you know that? This is your third day with me—and I must say you've been very good, very little trouble."

The man was secured to an inclined board, tilted back at an angle of a few degrees, so Dyce's face was level with him as he spoke. The nearly vertical position was helpful in draining blood when the subject was comatose, Dyce had found. Gravity did the job when the heart weakened.

The man could see Dyce's face swimming in and out of his line of vision like a beach ball riding the waves.

· "I'm just going to empty this bottle for you," said Dyce, dropping out of sight. "It's nearly full; you're doing very well, very well, you'd be surprised."

Dyce straightened again and held the bottle of blood in front of the man's face. "See?"

The man's eyelids fluttered and his eyebrows arched upwards. Dyce laid a hand on the man's cheek.

"Now, Bill . . . I'm sorry, I don't remember your real name. Is it all right if I just call you Bill? It's less confusing for me that way. You didn't like looking at that. I should have asked you first. It's funny how some people react to the sight of blood. Frankly, I'm indifferent to it myself. It makes some people queasy, though. I realize that, and it looks like you're one of them. Sorry, I won't do that again. It takes a while for us to get to know each other, after all. I can't be expected to guess your likes and dislikes right away."

The man had broken into a sweat. He felt the stirrings of nausea in the pit of his stomach and tried to swallow to fight them back. He was afraid that if he threw up he would choke on his own vomit. The object in his mouth depressed his tongue and made it very difficult to swallow and he thought for a moment he would choke to death.

Dyce stroked the man's face with a dry cloth, then put something very cold on his temples.

"It will pass," Dyce said comfortingly. "You're fine, you really are. There's no reason to be upset. Just breathe deeply. That's it, breathe deeply."

Dyce gently massaged the man's throat with one hand while running the ice cube across his forehead to the other temple. Droplets of ice water ran into the man's hairline.

"It's just your imagination that has made you feel upset. You don't need your tongue to swallow, you know. You just think you do. Relax those throat muscles, just relax them. That's it, let them go. Now swallow. There, you see? You mustn't let your imagination run away with you like that. You're perfectly all right. I won't let anything happen to you, you know that, don't you?"

Dyce wiped the man's forehead dry and touched his hair, fluffing it with his fingers.

"I'm here to help you. You know that, don't you? Don't you? Think how silly I'd be if I let anything happen to you. Now, I'll just pour this out and be right back and I'll have a little treat for you, all right?"

Dyce poured the contents of the bottle down the drain of the kitchen sink and rinsed it out, then went to his bedroom. The room was dark even during the day; the sun was perpetually blocked by heavy brown drapes. Like all the windows in the house, those in the bedroom were covered by double-glazed glass and a board of sound-proofing material pitted by peaks and depressions like an egg carton. Dyce did not like the drapes. For several months he had been thinking of changing them for something brighter and more cheerful. The bedroom was gloomy, no matter how many lights he turned on, and he spent no time in the room except to sleep. There were times when he had long-term guests, such as the man in the living room, when Dyce considered moving the television set into the bedroom so he could have some privacy at night, but the tomblike quality of the room decided him against it.

In the top drawer of the heavy oaken bureau he found the stiff-bristled military hairbrushes and the matching hand mirror. The backings were made of thick, dull silver, and his grandfather's initials were engraved into the handle of the mirror and burned into the leather straps on the brushes.

Dyce slipped his hands through the straps with a sense of ceremony and felt the presence of his grand-father. The feeling came upon him as a flush, an overall surge of emotion that filled and dominated him. He stood for a moment watching his reflection in the mirror atop the bureau, trying to see if the strength of the emotion were visible to the eye. Heat was suffusing him and the pattern of his breathing had changed, his stomach had tightened, and tremors seized the base of his spine—but nothing was apparent in the mirror. His plain, everyday face looked back at Dyce, eyes a bit too close together, mouth a little crooked, one nostril higher and larger than the other, hair thin and getting thinner as his forehead seemed to grow larger by the month. To the eye there was no trace of the joy that made him shiver with anticipation.

He had to have a look today, he realized. It was early, maybe a full day premature and it might even diminish his satisfaction when everything was perfect, but he could wait no longer. He would have a look today, a preview, and let tomorrow take care of itself.

Dyce opened the oaken wardrobe with its simple, patterned surface—the pattern of the polished oak had been ornament enough in the days when his grandfather acquired the furniture—and withdrew the length of cream-colored silk, the pillow of the same material, the dark blue suit, the stiffly starched shirt, and his grandfather's favorite paisley tie. He hesitated over the hair pomade, the lipstick, the mascara, then decided to leave them in the wardrobe. It was only a preview, after all. It was always better to save the full treatment for the end. Dyce believed in deferred pleasure, although his needs sometimes overcame his patience.

HE had forgotten to replace the collection bottle; a few drops of blood had dribbled to the floor. Dyce wiped them up, then put the bottle back on the end of the plastic drip. This kind of mistake annoyed him and normally made him angry with himself, but now with the fever of anticipation, he scarcely noted his error.

"Sorry I took so long," Dyce said. "I had to get a few things together." He held the brushes up so the man could see them.

"Like I promised, a treat for you, then one for me, too."

Dyce stood behind the man and began to brush his hair.

"His hair was pure white and thicker than yours. You're a young man, but believe me, his hair was thicker even at his age. He used to say there was an Italian in the woodpile; he couldn't figure out how else to explain a head of hair that full. And with just a little wave, not crinkly at all, just a little wave—but so white. A hundred strokes a night, no matter what, that's what he said the secret was, one hundred strokes a night. It kept the scalp alive, he said."

Dyce pulled the brushes gently through the man's hair from brow to neck, one hand following the other. First the top, then the sides, then the top again. Dyce heard the man moaning softly in appreciation.

"Funny how it always feels better when someone else does it, have you noticed? It's never quite the same when you have to do it yourself. There's a girl where I have my hair cut who does the shampoo—I can't just go to a barber anymore, my hair's too thin, there's no Italian in my woodpile, I guess. I need a real artist to take care of it these days, and women just know more about these things. Actually, the person who does the actual styling is a man, but you know what I mean, he's used to working on women, but what was I saying? There's this girl who gives me a shampoo before the guy does the cutting and her fingers feel so good I want to propose to her every time I go in . . . I don't, though . . . His wife used to do his hair before she died, and then I took over. One hundred strokes a night, no matter what. It was practically a religious thing and that makes me what, an altar boy or something . . . There, that's more than a hundred."

Dyce stood in front of the man, admiring the results of his work. A tear seeped from the man's eye.

"I know I promised you a treat and that was it, but I think I'll give you another one, and then it's my turn."

Dyce pressed the syringe in the man's arm, studying the level in the cylinder carefully. Contented with the dosage, he held the hand mirror so the man could see himself. The second treat.

The man looked at the face of his own death. His skin was the ashen pallor of a corpse, more deathly pale than the tape that covered his mouth. His eyes were an impossibly bright blue in contrast with his flesh, and his hair, fresh from the brushing and crackling with static electricity, stood up like the caricature of a man in terror.

Behind the mirror, Dyce's face swam in and out of focus, nodding approval and smiling. The man closed his eyes and gratefully allowed the drug to lower him into unconsciousness as softly as a mother with a babe.

DYCE covered the man's face while he worked so that he wouldn't be tempted to peek and spoil his first viewing. He laid the board flat on the sawhorses that were draped with black felt crepe to hide their rough-hewn legs. The shirt, tie, and suit jacket were awkward to put on and the covering slipped from the man's face several times. He drew the creamy silk up to the man's waist and then crossed his arms, which had already been freed from their restraints, in order to put on the clothing. Working by feel, Dyce removed the tape and took the darning egg out of the man's mouth. With the pillow under the man's head, Dyce finally removed the covering from his face, carefully avoiding even a glance.

With Mozart's Requiem playing softly on the tape machine, Dyce selected a tray of spicy chicken wings from his freezer and heated them in the microwave. Working with his back to the man, he set up the television tray in front of his favorite armchair and put out his napkin and a fork for the simple tossed salad. The chicken wings he would eat with his fingers. Normally he would not eat during such an occasion, but since it was only a preview, he reasoned, and because he was very hungry and would not want to have to interrupt himself as long as the emotion gripped him, he would do it this way just this once.

Throughout his preparations he felt the excitement of anticipation stirring him. With an effort he made himself slow down and go through every step methodically. Finally, when all was ready and the microwave sounded its buzzer, he took his tray of chicken wings to the television tray, sat in the chair, and for the first time allowed himself to look at the man.

In the gloom of the living room, the pale face and hands seemed to be lit with an inner light. The man's features had relaxed under the drug and his expression was one of utter serenity. From this distance, Dyce could not see the man's chest move with his shallow breaths, but, of course, he knew. He knew, and that detracted from the pleasure somewhat. And the man's color was not yet perfect. It never was while they were alive, but it was close. The difference between what was and the perfection he could so easily attain detracted, too. Life itself was the problem; it refused to be completely disguised. But still, it was close. And as long as they lived, they did not decay.

"So beautiful," Dyce murmured in the gloom.

He sat perfectly still for a long time before he reached for the first chicken wing.

CHAPTER 2

SEVENTY-FIVE feet in the air over Route 87, clinging to a rock with all the dubious tenacity of a cookie magnet to a refrigerator door, Becker came to the conclusion that he must have been crazy. Would a sane man have decided to take up rock climbing at his age? Would a sane man have taken up rock climbing, period?

"There's a little depression just above your right hand. Not more than eighteen inches." The voice came from below, which meant it was Alan Something, the kid with the stringy hair. Alan could look at a bare rockface from the ground and see every handhold and piton strike all the way to the top, then leap at the rock as if it weren't going up straight as a plumb line, and scamper up it with the agility and contempt of a kid vaulting over the neighbor's fence. Becker didn't care for Alan very much; he was the expert who had convinced Becker to take the lessons.

"Just eighteen inches. But if you feel you can't, you

don't have to." That voice was Cindi's, the girl who had preceded Becker to the top in what seemed like a minute and a half, finding the holds, wedging the pitons into the cracks so Becker could secure his rope and have a "safe" trip up. Her hair was as stringy as Alan's, but on her it looked better. "No one will think any the worse of you if you don't want to try," she said.

"Except me," said Becker. His words were muffled by the rock against which his face was pressed as if he could somehow cling to it with lips and cheek.

"Just reach up with your right hand," said Alan from below. He was having a hard time concealing his impatience. Becker had been frozen in position three-quarters of the way up the one-hundred-foot palisade for almost a minute. To Becker it seemed the better part of a day. His left hand was extended to the side and down, gripping with only the fingertips an irregularity in the rock that was slanted toward the ground. His left klettershoe was firmly planted—or as firmly as anything was ever planted in a sport that sought insecurity as its challenge—but only his right toe had the slightest purchase on a nub of stone. If he reached for the next hold with his right hand, he would have to release his left foot, which was the only thing keeping him up in the air. The other two grips had as much purchase on the rock as tail flaps on a jetliner. They might steer him a bit but they certainly wouldn't hold him up.

"Your muscles will cramp if you don't move," called Alan.

"He's right," said Cindi in a softer tone. She was nearly as good in her way as Alan was in his, but with

none of his arrogance. Becker liked her, but didn't
want her to see him in this position. The muscles in his
left arm and right leg had been dancing for the past
several seconds already. He either had to move or be
kicked off the rockface by a muscle spasm. The question was, move where? Upward and onward to glory,
or the ignominious climb back to the base.

"What did you say?"

Cindi was on her stomach on top of the rock, leaning out as far as she could to watch Becker. If Becker
rolled his eyes upward, he could just make out the
bright red of her helmet. *Crash* helmet. If Becker kept
his eyes strained upward long enough to make out her
features, he got dizzy. It seemed a poor choice of
pastimes for a man with a tendency to vertigo, which
confirmed Becker in his suspicion that he was crazy.

"I can't hear you," said Cindi.

"Golf. I said golf," said Becker, turning his lips
from the rock so he could be heard. "I could have
taken up golf."

His right leg began to jerk involuntarily.

"What is he *doing?*" Alan demanded.

"He's joking!" Cindi called.

"Choking? I know that."

Cindi lowered her voice so Alan could not hear.

"Do you want me to come down and get you?
There's no disgrace in it. It happens all the time in the
beginning."

"Or tennis," Becker said. "I actually like tennis."
Tilting his head a fraction more, he could see what
Alan was referring to as a handhold. With luck,
Becker could get three fingertips on it. That would
give him three fingertips and the toe of his spasming

right leg to support his weight—to *lift* his weight—until he found something for his left side. Not only crazy but a danger to himself.

"I'm coming down for you," said Cindi.

Becker pushed off with his left leg and reached for the handhold. He caught it with the last three fingers of his hand as he straightened his right leg. The edge of rock sliced into his fingers as his body kept swinging to the right, pivoting around his right toe. His hip struck the rockface, his fingers leapt off the grip, and he fell headfirst toward the highway.

The nylon rope secured to Cindi's piton with a carabiner caught him after a fall of six feet, and he swung into the rock like a speeding pendulum. Becker took the blow with his head and shoulders, rebounded, then bounced in a second time with his helmet. Stunned, he hung upside down for a while before slowly righting himself. He dangled in space, the climbing harness digging into his thighs and buttocks. By the time his head cleared, Cindi was at his side and Alan was halfway up the rock.

"Are you all right?" Cindi asked. Becker tried to smile; he was not yet ready to speak. His back was to the rockface now and he saw the police car pull to a stop.

"How is he?" Alan called from below, climbing.

"All right, I think."

Alan was already analyzing the mishap and gave Becker the benefit of his thoughts as he moved upward.

"The problem was you're not ready for that kind of move yet. You shouldn't have tried it. That was an advanced intermediate move. You're not that good, Becker."

The cop got out of his car and leaned against it, looking up.

"You told him he could do it," said Cindi.

"I just told him where the handhold was. He's got to be the judge of whether or not he can do it."

Alan was just below them now. It seemed to Becker that the young man had made the trip up in three bounds.

Cindi was looking into Becker's eyes, swinging out from the rockface on the end of the rope she had secured atop the palisade.

"How do you feel now?"

"Stupid."

"That's a good sign," she said.

"You took the wrong route," said Alan. "That's where you went wrong."

"Where I went wrong was getting out of the car," said Becker.

"You're obviously all right," said Cindi.

"The route to the left is much easier. You should have gone that way."

"I went that way last week," said Becker. "I thought I'd try something harder."

"You got the stones for it," said Alan with a touch of admiration. "I don't know if you've got the aptitude, but you've definitely got the stones."

"You don't need stones for it," said Cindi.

The cop lifted his hand and waggled his fingers at Becker.

"Looking good," said the cop.

Becker put a hand over his crotch and tugged.

"And stylish, too," the cop said.

"Friend of yours?" asked Cindi. She pulled gently on Becker's arm and he turned, weightless, to face the rock.

"This has been cleared with the police," Alan called down. "We got permission already. We don't need any hassle."

"Who does?" said the cop. "I'm just watching. This is a spectator sport, isn't it? I've never seen anything quite as graceful as Becker there. I saw a pig on ice once, but that's as close as it comes."

"You want to try it?" Alan called heatedly.

The cop chuckled. "Just as soon as you put in a staircase."

"I don't like cops," Alan said in a voice markedly softer.

"Neither do I," said Becker. "That's why I resigned."

Cindi had placed Becker's hands and feet on secure holds on the rock.

"The next hold is eight inches down with your right hand. I can put your hand there if you like. We'll just take it one step at a time, and I'll be right here with you."

"You're sure this is the macho thing to do?" Becker said.

"Oh, please."

"Are you sure a real man wouldn't go right back up and try it again?"

"A real man would be home making soup and humping his woman," said Cindi. "He wouldn't have to be out here demonstrating his *stones.*"

Becker laughed. "I've got a new crockpot at home. Want to come over and check it out?"

"You must have hit your head harder than I realized," said Cindi. "What's it going to be? Down or dangle here and flirt?"

"Down, please," said Becker.

"THEY look like spiders," Tee said. He was officially Thomas Terence Terhune, but he had long since reduced it all to an initial.

They were sitting in the police car, watching Alan and Cindi clamber up and down the rock, retrieving their ropes and equipment.

"You, on the other hand, looked like a window washer."

"Thank you."

"What possessed you? There are so many nicer ways to kill yourself. That girl would probably do you in in about an hour in bed, for instance. Less, in the back of a car."

"Cindi's a nice girl," said Becker.

"So? Nice girls don't fuck? Is this a new thing? As I understand it, nice girls fuck nicely. Look at her arms."

Cindi was splayed across the rock as if she had been hurled there. The spandex of her climbing outfit seemed to accentuate her musculature rather than hide it.

"Look at any of her," Tee continued. "If she can do that on a mountain, imagine what she can do in bed. I like a bit of muscle on a girl, don't you? I remember when they first came out. I was turned off by the biceps, the Navratilova look, you know? But now, I like it. Hell, I like anything. Muscle, fat, body hair, you name it."

"You getting along all right with your wife, are you, Tee?"

"We get along fine. I don't bother her and she doesn't bother me. This kid, Cindi, she's attached to Spiderman there?"

"Alan's in love with himself, as far as I can figure out."

"He shows rotten taste, doesn't he? How about some coffee."

"You had enough rockface eroticism, Tee?"

The police car was already moving. Tee swung into a sharp U-turn and headed back toward Clamden.

"What do you think she'd do if I put a move on her?"

"Cindi?"

"Yeah, who else we talking about?"

"Probably call a cop."

"She can call me anything she wants," said Tee.

"How about correspondent?"

"You've got a cold streak, you know that, Becker? You're just not a fun-lover. No wonder people try to kill you."

"So finally we're getting down to business," said Becker.

TEE adjusted his holster to ride on the front of his thigh before sliding into the booth. Once in, he spent several seconds adjusting the flashlight, radio, and other equipment on his webbed belt until he was comfortable.

"Shit was designed for Robocop," he said.

"There's no way a human can sit down without feeling like an asshole with all this crap hanging down and sticking you in the kidneys. Makes me feel like a telephone lineman."

"It's very becoming, though," said Becker. "It gives you that heterosexual look."

"You don't think I need to add a nightstick? Kind of as an image enhancer? . . . Janie?"

The waitress passed them by without looking back.

"I always wondered what would happen to a cop if he fell into the ocean with all that hardware on. The hobnail boots alone would pull you down."

"I got my belt attached with Velcro," said Tee. "In case I have to punish a suspect in her bedroom, *rrrrip,* and I'm ready."

"You get a lot of that, do you, Tee? Consoling widows, comforting victims, that sort of thing?"

"Not yet, but I've only been a cop for fifteen years. How about yourself? Were you ever called upon—in the course of your duties—to stuff it to one of those ragheads or whoever you were chasing? . . . Janie?"

The waitress passed them again.

"I take it she knows you," said Becker.

"She wants me."

"You're a strange sort of chief of police, Tee."

"Why?"

"Your uniform fits, for one thing. There were no doughnuts in your cruiser, for another. I checked. A kind of suspicious trail of ants leading to the glove compartment, but no doughnuts."

"So let me get this straight," said Tee. He shifted his weight, tugging again at the belt. "You hang upside down on a rope, then swing into a rock with your head? This doesn't hurt?"

"Hurt? Why should it hurt? It's no worse than slamming your fingers in the car door . . . Miss?"

The waitress stopped abruptly in her passage.

"Two coffees," said Becker.

"Two coffees," said the waitress before moving on.

"I get it," said Tee. "Her real name is Miss, not Janie."

Tee grew quiet and Becker realized the waiting period was over. Real questions would be next, or requests. Becker did not look forward to either since they usually amounted to the same thing. Whatever Tee wanted, it would make demands upon Becker and demands were exactly what he had spent the last six months avoiding.

The two men sat in a strained silence until the coffee came and Janie had retired to the other side of the room.

"Tell me again exactly what it is you do?" Tee asked, trying to sound casual as he lifted the coffee cup to his lips.

"Again? I don't believe I ever did tell you exactly, did I?"

"Not while you were doing it. Now that you've stopped, why don't you tell me?"

"Is this an official question?"

"Come on, Becker. Don't give me a hernia over this. You're not doing it anymore, I'm not asking for any secrets. Just give me the outline."

"You know the outline."

"I asked around some, yeah."

"Who would that be?"

"Guy named Hatcher, at FBI. Says he knows you."

"Hatcher is an anal retentive."

"I know that—whatever that means. He's a little prissy, too, but he knows things—or can find them out."

Becker drank and looked at Tee over the rim of his cup.

"And?"

"Is this a guessing game? You going to make me tell you what I know and then you tell me if it's right?"

"It's your game, Tee. But I am curious to know what Hatcher found out."

"You worked for the government, all over the place. At one time or another since leaving the FBI you've been listed on the payroll of at least half a dozen agencies, including the Defense Department and the National Security Council staff. This within five years. Right?"

"Right. So?"

"So in each of these capacities you were authorized to carry a weapon, which means, to me anyway, that you were probably performing essentially the same job for each of them. And doing it well since you weren't dismissed from any of the agencies and obviously had no trouble finding a new place—in fact your GS rating went up each time you moved. You were making some pretty fair change at the end."

"You working for the IRS, Tee?"

"To me, the pattern looks like you were a trouble-shooter."

"Very good, Tee. No wonder you're a cop."

"Actually, I'm a cop because of you. Or partly

because of you. I'm serious about this. When you joined up with the FBI, that made you a hero to some of us. Not only a hero, but glamorous, too. It was an inspiration—don't grin, I'm serious about this—"

"This isn't a grin."

"—a kid from Clamden out doing battle with the bad guys, chasing Commies, whatever it was then. It made an impression."

"I joined the FBI because I didn't want to go to Vietnam."

"Yeah, well, that wasn't altogether stupid, either."

"I didn't want to kill anybody and I didn't want anybody to kill me."

"This was reasonable. Anyway, my point is, you were a factor in my applying for the FBI myself a couple years later. Did you know I applied?"

"No."

"I didn't pass the test."

"Many are called but few are chosen. You're better off."

"Yeah, well, I made my peace with it a long time ago. The feds don't get to wear these nifty belts, for one thing. My point is . . . I forgot my point."

"You want me to do something."

"Did I get to that part already?"

"I couldn't stand the suspense."

"I understand you're retired. You put in the twenty, plus you got a disability of some kind. That much Hatcher could find out. There's a whole lot of other stuff he couldn't find out. Which is surprising since that's his job and he's authorized to do it. Find out stuff. It seems your personnel file is full of No

Access signs. Even for someone with Hatcher's clearance."

"Hatcher is not very bright."

"Well, neither am I, John. That's probably why Hatcher and I get along so well . . . Look, I don't know what kind of work you did and obviously you don't want to tell me. I assume it's either something very hush-hush or it's something messy. Either way, it doesn't matter. You obviously know things. You got access, you know how to do things . . . John, I need your help."

Becker placed a napkin under his cup to soak up the coffee that was pooling there.

"I want you to help me find somebody."

"A missing person?"

"Sort of, yeah. Yeah, a missing person."

"Somebody from here?"

"Yeah."

"Tee, you're a cop. You're the chief of police."

"I'm a *Clamden* cop, John. I'm not even a Hartford cop. How big was Clamden when you left—what's that, twenty-two years ago? Maybe twenty-seven thousand, twenty-eight? We're now thirty-five thousand. That's how much things have changed in two decades. I know how to work this town. I'm good at it, but that's all I know."

"Who's missing?"

"My nephew. My wife's nephew to be precise. Mick Seeger."

"Little Mick?"

"Not so little anymore. Mick's twenty-eight."

"Christ, how old are we?"

"Whatever it is, I'm still two years younger than you."

"The whole world is two years younger than I am. How long's he been missing?"

"He's been gone for a week."

"That's not missing; that's just absent."

"Well, I'd agree except he's not the only one. Two months ago Timmy Heegan disappeared. Timmy's twenty-six. Six months before that, Larry Sheehan, age thirty-two."

"People do this sometimes. . . ."

"I know people do this, John. But none of these guys was young enough to run away, they weren't thumbing their nose at mom and pop, they all had jobs, Mick has a baby."

"Debts, marital problems . . ."

"John, I admitted I'm not a supercop, but give me some credit. In Clamden over the past four years, six men have disappeared. Statistically curious, but not phenomenal, I agree. But in Branford, six miles from here, five men in the last three years. In Guileford, eight miles away, three in the last eighteen months. In Essex, one, three months ago. That's fifteen men in four years within a radius of twelve miles. None of them had been recently fired, divorced, involved in any great scandal or was in any particularly heavy debt. I'm not saying they hadn't had fights with their women, those that had women, and I'm not saying they were all happy in their work, but fifteen in four years from an area with a total population of just over a hundred thousand—Hatcher tells me that's statistically significant."

"Hatcher would know. This is why you were palling around with him?"

"He doesn't like you, either."

"But the Bureau can't help you, right? No federal crime involved, no apparent crime of any kind. Have you tried claiming this is a civil rights case? We've shoehorned a lot of things in that way."

"First of all, I've got no reason to contend anybody's been deprived of anything, but more to the point, all these men were white . . . John, one thing Hatcher said—he said it was just rumor, but he seemed to believe it—he said you were assigned to a case where you heard some raghead was sent over here to assassinate the President. He said you had practically nothing to work on but somehow you found this character in New York and took care of it."

"Took care of it?"

"Well . . . killed the guy . . . That's what Hatcher said."

"Interesting."

"I don't know that he said killed. That was the implication. One guy. You had squat for information and you found this one guy in New York City. How'd you do that, John? Was the guy painted green or something?"

"Hatcher put this forth as rumor, is that it?"

"He was impressed. It's true, John. He didn't understand how you did it. He said you worked with a Ouija board or a crystal ball or something."

"Or something. What else did Hatcher tell you?"

"Nothing. But I did get the impression that he

thought you were damned good at what you do—and
that he was scared shitless of you."

"I'll tell you about Hatcher some day."

"Will you help me, John?"

"Have you noticed how you call me 'Becker' when
you're ragging me, and it's 'John' when you want
something?"

"Do I do that?"

"If those are the rules, I prefer 'Becker.' "

"Just take a look at it, that's all I'm asking. I'll get
you the sheets. I'll bring them to your house; you
don't even have to come to the station. Just look at
the sheets; maybe you'll see a pattern, something I can
start with."

"Your computer will show you patterns."

"My computer? This is Clamden. My computer
shows payroll and traffic citations."

"Tee, I'm retired. I retired for two reasons. One, I
didn't want to do it anymore. I didn't want to do it
full-time nationally, I didn't want to do it part-time
locally. I didn't want to do it for pay and I don't want
to do it for a favor. Two, I retired for my health."

"I didn't know you were sick."

"I'm sick of doing it. It's not good for my health."

"You got a condition, John?"

"Well, okay, if that's your understanding of the
term 'health,' then, yeah, I've got a condition. I didn't
quit and come back to my hometown just so I could
start aggravating my condition."

"Tell you what, Becker. Why don't you not do it."

"You think?"

" 'Cause I wouldn't want you to aggravate your
condition. Putting in an hour of your time? That

would be asking too much of a man in your delicate condition, I can see that. So why don't you just say no and we'll both feel a whole lot better about the whole thing. I'll just tell Mick's wife you're unable to assist us in this matter due to failing health."

"Thanks for the coffee, Tee." Becker slid out of the booth.

"The rock climbing is for therapy, then, is that it?"

"As a matter of fact, it is . . . I just realized you don't pay for the coffee anyway, do you?"

"As a matter of fact, I do. Wouldn't want anyone to think Janie was trying to exercise undue influence."

"As I said, you're a strange chief of police, Tee."

CHAPTER 3

PICKING his way between the frozen-food freezers, selecting the entrees he would need for the week, Dyce was struck with a sudden sense of self-disgust. He had promised himself he would stop this whole business, and here he was at it again. He didn't feel that it was *wrong*. He never had conflicts of right and wrong, didn't think in those terms, but he did think it was self-indulgent and worse, stupid. Dyce prided himself on being an intelligent man, more intelligent, in fact, than any of the half-wits at work including his boss and that snake charmer, Chaney. Dyce had based his life on an intelligent approach to things. It was important, after all, to give the appearance of conformity and rationality.

Not that I don't have emotions, he thought. He had been accused of being emotionless more than once, and the charge rankled because, of course, he had more emotions than most people. I feel things more deeply than others, he thought. I have a greater range of emotions and they move me to a greater degree. I feel things with the same sensitivity as the great musicians. He felt a particular affinity to Schubert and could not listen to anything by that neurasthenic master without being stirred to the soul.

The problem, the reason for the charge, was that Dyce controlled his emotions; he did not spill them all over the sidewalk for the world to see like some people he knew. There was a proper place for their expression, but that place was internal. But now with this business, he was not controlling them well enough, and he was ashamed of himself. The men had become more frequent. After each one he vowed he would quit. It wasn't sensible, it would only lead to trouble. But then, after six months, then four months, then two, he would do it again.

He selected frozen lasagna, a favorite of his, and, to balance the cholesterol indulgence, a package of frozen spinach. Dyce made it a point to eat spinach regularly: because it was good for him, and because he didn't like it. He made a casserole of canned beans and spinach and garlic that he could practically feel scouring out his veins and arteries of any offending plaque.

He had to stop; it was going to be dangerous, there were too many and eventually he would make a mistake. Not from stupidity but from impatience. And from the odds. Dyce understood odds. He knew them backwards and forwards. He could calculate the chances of dying in a hurricane in a wood frame house as opposed to a brick house. He could figure the chances of having a heart attack while jogging— they were high—as opposed to dying within six months of having stopped—they were low. He could deduce the likelihood of dying of an aneurism while conducting a symphony orchestra or buying it during sex. Dyce knew a great deal about dying, certainly more than anyone he knew.

He also knew that the statistical probability of dying in his living room if you were a young man within a four-town area was becoming dangerously high. Dangerous for Dyce, that is. He had already pushed things too far for the sake of convenience. If he continued this business, he was going to have to start seeking men farther afield. And for the fifth time in the past year, he promised himself he would now stop. Clean up the mess at home, and then call it quits.

He became so agitated while contemplating his shortcomings that he barely spoke to the blonde girl at the checkout. When he reached his car he realized that he had been thinking so much about himself that he had forgotten to buy bread. He returned to the store and selected a loaf of country oat after tantalizing himself with a box of glazed doughnuts that rested within arm's reach of the bread. Sugar was a problem for Dyce. He tried to avoid it because he overindulged once he got started.

It was unlike him to be rude, so he made a point of getting on the blonde girl's line again, but as he arrived, she was transferring her cash tray and handing the register over to an acned boy. Dyce watched her go. She did not look his way and seemed preoccupied with her own sorrows. Her eyes looked as if she had been crying again. Dyce wanted to tell her he was sorry for not having spoken to her earlier. It was not the kind of gesture he would make, although he often had the impulse.

When he reached his car, the girl was fumbling with her keys, trying to get into the car next to his. She dropped the keys and left them there, leaning her head on her arm atop the car, as if dropping them was the final straw.

Dyce picked them up but when he said, "Here, Miss . . ." she did not take them.

He read the name stitched into her uniform. Helen. What an old-fashioned name, he thought with approval. Dyce had no patience with the fashionable Michelles and Heathers, or the handrolled Lareenas and Berthines. She seemed a decent, old-fashioned friendly girl, and he was glad she had a name to match.

"You dropped your keys, Helen."

She turned at the sound of her name and stared at him for a moment. Tears were rolling down her cheeks. Dyce noted that there was no mascara. He didn't like mascara on the living.

"Oh, Mr. Dyce," she cried and suddenly lowered her head to his shoulder.

She told him through her sobs that she hadn't realized it was him. Dyce patted her back gently and looked around the parking lot to see if he was being observed. He rather wished that someone was watching. Clearly here was a girl, a woman really, who didn't think he couldn't understand emotion. Here was somebody who didn't regard Dyce as a robot or number-chasing nerd. He hoped someone would be a witness.

She pulled away, wiping at her face with her hand,

then the back of her arm. "I'm sorry," she said, sniffing loudly.

"No," he said. "No, no."

"I just . . . I have no right, I just . . ."

"No, no. No."

"You always seem so kind," she said. She sniffed again, then laughed at herself. "Listen to me snorting away."

"No, I'm glad . . . Can I help?"

She tried to smile but her tears welled up again and the smile bent downward.

"I've had a death," she said. She shook her head, paused, shook it again and tried once more to unlock her car.

Dyce steadied her hand with his own, surprised at his boldness.

"Listen," he said. "Listen . . ."

"I can't . . . You're so kind . . ."

"Listen. Let me buy you a cup of coffee."

Helen dropped the keys into her purse. Dyce found his arm across her shoulders as they walked across the parking lot to a coffee shop.

They slid into a booth that had just been vacated by a police officer. Helen nodded as if she knew the man.

"My mother," Helen said. She started crying again, but softly now that they were in public. When she was finished, she blew her nose in a paper napkin.

"I know," said Dyce sympathetically.

"I can't seem to get used to it. It wasn't a surprise. I mean, I knew she was going to die, she'd been sick for so long, but somehow you're just never ready."

"I know. I know."

"It's been a week, but I just can't get used to the idea that she's not here anymore. I dream about her, I see her. I mean, people—women—will come into the store and just for a second I'm positive it's her. And then I'll go along for a while and be fine, I'll actually think I'm fine. Then all of a sudden, for no special reason, I'll just burst into tears, just like now."

"I know," said Dyce. "I know."

"Mr. Dyce . . . I was lucky it was you there in the parking lot. I mean, when I get like this, I don't know if I'm coming or going. If a stranger had picked up my keys—well, I mean, we don't know each other very well, but somehow I feel I know you, you know? You're always so friendly, you take time to say a word, you always seem to have a comment about something, the weather or something, you know? Some people will not give you the time of day in those circumstances. They just want me to bag them up and take their money and run and . . ."

"Did you see her?"

"Pardon me?"

"Did you see your mother after—at the funeral. Was it open casket?"

"Oh. Yes, I saw her. Of course. I think an open casket is important, don't you? People want to say good-bye."

"Wasn't she beautiful?"

"Why yes, yes, she was. She looked so natural, and so peaceful."

"I know."

"She wore this lovely soft white silk blouse with a lacey collar she liked so much. She looked so . . ."

"I know. Beautiful."

"Mr. Dyce, you are so sympathetic."

"I lost my father," he said.

Helen touched his hand. "I'm so sorry," she said.

Dyce wished there was a witness to this. A young woman was holding his hand in public.

"I was just a child."

"Oh, you poor man."

"He was very young, about the age I am now."

"It must have been awful for you. It's bad enough to lose a parent, but for a little boy . . ."

"We had the casket in the living room."

"In your house?"

"In my grandfather's house."

"I didn't know that was . . . can you do that?"

"We kept him for three days. My grandfather thought he would rise."

"Rise. Rise?"

"I was very small and couldn't see up into the casket, so my grandfather would lift me and hold me over my father. So I could see."

"Uh-huh."

"So I could see how beautiful he was."

"That must have been . . . you must have loved him very much."

"He was my grandfather."

"I meant—well, of course you loved them both. How did he die so young?"

Dyce removed his hand from Helen's grasp. He folded his hands in his lap.

"You knew my name from my checks," he said.

Helen was startled by the abrupt change in Dyce's attitude.

"Have I said something? I didn't mean to press you about your father . . ."

"There's no other way you could know my name. You never asked me. No one else in the store knows me."

"I suppose I must have seen it on your check. I don't remember. I've known it for a long time; I was interested, you were always so nice—I hope I haven't done anything wrong."

"It's all right. I was just curious how you knew. Of course it's on my checks."

"Mr. Dyce, you've been so kind, I wouldn't do anything to upset you for the world. It's not often you meet someone who's kind. Most people only have time for themselves. You wouldn't know that because you're not that way, but most people couldn't care less about somebody else's troubles. And I have certainly had my share of troubles. Even the girls I work with, they're not bad people, but I can see them rolling their eyes whenever I feel sad now. It's only been a week, but I can see them thinking, why doesn't she get over it already? Well, I'm sorry, it's just not that fast."

"You never get over a death," said Dyce, loosening again. "If they expect you to get over it, then that person didn't mean anything to you. And if that person didn't mean anything to you, there's no reason to mourn in the first place, is there?"

Helen noted his renewed animation with relief. For a moment she feared that she had lost him, that she had said too much, or the wrong thing, or the wrong way. She realized that her desperation drove them off—calm and an emotional distance would work better. Men were lured to the elusive ones. They seemed to want what didn't want them, but if she possessed either calm or emotional control, she wouldn't be alone and lonely to begin with. It wasn't her looks that caused the problems. There were women at the store so ugly they shouldn't be let out of the basement who had husbands, boyfriends, lovers. Melva, who had warts and an odd upper lip, had gone through at least three men in the past six months that Helen knew of. Helen wasn't beautiful, but she looked all right. Given time and the right accessories, she thought she made quite a nice appearance. It wasn't her looks; it was her horrible need that repulsed them. Even now she knew it was not her red eyes or runny nose that had driven him into that frightening moment of resistance; she had tripped over something, some subtlety of discretion that other women stepped around with the surety of tightrope walkers.

"You wouldn't mourn a stranger, would you?" Dyce demanded.

Helen was not sure of the implications of the questions. She shook her head slightly, which she hoped indicated encouragement as much as an opinion.

"Why would you?"

"I wouldn't."

"Of course not. If a stranger dies, it's nothing more than flesh. I don't mean to sound indifferent, Helen, but really, who could care? We all must die, some earlier than others, but that doesn't matter. But if it's a loved one. If you lose someone you love . . ."

The sound of her name thrilled her. He had not glanced at her name tag; he had simply said "Helen" as if the word were always in his mind. She wondered if he had been fantasizing about her as she had about him. There was a need in Mr. Dyce, she could sense it. Perhaps a need to match her own.

"You are very sensitive," she said. It was hard to hold his eyes. They kept moving around the room, but they would light on her sometimes, and when they did, Helen gave him her most sympathetic smile.

"I respond to that," she said. "I mean, that is something we have in common. I'm sensitive, too. Most men are afraid to be sensitive."

Dyce sipped his coffee and when he returned the cup to the saucer she had moved her hand so that it was impossible to avoid touching it again. Tentatively, startling himself, he brushed it with his fingers. Her hand turned over immediately and clutched his with a palm that was warm and moist.

"Can I tell you something? I think you'll understand. My mother has really been gone a month. I told you a week because I thought it would sound silly for me to be acting this way after a month, but now I think you would understand."

"Yes," said Dyce.

"I knew you would understand. I'm not a liar, though. I don't tell lies. This was just—you know."

"Yes."

"What you said about love. I agree with that, I believe that, but can I ask you a question?"

Dyce nodded. Her hand was soft and fleshy, like her face, but her touch was no longer just sympathetic. Somehow her fingers had become entwined with his own. As the waitress passed, Dyce thought she must see them as lovers. He wondered if Helen understood the implications of holding his hand in this way. She seemed so naive and trusting.

"Do you think it's possible to love someone too much? Because that's how I love. Completely. I give myself completely. Is that wrong?"

"No," said Dyce. "Love is forever."

She squeezed his hand so hard it hurt.

CHAPTER 4

"So it started when, exactly?"

Becker stopped pacing and looked out the window. He had to part the vertical blinds to see the building opposite his, where the blinds were discreetly closed. If he looked far enough to the side he could just glimpse a sorry-looking acacia sapling bound in a cement pot the size of an oil drum. Beautification was not the highest priority in the Bureau complex. The window covering was a muted purple, just about right for a remembered dream and thus appropriate for a shrink's office, even if out of place in an FBI office. This, however, was both.

"It started with my mother. At least that's standard theory, isn't it? She weaned me too early, and I shall never forgive her for it."

Gold drew a line down the margin of his notepad. "Is it me you dislike, or this process?"

"Aren't you part of the process? Don't I transfer my love and hostilities to you and allow you to soak them up like a saintly sponge?"

"In your case we can skip the transference if you like." Gold drew a serpentine curve the length of the first line, intersecting it at regular intervals. "I'd rather not be the object of either your affections or your hostilities. Besides, this isn't Freudian analysis. It isn't primal scream therapy, either. For that matter, I'm not terribly interested in your relationship with your mother."

"What are you interested in?" Becker asked.

"We just want to know why you felt you had to quit."

"We?"

"They want to know. I'm supposed to find out. You're supposed to tell me. It's a team thing."

"Why do they care?"

"Naiveté doesn't suit you, Mr. Becker. You're too valuable for them to give up without an effort."

Gold began to fill in the parabolas created by the intersecting lines.

"I retired because it was time." Becker was pacing again.

"You're still a relatively young man. You were in your prime, you were in heavy demand."

"It was time for me."

"But why?"

"You ever been shot at, Gold?"

"No."

"Stabbed? Or even threatened? Ever have a terrorist point a gun at you, wave a grenade in your face, threaten to kill you and a hundred other people?"

"You know I haven't. Is that supposed to justify you or put me in my puny civilian wimpish place?"

Becker felt suddenly weary and ashamed. He sat heavily on the sofa.

"I'm sorry, Gold. I didn't mean to be attacking you personally. I've got nothing against you. I know you didn't ask for this job."

"As a matter of fact, I did."

"You did? Why?"

"I thought you'd be interesting. You're something of a legend in certain circles, you know." Gold tapped his pen on a folder on his desk. "Your history is fascinating."

"Glad to ease the boredom of your days."

"Did you think therapists don't have favorites? I haven't been shot at, thank God, but I have sat through some of the dreariest, mind-numbing sessions that would have killed a lesser man. Your colleagues are a pretty humdrum lot, Becker."

"What makes you think I'm not?"

"Are you fishing? I don't know if you are or not since you won't talk to me, but my instinct tells me you are. It also tells me that you quit because you're suffering from a very rare disease in this day and age."

"I'm supposed to ask what."

"It would help the flow."

"What does your instinct tell you I'm suffering from?"

"A conscience. I think you quit your particular brand of work because you had a crisis of conscience."

Becker laughed. Gold thought it was not a pleasant sound.

"Well, thank God," said Becker. "I was afraid you were some sort of genius who could cut right to the heart of it and find out what I was really like. But I guess we have to do it the hard way after all."

"What's the hard way?"

"With me stalling and covering up and misleading you every step of the way."

"That sounds about right," said Gold. "So why not tell me how it started?"

"That should be in my fascinating file."

"It would be revealing if *you* told me when it started."

"When I *think* it started. The final decision will be yours, of course."

"Who knows you better than I?"

Becker laughed again. "Nobody."

Gold waited, drawing horizontal bars where the serpentine line met the vertical.

"I'd been in the Bureau for about eight years," Becker said. "Routine work for the most part, nothing to set the world on fire. I don't think I had any particular desire to set the world on fire, for that matter. I was basically just learning the job and I don't know that I'd shown any greater aptitude for it than anyone else. My job evaluations should be on your desk, so in this case you know more about me than I do. Have you looked at them?"

"Of course."

"And?"

"Average, I'd say. Some of them thought you were a bit brighter than average—which your test scores confirm, by the way—but no flashes of brilliance in the beginning. Just another agent."

"That's fair . . . So. I was assigned to New York, working a counterfeit case, when a hostage situation

developed in a bank robbery. Very bizarre situation.
The cops had caught these two guys in the act, but the
guys had the bank employees as hostages and they
were demanding a plane to Libya. The television people found out about it and there was this freak-show
atmosphere with the negotiations being held on cam-
era and the media putting in calls to the clowns in the
bank. A very weird situation. I was sent over to help
Terry Dwyer who had taken over the negotiations
from the local cop who had been giving away the
store. This had been going on for hours, so we had
time to prepare the limo that was supposed to take
them to the airport. I wasn't the only agent there, of
course. There must have been a dozen of us, some of
us with our badges showing, some dressed as cops, a
couple in paramedics uniforms.

"The plan was to have Harper drive them since he
was experienced at this, but all of us had been briefed
just in case. One of the two clowns, the one who did
all the talking, came out into the street and inspected
the limo—this whole crowd of spectators standing
behind the barricades and cheering for him like he
was a hero of some kind. I think they thought he was
Jesse James and not some doped-up moron who got
caught with his dick in his hand. He was eating it up,
of course, and playing to the crowd, so we knew he
was going to make a mistake. We weren't really worried about—Tony, his name was. It was his partner,
Sal, who had us scared. A silent partner. The guy
never said a word, but you could tell by his eyes he
was dangerous. Stupid and scared silly, but God, was
he paying attention. Tony was distracted, but Sal
knew exactly where everyone was and what they were

doing even if he wasn't smart enough to know what was really going on.

"Anyway, the point is, Tony didn't want Harper to drive. He knew that he was no good just by looking at him—you know, Harper?"

"Is he the one who looks like the loser in a head-butting competition?"

"Not the kind of man you want working under-cover, unless you're investigating a convention of hit men. So anyway, the clown who thought he had brains . . ."

"Tony."

"Tony. He doesn't want Harper and he does this eeny-meeny-miney-mo business with the rest of us. I was one of us whose badge was showing, and he picked me. Said at least he knew who I was. I didn't even know who I was at that point, so what chance did he have? Anyway, he patted me down and patted Terry down and off we go to the airport, me driving, Tony next to me, Terry Dwyer next to him in the front seat because Terry has developed this "rapport" with him. Sal, with the eyes, is sitting behind me with an assault rifle pointing at my head as if I was going to suddenly drive him straight into the holding cell at the next precinct.

"I told him, 'Sal, if we hit a bump and you pull the trigger, we're all going to die.' He just stared at me for about a minute. His eyes were as big as a deer's and just that frightened, but boy, let me tell you, he *saw* things. He wasn't like his pal, Tony. He didn't have any illusions that he was center stage in a drama starring himself. He knew he was in the middle of a police convoy on the way to the airport with about a thousand locals and feds and several SWAT teams all waiting for a chance to jump on him. Finally he pointed the gun down, but I had to keep checking him in the mirror all the way to the airport because his instincts kept telling him to hold that gun on my head and it just kept drifting up. He had great instincts. He was just too dumb to trust them.

"The plan was to take them when we got to the airport and they thought they'd made it and relaxed a bit. Dwyer was going to freeze Tony in place, which shouldn't have been a problem because he was waving to the crowds along the way, and I was going to get the .45 that was under the door covering—the armrest was rigged to come down and I could pull it out and take care of Sal. But halfway there, Tony got a little bit smarter. I don't know what it was, but suddenly he tells me to stop and he opens the door and kicks Terry Dwyer onto the highway and off we go again. So much for the rapport. Maybe there weren't enough cameramen on the highway, so Tony had a chance to remember he was in deep shit. Whatever, all of a sudden I have Tony's shotgun in my ribs and Sal's got the Kalashnikov right back where it belonged.

"We get to the airport, and I am driving very carefully now, believe me. I keep working on Sal, asking him to keep the AK-47 pointed away but he's not buying it anymore, and when we hit the tarmac with all the airport lights and about a thousand more cops and the roar of the jets and the hostages in the back starting to wail because it looks like they're going to have to escort our boys to Libya, old Sal's discomfort level goes up about ten more notches. If I had sneezed, he would have blown my head off."

Becker stopped abruptly and returned to the window. After staring blankly for a few moments, he turned to Gold.

"That should do it for today," he said.

"What happened just now?" Gold asked.

Becker said, "This has been at least an hour; that's enough for now."

"What made you stop? What did you remember?"

After a pause, Becker said, "I saw Sal's eyes. In my mind, I saw them very clearly. Clearer than yours. I haven't had any reason to study yours."

"And?"

"You know the most distinctive thing about his eyes? It wasn't that they were scared or concentrated or dangerous. They were trusting. They didn't trust me, or the situation, but you could see that this was the kind of guy who would normally trust people, things, life. He trusted his nitwit friend, Tony. He trusted in the ability of the assault rifle to intimidate me and everybody else. It wasn't that he expected events to take an orderly progression; he'd been on the short end all his life, but even on that end, there were things you could trust. You could trust that might makes right, for instance. You could trust that a man with a weapon in his ribs and an automatic rifle point-blank to his head is not the man who is going to try anything to harm you . . . Once a man trusts you, once he thinks he knows what you're going to do, he's yours."

Becker started toward the door.

"What did you do?" Gold asked.

"It's in your file."

"The file just says you shot him."

"That's all I did."

"But why?"

"Why? He was in the act of committing a felony with a deadly weapon. He was kidnapping eight American citizens, he was . . ."

"But why you?" Gold interrupted.

"I was supposed to."

"If Dwyer had been with you to take care of Tony. But even then you had contingency plans; there were snipers all over the place. The copilot was an armed agent, so was one of the stewardesses . . ."

"That's not all in the file. You did a little research."

"I told you, I wanted the assignment. Why did you go ahead with it? You could have just let them get out of the limo, and no one would have blamed you. Why did you do it?"

Becker grinned at him from the doorway. "You're going to have to work harder than that," he said and left the room. He eased the door closed behind him.

Dyce was startled to find the man lying in his living room. His mind had been so filled with his encounter with Helen that he had forgotten about the presence of the man. Even his resolve while shopping that he would not do this again had slipped his mind. The girl—woman—he did not know what to call her, how to think of her. She was probably not as young as he thought; women weren't for some years. It was only when they reached their forties that women began to look their age and men looked younger. But there was something so trusting and simple about her character

that he suspected some part of her would always remain a girl.

And she liked him, she clearly liked him. He was no
expert, but he could see that. He wasn't entirely certain how it made him feel to have her respond to him
so unambiguously, but he was certain he hadn't mis-
read her feelings at least. There had been mistakes in
the past. Dyce had allowed himself to become in-
fatuated with girls who did not reciprocate, girls who
ultimately weren't worthy. Such episodes always left
him feeling ashamed of himself for being so gullible,
and renewed his resolve to remain alone. But he was
not mistaken about Helen, that much was certain.
She had remembered his name, she had thought
about him—she had told him that!

Working in a state of distraction as he thought
about his meeting with the girl, Dyce prepared himself for what he had to do. It was time, in any event,
whether he had resolved to stop or not, whether he
now had new interests or not. The man had been dead
for three days, and it was time to get rid of him. His
coloring had begun to change and the odor, despite
repeated washings, was getting hard to ignore.

Dyce lit the incense that he had placed in saucers
around the room. He did not like the smell of incense,
but it was more effective than the modern deodorizers
and Dyce didn't approve of using aerosols anyway
because of the ozone layer. The incense, however,
added smoke to the already-murky aspect of the
room and gave the whole proceedings an oriental feel
which he thought was inappropriate. It would take
several days to air out the house after he was done,
which meant removing the soundproofing from the

windows, a step that made Dyce nervous even when there was nothing to hide. Disposal had always been a problem.

The man's body was surprisingly heavy in comparison to his ethereal appearance. He should have weighed no more than a ghost, but his body seemed to struggle against Dyce's strength as he carried it to the bathroom, as if it wanted to remain in the place where it had spent the last ten days, alive and dead, or as if the body was resisting the final insult that awaited it in the bathtub.

Setting the showerhead to a fine spray, Dyce adjusted the pressure so that the body was enveloped in a lukewarm mist. The trick was to make the water warm enough to aid in the dissolution of liquids but not so hot that it would burn Dyce, who would be working in the mist. With the water running, Dyce filled his thirty-gallon, restaurant-sized stock pot halfway and turned the stove burner to high flame. If his timing was accurate, the water would be aboil by the time he needed it.

When Dyce returned to the bathroom with his knives, the mascara was running down the man's cheeks and coloring the stream of water that swirled down the drain. In the brighter light of the bathroom, the lipstick on the man looked harsh and cheap and shameful, as if he were a transvestite who had been caught in mid-transformation, frozen forever in his gender confusion. Dyce felt a moment's disgust as he regarded the man. He was not worthy, after all. Dyce had been wasting his time admiring the beauty of the man. He felt momentarily soiled and ashamed, as if he had just discovered he had made love to a harlot with a virgin's mask. You are better than this, he told himself. You deserve better for yourself, and you must stop acting this way.

He undressed, kneeled, and leaned into the shower's spray. Droplets formed immediately and dripped from the blade of the chef's knife. Filled with resolve to make this the last time, to change his life and live in a better, purer, more self-sufficient way, Dyce set to work.

HELEN was frantic. She knew she shouldn't do it, she knew it was precisely the kind of thing that drove men away, but she couldn't help herself. She actually said it to herself, *I can not help myself,* as if it were permission. She liked to think of herself as someone who was swept along by irresistible forces, a victim of her own tempestuous emotions. The winds of compulsion blew and raged and she was cast helplessly before them, rudder broken, the sails of her spirit swollen to the ripping point by the great force of her wild passions.

At the same time she knew perfectly well that it was this same compulsive behavior that frightened men away. In her sober moments she yearned for some measure of self-control that would keep her from hurling herself off cliffs of impulse, into the arms of strangers. But when the turmoil of passion gripped her, she forgave herself everything. She felt she must continue to throw her heart until someone caught it.

She had found his house with no problem but she hesitated at the door, trying to calm herself a bit, at least. Sometimes when she felt this way, it was all she could do to breathe, and her body would quiver with

excitement. Surely, surely, the world could sense the
urgency and rightness of what she did when it sent
such strong vibrations to her.

There were no lights coming from the house, but
his car was in the garage so he must be home. She did
not know much about him, but she was certain Mr.
Dyce was not the kind of man to be off with friends
on a week night.

Glancing at the other houses on the block, she
confirmed that it was not too late to call. The whole
row of houses, each with its little lawn and full front
porch, was lighted brightly, almost festively. Greenish
pictures jerked and shifted on television screens and
bulbs shone from upstairs bedrooms, kitchens, living
rooms. People moved openly and in silhouette behind
screens, and at the end of the block two children were
still at play, yelling at each other in the night.

It was a family neighborhood, a sane place, secure,
not affluent, exactly, but certainly comfortable. A
strange location, perhaps, for a single man, but a sign
that he valued the right things in life. For a moment,
Helen wondered if maybe Mr. Dyce had a family after
all, if the lights were out because he and Mrs. Dyce
were making love, if even a family of children, in-
laws, pets awaited on the other side of the door. He
didn't seem to be connected to anyone. He had not
mentioned anyone at the coffee shop when she had
given him the opportunity; he had all the earmarks of
a lonely man. Helen could not believe that she had
misjudged him so completely. His compassion was
real; there was no mistaking that, and she would rely
on that if nothing else. If she had made an error in
coming here, at least his compassion would keep her

from suffering too much for it. She knew she could count on him.

She rang the bell, waited, then rang it again too soon, unable to stop herself. There was not a sound from the house, and she decided that the bell did not work. A large iron knocker was in the middle of the door, a decorative relic from a pre-electronic time. She opened the screen door and lifted the knocker and let it fall against its metallic stump. That was not loud enough, so she rapped it several more times, holding it in her hand.

Nervously, Helen watched the neighboring houses to see if there was any response to the knocking, which seemed to clang like a shovel slammed against a car. She could hear nothing from within the house, even with her ear pressed against the door. It occurred to her that Dyce might be injured, he might be lying on the floor, unable to respond, the victim of a stroke, a heart attack. She could almost see him groping toward her with outstretched hand, mouthing her name and a cry for help.

Helen tried the door knob. He would want to know she was here. He would not want to miss her because he couldn't hear. Perhaps he was listening to music with earphones on. What sort of music? she wondered. The knob twisted in her hand, but the door did not budge.

Her hand was still on the knob when the door opened suddenly and without a sound of warning. Dyce stood there in a bathrobe, blinking at her, looking startled.

"Oh, Mr. Dyce," she said, "I'm so glad you're here. I hate to bother you but I was so unhappy, I just started thinking about my poor mother again and I couldn't stop and it was driving me crazy and I knew you would understand . . ."

She brushed past him and into the house before he spoke. He reached out as if to stop her, then relented. She knew he would want to see her. She waited for him in the little foyer just inside the door. From where she stood she could see into the living room and a portion of the kitchen and her eyes roved curiously as she spoke.

"I just had to come. I knew I shouldn't, but then I said to myself, Mr. Dyce will understand, he has been through it . . ."

He still had not spoken. His hair was wet and plastered to his forehead and his face dripped water into the bathrobe. There was something perplexed about his expression, as if he could not believe she was there—or worse, did not remember her.

"I got you out of the shower," she said.

"Yes," he said, breaking his silence for the first time. "Yes, I was in the shower."

"I knew you were here but just couldn't hear me," said Helen. The shower was running in the background and she could hear water boiling and a lid clattering in the kitchen. The shower explained why he hadn't heard her, but the house seemed alive with noise and Helen wondered why she had heard none of it from the porch.

"What do you want?"

"I had to see you. I just didn't know where else to turn, I didn't know who else to go to, this is a lovely house . . ."

She entered the living room and swept the panorama with a little turn of admiration. "Oh," she said. "It's so nice. You've done this so nice. And it's so much bigger than my place. Look at those curtains. It's unusual for a man to have curtains, I mean, such nice, big ones like that. I mean, men tend to just live with what they have, don't they, but floral curtains— someone must have put a lot of thought into that, I bet."

Dyce moved to the other side of her so that he was standing between her and the hall leading to the bathroom. He could not imagine what was going on with her or why she was here. What did she mean about his curtains?

"It's lovely, it really is. And what is that you're burning? Incense? Is that incense?"

She leaned over one of the saucers and waved the fumes to her nose.

"I never really knew what incense smelled like. That's such a nice touch, it really is, Mr. Dyce. You've done everything up so nicely."

She ran a finger across the table draped with white silk.

"Did you have help?"

"What?" Dyce asked dully. His mind was racing with priorities, possibilities, and necessities. Nothing she said made any sense to him.

"Did you have help decorating at all?" Helen swept an arm around the room. Dyce followed it, trying to imagine what she saw.

"It looks like a woman's touch."

"I don't know what . . . what did you want?"

"I just had to see you tonight. I'm sorry, I would have called, but you only had your address on your checks, not your phone number. I just felt so awful. I know we don't know each other very long, but I feel that I *know* you. Am I wrong? I feel I can talk to you in a way I can't to anybody else. There's something between us. I know it, I just know it."

She stopped speaking abruptly and stood in the middle of the room, trembling. She had said it. This was the moment: He would either laugh at her or throw her out, or, worst of all, treat her with pity.

Dyce's expression was still one of confusion, but she noticed his chest was heaving as if he were reacting with strong emotion—or struggling to control himself.

"Would you like me to go now?" she asked at last.

"I don't think I can let you go," he said.

"Oh, Mr. Dyce!" She took a step toward him, then stopped herself. It was better to let them make the first move, if they could ever be coaxed into making it. But he cared, he clearly cared!

"I'll wait here if you want to turn off the shower," she said, seating herself in the overstuffed chair that she knew must be "his."

"Yes," said Dyce. "The shower." He left the room, then came back almost immediately. He gave Helen a very peculiar smile.

"Don't go away," he said and for the first time that night there was animation in his voice.

"I won't."

"Because I think we have to talk," said Dyce.

She smiled at him, then lowered her eyes. When she looked up, he had gone. Realizing the chair was a mistake because it would not allow him to sit beside her, Helen transferred to the sofa. Like all the other furniture in the room, it was heavy and old, as if it had come from a different age. She sank into it and caught a whiff of mildew. The living room itself was the dumpiest thing she had ever seen, Helen thought. The curtains looked as if they'd been made by hand by somebody's grandmother. There was practically no light in the room, and what was that thing with the white silk on it, some kind of altar? And the smell! No wonder he was burning incense, although she wondered if that might not go with the altar in some way, too. She hoped he wasn't religious in some obsessional way. She could deal with it if he was because she had been that way for a time herself. She understood it, but the memory of her days in the commune still rankled, and she didn't want to be reminded if she could help it. God was all right; it was the people that troubled Helen.

Impatiently she got to her feet and made a circuit of the living room. A little light would do wonders, she decided. Preferably sunlight. The cobwebs on the ceiling caught her attention. She wondered if smoke from the incense turned them that black. At least he seemed to be clean in his personal hygiene. Had he decided to finish his shower? The water was still running. How long could it take to turn it off?

Pausing by the foyer entrance, Helen thought of extinguishing the fire under the rattling pot on the stove. What could require such a violent, prolonged boiling? Was that the source of the stench? It was all she could do to keep herself from going into the kitchen and taking charge.

• • •

THE bathroom was filled with mist and the mirror was filmed over so that Dyce could not see his reflection. He wanted to know how he looked, what she might have seen. His brain was careening; he could not think clearly what to do. How much did she know? Did she know anything? Why was she here, could he believe her reasons, was there something else, what had he left visible in the living room? And if she did see anything, what conclusions could she reach? It all seemed an impossible maze. He needed time to think.

After a few minutes, Dyce remembered to turn off the shower. He pulled the shower curtain closed, put down the toilet seat, and sat on the toilet. The mist settled on his cool skin and soon rivulets of water ran down his face and his naked legs, but he did not notice.

It did not occur to him to kill her. Dyce did not think of himself as such a person. He was not a man of violence. The things he did with the men were not done from malice or panic or ill will of any sort. He did them because they needed to be done, but that was only one small segment of his life and certainly not the dominant part of his personality. That was not the way he lived his *life,* for heaven's sake. It was not the way he would solve his problems. He would have thought less of himself if he did.

HELEN could contain herself no longer. The noise from the pan lid in the kitchen was driving her crazy and was probably dangerous. Fires could get started that way. She was doing him a service. Helen went into the kitchen.

It was the largest pot she had ever seen in a home.

Fire had blackened the aluminum halfway up the sides, and the carbon was thick enough to scrape off with the edge of a spoon. Two burners were going at high flame underneath the pot, and scum and foam were pushing at the lid and oozing from underneath it. The bubbles of scum came out rhythmically, like gulps or gasps for air that were cut short by the weight of the lid bearing down again. Some of the foam would drift down the side of the pot to meet the flames and then vanish in an angry sizzle of steam as the fire emitted momentary sparks of yellow and green. The smell of it was horrible.

Helen reached for the burner but turned, frightened, as she realized someone was behind her.

"Oh!" she exclaimed. "You frightened me!"

"Don't turn it off," Dyce said.

"It's boiling over. It will be ruined."

"It won't be ruined," he said.

"What on earth are you making?"

Dyce took her by the hand and led her from the kitchen.

"It's not important," he said. He preceded her to the couch, still holding her hand, then sat, pulling her gently down beside him. His manner had changed dramatically. For the only time since Helen had known him, he appeared to be in charge of things. She definitely felt he was in charge of her. Wonderfully, masterfully in control.

"I was just trying to help," she said.

"I understand," he said calmly. He sat facing her, one leg draped over the other and resting on the floor. Helen realized that he had put on pajama bottoms, but his torso was still bare beneath the robe. The skin of his chest was smooth and hairless.

"Tell me what brought you here," he said.

Helen pulled her knees up under her. She felt so comfortable with him when he spoke to her like this. So secure. She was his, if only he knew it. Helen was glad the lights were dim because she had applied the purple eye shadow during her frantic phase and she thought she might have overdone it.

"I wondered at first if you knew who I was," she said. "I mean, seeing me out of context, sort of. Without my uniform." She was wearing her robin's egg blue blouse with the scoop neck that accentuated her cleavage. She could see his eyes wander to the edge of the neckline. She leaned forward, revealing just a bit more of her flesh.

"I knew you . . . Helen. My mind was elsewhere for a while, that's all."

"I understand," she said. "You weren't expecting me."

"In a way, I think I was," he said.

His arm was resting atop the back of the sofa. With a show of pushing the hair from her face, Helen moved her own arm to the sofa back and let her hand come to rest inches from his fingertips.

"I've been thinking about this afternoon, so much," she said. "So much."

Dyce moved his fingers the few inches until they touched the tips of hers. Helen could feel the electricity of it. She gasped slightly, then laughed nervously.

Dyce smiled at her again with that peculiar smile. His eyes were alive with a life of their own.

CHAPTER 5

S HE just started talking on the telephone, assuming she would be recognized. It was one of Becker's pet peeves and he played with the notion of asking who the hell she was. There was no particular reason for him to recognize her voice—but he did. And how had she known he would? Or did she usually start like this, as if she were always in mid-conversation?

"I've been trying to reach you for the past day and a half. I just wanted to make sure you're okay."

"I'm fine. I was in Washington, yesterday."

"Really? Washington?"

She paused, waiting for him to explain, which also annoyed Becker.

"I went there to see a shrink."

"That's a long way for a shrink."

"He's a special shrink."

"Does that mean you're a special guy, or that you're especially screwed up?"

She had seemed so sympathetic when he was dangling upside down on a rope. Maybe that brought out the best in people. On the other hand, she had taken the trouble to find out how he was feeling. Nosy but concerned. Not the worst trade-off, he thought.

"It means I'm screwed up in a special way. How about you?"

"Just the usual way, I suppose, but I'm kind of proud of it."

"Let me guess," he said. "Does it have to do with the way you relate to other people and your feelings of guilt and aggression and codependency and your inability to form a truly lasting bond with another human being?"

"No. My fear of heights. Alan and I are going up again today. I just thought I'd let you know if you wanted to join us."

"I got the impression last time that Alan was a little annoyed that I spoiled the party."

"Alan was just upset because during your three minutes of crisis he wasn't the center of attention. We're starting around two so the sun won't be in our eyes. Okay?"

"If I'm not there, start without me."

"We will." She hung up without saying good-bye. Another thing that annoyed Becker.

ALAN had found a new route that obliged him to hang upside down for a distance of five feet before restoring himself to the merely vertical. Going straight up at ninety degrees was bad enough, but one hundred twenty seemed to be pushing beyond stupidity into lunacy. Becker was not even sure that a fly could handle an outcropping like the one Alan was negotiating as Becker arrived. Cindi was halfway up the rockface, spread-eagled against the stone as if she'd been staked out for torture, but calmly watching Alan perform. Becker was relieved to see Tee's cop car parked alongside the highway; if he talked to Tee long enough maybe Cindi and Alan would get to the top and Becker could tackle the more conventional route up. If he went up at all. His bones ached just thinking about it.

As he approached Tee, Becker realized there was someone else in the car.

"Mick Seeger's wife," Tee said with a great show of innocence.

"Oh, subtle. Widows and orphans."

"I didn't know you'd be here, did I? We were just passing by. I saw your friend hanging up there like a chandelier; it's free entertainment, and I don't know how it's going to come out. I didn't think you'd be here after that spill."

"Uh-huh. How long have you been waiting?"

"Just got here. Swear to God, John . . ."

"Good thing God isn't listening to you anymore, Tee. You'd be in big trouble."

"Laurie, come on out here and say hello to John Becker. John's the man I was telling you about."

"Oh, thank you, Mr. Becker. Thank you so much."

She was about Cindi's age, maybe a year or two younger, but she seemed to be from a different generation, one in which innocence still existed. Mick Seeger had married a baby, thought Becker.

"I've been so worried, I just can't tell you. Mickey and I haven't been apart for even a day since we got married and now . . ."

Her face quivered with the effort to keep from crying. Becker thought she was the kind of woman for whom tears were never very far away.

Becker looked angrily at Tee, but the policeman was innocently watching the climbers.

"Tee tells me you're so good at it," Laurie said.

"Tee doesn't really know what he's talking about."

She laughed, as if the notion of Tee not knowing everything were hilarious. So young, Becker thought. Married, a mother, and so young.

"Have you been watching these climbers long?"

"Not long," Tee said quickly.

"Only about twenty minutes," said Laurie. "Tee said you'd be here soon."

"I was driving Laurie to the gynecologist. My wife and I didn't think she should be alone at a time like this."

"Nothing wrong at the doctor's, I hope," Becker said, knowing he shouldn't.

Laurie looked shyly away. "No," she said.

"Laurie's pregnant again," Tee offered happily, watching Becker.

Becker rolled his eyes to the sky. It was bad enough being manipulated, but Tee was so clumsy at it he made Becker feel like a puppet with some strings broken. Tee was tugging like crazy at the ones that remained.

"Oh, I wish you hadn't told him, Tee," Laurie said. "I wanted Mickey to be the first to hear the good news."

"Sorry, honey," said Tee. "But Mickey will be just as happy to hear it."

She started to cry again. "I just hope he isn't hurt.

If he doesn't want to be with me anymore, I can . . . I just can't stand the idea of him being hurt somewhere."

"I'm sure he's okay, Laurie," said Tee.

"Maybe he just lost his memory. That happens, doesn't it? People just forget who they are for a while? Doesn't that happen, Mr. Becker?"

Not in my experience, Becker thought, not that he cared to share that with Laurie, particularly given her condition.

"That happens sometimes," he said.

"Do you think it will take you a long time to find him?"

"That depends on Tee."

"On Tee?"

"He hasn't given me the records I need to get started," said Becker.

"Tee-ee!"

"They're in the car," said Tee, grinning and opening the back door of the sedan.

Laurie touched Becker's arm. "I don't know how to thank you," she said.

"I haven't really done anything. I may not be able to."

"You will, I know you will. Tee says you're the very best there is."

"It isn't a good idea to believe absolutely everything Tee tells you."

Laurie strained up on tiptoes and kissed Becker on the cheek.

"Thank you, Mr. Becker. Thank you." She was crying again as she got into the car.

Tee tucked a file folder into Becker's hands but avoided his eyes.

"I'll call you," said Tee.

"No. You won't. You'll leave me the fuck alone until I contact you. In fact, you'd better give me plenty of room for quite some time, Tee."

"Gotcha."

"Yeah, you got me, but I don't like the way you did it."

"I understand," said Tee. "You're a good man, John."

No, thought Becker as Tee's police car pulled away. No, I'm not, which is why I couldn't tell that child I wouldn't do it. Maybe a good man could have been honest enough to break her heart. But a bad man could not take that chance, Becker thought. It would be entirely too revealing.

Alan had reached the top of the palisade and now Cindi was creeping her way under the overhang. For a moment her face was turned directly toward Becker and he thought she smiled at him. With a movement, he realized it was a grimace. Even an expert was struggling against her fear on this particular route.

Becker felt the file folder in his hand and was suddenly glad for it. At least it was something he could handle. I'm like an alcoholic with a bottle in front of me, Becker thought. Sure, it will kill me, but at least it's something I know how to do.

He waited until Cindi had pulled herself around the overhang and was pressed safely—or as safely as her ego would allow—against the vertical face before driving off.

•   •   •

THE contents of the file were spread across the dining room floor in a semicircle around Becker's chair so he could see them all by twisting his head. The dining table was littered with more papers and scraps of scribbled notes surrounding the computer and its terminal.

"Technically, that's police property," said Tee, gesturing at the strewn files.

"So?"

Becker was bringing his aging computer to life. The seconds it took to perform its more complex functions had come to seem interminable to Becker.

Tee was standing in the doorway leading to the kitchen, drinking a beer he had taken without comment from the refrigerator. It was a bottle from the same six-pack he had brought to Becker's house two days before. Leaving beer and finding it untouched later was something novel in Tee's experience.

"So you should treat them with respect."

"I give them all the respect they deserve. It's pretty slack work, Tee."

"We don't have the Bureau standards in Clamden."

"No, you don't. I spent the last two days running around and filling in the gaps."

"Sorry. I spent the last two days holding Laurie's hand and maintaining law and order."

The computer signaled its readiness and Becker gave it new instructions. The screen filled with columns.

"How do you get it to do that?" Tee asked. "Do they sell a missing-persons software?"

"I programmed it myself."

"You did? Jesus. How do you know how to do that?"

"What age are you living in, Tee?"

"The Iron Age, isn't it? I don't know how to smelt ore, though. Fortunately, you do. Did you find out anything?"

"Would I ask you over for social reasons?"

"My wife has been asking me the same thing. About you, I mean. She thinks you don't love us enough. You've got the house, you've got the refrigerator. Why don't you entertain? Why not have friends over, Gloria wants to know."

"I have no friends."

"You've got at least one."

"And he takes advantage of me."

"I meant the human fly, what's her name, Cindi. I ran into her in the Crossroads the other night. She asked about you."

"The Crossroads?"

"A restaurant, bar, whatever. It's where you single people go to arrange your nasty liaisons."

"I know what it is. What were you doing there?"

"Official drinking. She's gorgeous, you know, if you take her out of her climbing gear—and wouldn't I like to. She was asking lots of questions about you: Are you married, why not, what are your sexual preferences, how do you spell that—that sort of thing."

"What is it about marriage that makes you so horny, Tee? They have an operation that will cure that problem right up, you know. Your local vet could probably take care of it for you."

"I don't think so. My local vet's a man." Tee drained the beer and crushed the can in his hand.

"Whew," said Becker. "How do you do that?"

"Scary, isn't it?"

"Now, Chief, if your testosterone level has settled down, tell me about Mick. Did he fool around, too?"

"I don't really fool around. I just want to. No, he didn't. Not that I know of."

"Would you know?"

"I think so. We talked a lot."

"At the Crossroads?"

"Yeah, some. I'd see him there sometimes, having a beer after work, you know. He'd be at the bar, though. He wasn't off in a corner with a girl."

"That's the last place he was seen before he disappeared."

"I know. Nothing unusual about his being there, though."

"There was nothing unusual about him at all," said Becker. He pointed to the screen. "There was nothing unusual about most of them. At least not at first glance. Or second glance, either. You've got to study it for a while. First of all, it's not fifteen men missing in four years. Not for our purposes. Under normal circumstances in a population of one hundred thousand in this kind of New England situation— nonisolated, small communities, close to major cities—you'd lose five or six in four years. Running out on their wives, skipping out to avoid alimony and child support, just starting over, whatever. So what we have is an aberration of nine or ten disappearances, not fifteen. The question is which nine or ten are unusual, which of them make a pattern. You can't begin until you see a pattern. So I had the computer try to eliminate the five or six normal disappearances for me, and it went at it a number of ways; annual income, marital status, number of kids, type of work, age, place last seen, you name it. It took awhile because I ran out of questions to ask the computer. Then it took awhile longer because I had to find out more about the missing men, which meant interviewing a lot of people."

"I could have helped you there."

"Not if you didn't know what questions to ask, and I didn't know until I was halfway through the process, and then I had to go back and ask some more. I stumbled on it when I was checking out this guy named Jensen from Guileford. Salvatore Jensen, strange combination. But half the people I talked to about him didn't know him as Jensen; they knew him as D'Amico. He was born Sal D'Amico, became an actor and changed his name to Sal Jensen because there was another actor in Actors' Equity named Sal D'Amico and they have a rule about that kind of duplication."

"You mean all these guys changed their names? Because Mick didn't."

"D'Amico is the only one who changed his name, but it was how he changed it. He did what a lot of actors do, they tell me. He didn't just make something up the way they used to do in Hollywood. And he didn't just add a middle initial—apparently all the actors with middle initials? It's because someone else has registered their name."

"I didn't know that."

"No reason ever to think about it. It's only an actor's problem. But what D'Amico did that was significant was to take his mother's maiden name, Jensen. Do you know Mick's mother's maiden name?"

"Her maiden name? That's Gloria's brother's wife, Julie, and she came from Hartford and they'd already been married for about ten years before I even met Gloria—I don't know. I can find out."

"It's Peterssen."

"Right. That sounds kind of familiar. I think I met her father in Hartford once. So, it's Peterson. So what?"

"No flash of insight? No light bulb over your head?"

"Give me a break, John. If I had flashes of insight, would I stand here and let you insult my stupidity?"

"They are both Scandinavian names. They are all Scandinavian names."

Becker pushed another key and eight names came up on the screen.

"Eight of them," he continued. "Eight of them with mothers with Scandinavian names. Not their own names. Their mothers. Only two of them had Scandinavian names themselves."

"Wait a minute. Peterson could be English, couldn't it?"

"If you say it aloud, yes. The s-e-n ending and the s-o-n ending sound the same. You have to see it written to know the difference. And s-e-n is Scandinavian. Primarily Danish or Norwegian, although it could be Swedish as well. With two esses it could also be Icelandic."

"Icelandic?"

"Look at the names, Tee. Peterssen, Jensen, Cederquist, Nordholm, Dahl, Lind, Hedstrom, Nilsson.

Each of those is definitely Scandinavian. Not maybe, not could also be German or Dutch or English. Definitely Scandinavian."

"How do you know this crap?"

"I have a library card."

"So what's going on? There's some secret meeting of Danes and everyone is sneaking out to it, or what?"

"They're not going on their own. Someone's taking them."

"How do you know that?"

"I don't believe in cabals, Tee. I don't believe in secret summonses or mysterious inheritances or a gathering of the trolls or aliens. I don't look for fancy explanations. Maybe it's just a predisposition because of my training, but this stinks all over the place. If they have anything else in common, I can't find out what it is. They range in age from twenty-five to thirty-six, they're male, they live around here, and that's it."

"Except for their mothers."

"Except for their mothers' *names.* The mothers don't have much in common, either, although I need to look at that further. It's not as if they just got off the boat from Copenhagen. Most of the families have been here for many generations. Their only link to Scandinavia is the surname."

"Who would care if they had Scandinavian names? What difference does it make?"

"I have no idea."

"And who would even know the surnames?"

"Bingo, Tee. No wonder you're the chief. Who would know the names? You didn't know your nephew's mother's maiden name. And not only know the names, but know them correctly, by spelling. Someone with access to records, obviously. And what kind of records have women's maiden names?"

"Marriage records."

"Correct, but marriage licenses don't tell you if the woman has or had or will have a child."

"Hospitals, birth certificates."

"Which will tell you a child was born, but not if he's still alive at least twenty-five years later, or if he lives around here."

"We need something where a woman with a Scandinavian last name tells you she's got a son at least twenty-five years old?"

"Or vice versa. A form of some kind where the son gives his mother's maiden name."

"Hell, John, that could be credit-card applications, job applications, a lot of things."

"Except I'm sure these men didn't all apply for the same job. The army takes that kind of information, but only two of our men were in it."

"Social security?"

"No."

"The goddamned census, I don't know, what?"

"The census is an idea, Tee, although I don't think they take that kind of information, but I'll check it out."

"You know the answer already or you wouldn't be jumping me through the hoops. Where would you get the information?"

"Insurance. There are other ways, but they're harder and not local. The same insurance salesman could easily cover our four towns. And he doesn't even have to sell you a policy to get the information.

They offer to see if they can beat your present insurance rate, you know. Just fill out the form and they'll get you a free quote, no obligation to buy."

"I always knew I didn't like insurance salesmen. So we have to find out if the same insurance salesman talked to all of these men who disappeared?"

"To begin with, we have to see if the same one talked to even two of them. That's something to start with, but it won't be easy to find out. Would your wife remember if you had a talk with an insurance salesman six months ago? A year ago? We don't know how long this guy waits once he selects his victim."

"Victim? You're sure that's what's going on?"

"Nope. I'm still hoping it's a case of mass amnesia. But in the meanwhile, I'll stay cynical."

"But why the mothers? Wouldn't it be easier to just pick men with Scandinavian names, if that's what you were after?"

"Easier, but it would make for an obvious pattern. I only stumbled onto this because of the actor. It wouldn't show up in a routine scan of the victims' case studies. It didn't for you, did it?"

"You think Mick's dead, then?"

"I think we should start checking out insurance salesmen."

"Damn it, Becker, I'm not Laurie! Tell me what you think. Is he dead?"

"Did you get a ransom note?"

"Of course not. Why would anybody kidnap Mick? He doesn't have any money . . ."

"You've checked hospitals, traffic fatalities . . . It's not just Mick, there are eight of them. Christ, Tee, you brought this thing to me yourself. What did you think it was? Things like this go on. All the time, all over the country. Read the newspaper; there's a new case every other month. The Hillside Strangler, the Atlanta murders, John Wayne Gacy, Ted Bundy. There's some farm couple in Missouri in their seventies who killed at least twenty and counting. Sometimes I think it's a national competition. And the newspapers are just interested in the big numbers. You never even hear about the creep in Arizona who got caught after three, or the one in Baton Rouge who . . . Maybe I'm wrong, Tee. Give me another explanation."

Tee was silent for a moment. Becker looked away, giving him the time in privacy.

"Okay," said Tee at length.

"Sorry. Maybe I'm wrong."

"Okay."

"It's my experience, Tee. My training. I look for the worst."

"I accept that it's not UFOs . . . It's just that Mick and I . . . okay."

"It's not just about Mick, Tee."

"I know."

"It's happening faster, his pace is accelerating. He took the first four in thirty months. He took the last four in eighteen. The time between Timmy Heegan and Mick was only two months. His appetite is getting ravenous, the need is consuming him."

"The need?"

"That's what it is. That's what it becomes. Maybe not the first time; that could be accident or fluke or experiment, but after that, you start to want it—if you're that kind of person. After awhile you need it, you need the rush of adrenaline or the sexual thrill or whatever it happens to be in your case. Like any addiction, you need more and more. The more you get, the more you need, until eventually, like any addiction, you overdose . . . Killing grows on you."

Tee noted the intensity with which Becker spoke and looked away from it. There were some things he didn't want to witness and some he didn't want to know.

"Well, so. Insurance salesmen. How much time do you think we have until his 'appetite' makes him take somebody else?" asked Tee.

"Mick disappeared fourteen days ago. I'd guess we have a month, maybe less."

"Unless he stops."

"Stops?" Becker laughed. "He's in too far to stop. It's in his blood, in his gut, it makes him dizzy with desire. He can hear it like a howling in his ears."

Tee watched Becker with growing unease. He did not want to know how his friend knew such things.

CHAPTER 6

D YCE made his way through the pillows as he ma-
neuvered across the bedroom, taking care not to
step on them, even though they were everywhere un-
derfoot. Helen filled her bed with pillows when she
was not in it, at least ten of them arranged together
like children propped against the headboard. Two of
them were for sleeping, but the others—a motley
group of calico-patterned cats, gingham dogs, hand-
stitched samplers with pictures of cottages and comforting proverbs, and compact, satin-covered
cushions suited for a doll—were lined up for decora-
tion or solace, Dyce did not know which. When they
got into the bed, usually with much display of sexual
urgency, Dyce would sweep as many of them to the
floor as he could take with his arm. Helen would
remove those from her side of the bed rapidly, but
with care. He knew she did not approve of his style of
inconsiderate dumping, but she never mentioned it.

Later, if they were out of the bed, even for a few

minutes, she would line up all the pillows again. It made no sense to him, but he had decided it was a female crotchet, one he couldn't expect to understand but must learn to tolerate if he was to exist in her world.

"It's all right," Helen said. "It doesn't matter to me."

Dyce pushed a red and white checked cat out of the way with his foot. Someone had sewn plastic whiskers onto the pillow's face and they pricked his foot as he brushed against them while digging with his toes for his underpants that were buried under the cushions.

"I love it just having you hold me. We don't have to do anything," she said. She always said the same thing, and it sounded more accusatory to him every time.

"Don't be upset. I don't mind, really I don't."

"I'm not upset," he said. He found the underpants and lifted them with his toes, keeping his back to her. Dyce was shy about letting her see him naked as long as he was flaccid. A natural modesty was compounded by his impotence. Helen, on the other hand, seemed to have no modesty at all. She paraded nude with as much indifference as if she were clothed. In his opinion, she didn't look that good, either. Her breasts were full, he liked that, but so was the rest of her. Dyce had expected filmy peignoirs and full slips of the type he saw on television. He had not been prepared for this all-out assault of flesh and naturalness; it was not femininity as he thought of it. It was woman, but it was not feminine. Dyce would have preferred something with the lights out, something with soft music and gentle touches, perhaps some coy resistance on her part, a sense of conquest on his.

Instead, he was assailed by a woman who seemed to want to consume him, smothering him with her body and her mouth and her desire. Dyce felt overpowered by it all but did not know how to tell her so. His impotence was her fault, he knew it. He had done fine that first night when she burst into his house. With their clothes on and the unfinished business in the bathtub and the sound of the pot boiling in the kitchen and the air crackling with danger, he had performed like a champion. Helen had acted properly then, too, protesting that no, she mustn't, and Mr. Dyce, it was too soon, and then, fairly swooning as she succumbed, oh, Mr. Dyce, Mr. Dyce! Afterwards he had escorted her to the door and out to her car and there was no question who was the master of the situation.

Later, he had been amazed at himself. He was a stallion, a champion, virile as a bull, cunning as a wolf. A small twinge of guilt for taking advantage of the girl had nagged at him. She clearly did not know what she was in for when she came into the lair of Roger Dyce; she had not been prepared. He had swept her along on the torrent of his passion and overwhelmed her. But his guilt was more than overcome by his pride. He had been faced with a dilemma and had dealt with it as masterfully as anyone could have.

But that was then and there. Since then they had been on her ground, in her tiny apartment, so small he could hear her going to the bathroom while he lay in bed two rooms away, and she had been acting as if *she* were the master. It was no wonder he could not perform under such circumstances. It was her fault.

Dyce stood in the bathroom and regarded his reflection in the full-length mirror on the back of the door. His body was smooth and virtually hairless except for the pubic area and the tops of his thighs. He took hold of his pathetic member and shook it angrily. Perhaps this was all a mistake, perhaps his involvement with Helen was an error in judgment. A tactical move that had dragged on too long. And was it really even involvement? She seemed to think it was; she spoke of them as if they were a permanent couple, already fixed and immutable. She regarded them as deeply in love, as needing each other, as being the answer to each other's prayers. Dyce was not certain when all this had happened. One minute he had sat next to her on his own sofa and touched her hand and she had moaned and thrown her head back, and then his hand was on her breast and she was pleading with him to stop but too powerless to stop him even though her hand was atop his. The next thing he knew he was here, in this minuscule boudoir filled with pillows and a plump, naked woman who kept insisting that she didn't think him any less a man because he couldn't have sex with her. She spoke of togetherness and intimacy and cuddling and kissing, which sounded to his ears like so many gnats buzzing. He wanted her to turn the lights out and act more like a virgin, and she wanted to act as if they were an old married couple. And she wanted to watch him, as if he might dematerialize if her gaze faltered. She was perpetually probing. It seemed he could not say or do a thing without Helen's instant, often lengthy analysis. Because they didn't speak the same language, Dyce spoke less and less.

The differences between them were evident even here in the bathroom. The apartment was really a converted loft over what had once been a stable and was now a garage. Everything in the place was cramped and antiquated and the bathroom was no different. The room was not much bigger than a large closet to begin with, and an old claw-footed tub took up most of the room. What space was left she had crammed with shelves that groaned with powders, oils, unguents, creams, scents, and sprays. What a nudist like Helen was doing with all these cosmetics was more than Dyce could divine.

His eyes caught the can of talcum powder on the stick-on shelf over the bathtub. He had noticed it on previous visits but had not dwelt on it. That was one of the positive aspects of their relationship: He had not thought of the other thing since their first time together. It had been well over three weeks now and it had not even entered his mind. She was good for him in that way. She would keep him to the straight and narrow.

He had the talcum powder can in his hand and did not remember reaching for it. He should put it back, he knew he should put it back.

Dyce looked at himself in the mirror again. He shook his member but felt nothing, not a stirring. His gaze shifted to his face, then to the talcum powder in his hand. The lid was open. He shook some talc from the little holes into his palm. His breath caught in his throat, then shivered out.

•　　•　　•

HELEN lay atop the covers, clutching a pillow to her chest. The air was just cool enough on her skin to make the goose flesh start on her thighs, a not uncomfortable sensation. Her eyes were on the ceiling where a hairline crack in the plaster spread in all directions like a spider web, but her ears were on the bathroom. He was so quiet.

Helen hated silence. It only reminded her that she was alone in life. She talked too much, she knew it, and when there was no one else in her apartment, she talked to herself. She sang with the radio and had conversations with the television. When she read her magazines she did it with the radio or stereo or television playing. Her place was never quiet except when he was there. He was so quiet in everything he did.

She thought of him as "he." She called him Roger, now, but the name did not fit him somehow. He could no longer be Mr. Dyce, of course; they were too intimate for that, but still she felt that the formal appellation fit him better than Roger. In her mind, he was "he" and "him," and the two words filled her brain so that she could think of little else.

He had been in the bathroom so long she began to worry. The withdrawal seemed symptomatic of the relationship as a whole. She was losing him, he was pulling away from her. She could sense it but did not know what to do about it. His impotence was part of the problem, she was sure of it. God knows she had tried, she had done everything she could think of, she had been positively brazen about it, flaunting herself, pawing him like a whore, but he had managed it only the first time. Of course she didn't want him to brood about it since that would only make it worse, so she had reassured him constantly that it didn't matter to her. It did matter, of course. She nearly ground her teeth with frustration as she lay next to him or on him or under him without so much as a suggestion of satisfaction. There were other things he could do to make her happy, but she sensed that even a hint would horrify him. He was so innocent, and so annoying. And yet he was her man, and she would cling to him no matter what. They were intended for each other; she knew that much even if she did not know what was wrong.

He had been gone too long and the apartment seemed to shrink in on her with the silence.

"Are you all right?" she called.

There was no answer. Perhaps he had fallen and hit his head on the tub.

Helen got out of bed. From the doorway to the bedroom she could see across the living room to the bathroom door, which was open a crack.

"Roger?"

If he had wanted privacy he would have closed the door. One of the pillows was in the doorway of the bedroom. Helen hugged it to her for a moment before deciding.

She crossed the living room, a distance of no more than fifteen feet, and stopped in front of the bathroom door. She listened.

At first she heard nothing at all except her own breathing. Holding her breath, she leaned closer. A strange sound, one she could not identify, something being softly patted, something like a swish, then nothing.

Then more, a high moaning, faint but definitely a

moaning, like a child holding back a whimper. He was hurt, she knew it. She could picture him lying on the floor, blood on his head where it had struck the bathtub.

"I called but you didn't answer," she said even before she opened the door in case he wasn't hurt.

An apparition stood before her. There was no light on in the bathroom and he shone like a ghost in the gloom. He was chalky white from head to toe. Deathly white. For one irrational moment she thought he was a standing corpse.

His eyes were wide and staring and his lips were peeled back from his teeth. She stood right in front of him and yet she was sure he did not see her. He had been looking at himself in the mirror and his mind was still fixed there, staring at his sepulchral reflection.

He moaned once more, almost a pleading, and it was then that Helen noticed that his penis was hugely erect.

"Roger?" she said, not knowing what world he was in at the moment.

He shook his head as if trying to clear it and powder floated off. Dyce struggled to focus on her, but Helen could not keep her eyes off the pure white of his stiff penis. The powder was smooth and uniform and had not been touched since application.

In the darkness its size was accentuated by its pallor. Helen thought it shined. She took one step toward him and he threw his arms around her, yanking her into his body. She groaned with gratitude as she felt the rigidity ram against her.

•   •   •

BECKER sat at the corner of the bar so he could watch the door and see when his man was leaving. He had no need to watch him directly or to keep tabs on him in the mirror; the guy was not about to exit through the toilet window or the kitchen. He had no reason to know that Becker was tailing him, no reason to be suspicious of a thing.

Right now the man was sitting quietly at a table for two in the singles hangout called the Crossroads. Insurance literature was spread out on the table in front of him, and the man was studying it as he sipped a cup of coffee. He had a settled-in look about him as if he were here for the balance of the evening.

Becker had got onto the man initially when Laurie Seeger produced his business card from a desk drawer where Mick had presumably tossed it. Mick had purchased a life-insurance policy just before the birth of their first child three years earlier. Recently, Mick had contacted the insurance agency to increase his policy. The man who had sold him the original policy had since retired, but the new man who was now sipping coffee in the Crossroads had called on Mick and serviced the new requirement. It was, as far as Laurie knew, their only contact.

But it was not the insurance man's only contact with one of the missing men. Marley of Guileford, mother's name Cederquist, had taken out a policy from the same man two years earlier. None of the others had, but Vohl of Branford, mother's name Nordholm, received a brochure from an insurance company the day before Becker's second visit to Mrs. Vohl. The brochure was still lying on the kitchen counter, unopened, and on the brochure, stamped by hand in the bottom corner, was the name of the man's agency.

Three of eight was pressing coincidence to the point of probability. Becker had watched the man for two days now in a sporadic pattern, checking in on his activities now and then, never staying long enough to draw attention to himself. He did not expect to catch the man in the act; rather he wanted to get a feel of the man, to fill his nostrils with the man's scent, and to get a sense of his pattern so that any aberrance would send off a warning signal.

The bartender placed another diet soda in front of Becker.

"From the lady," said the bartender.

Cindi lifted a glass to him from the back of the room and Becker rose to join her. The insurance salesman cast him a casual glance as he passed, but Becker did not look back.

"We've been watching you," Cindi said, "wondering if you'd ever turn around. Most men scope out a place. What's the matter, not curious?"

"Who's we?"

"Alan's in the john. What's the point of coming to a place like the Crossroads if you don't check out the action?"

"I had this silly idea about getting something to drink," said Becker.

"Yeah, I usually come to a singles place if I feel like a Coke, too. A buck and a half seems like a fair price for half a can."

She was still wearing her spandex climbing outfit, but the front zipper was open far enough to suggest cleavage and her hair was flowing freely over her shoulders. Becker had not realized she had such a full mane of it.

"Are you a detective of some kind?" Becker said.

"I notice things," she said, then grinned.

It was peculiar, Becker thought, but it seemed that he could see her better in the half light of the bar than in the full sunshine. There was a sprinkling of freckles across the bridge of her nose and her cheekbones. Not enough to even qualify as a dusting, a countable number. Her teeth were unnaturally bright when she smiled because of the fluorescent lighting, and her last swallow of beer had left her with a foam mustache just on the corners of her mouth.

"I notice you've been climbing again," said Becker. "Or else you've got a very limited wardrobe."

"Right on both counts. We tried a new face today. It's about a quarter mile farther north than the last one."

"How is it?"

"Kind of tough. We missed you."

She seemed a little older than she had on the rocks, too, for which Becker was grateful. He had trouble finding himself attracted to women who were too young for him. Cindi, if one were liberal enough about these things, was just old enough for a man his age. Her bottom teeth were not quite straight, as if orthodontia had been abandoned before it could take full effect. A restless, impatient girl who did not wear her retainer often enough or long enough.

"Do you do anything else for fun, or just climb rocks?"

"Now that is a lousy come-on for a man of your age and experience," she said.

"I'm out of practice."

"That might be marginally in your favor," she said.

The waitress stopped at the insurance sales a n's table and spoke to him. The salesman shook his head and the waitress moved off. Becker watched him from behind as he rearranged his papers, put some in his briefcase, then checked his watch.

"So he finally looked," said Alan as he slid into his chair. There was an extremely loose, limber quality to everything he did. A natural ease in his body that was completely lacking in his social manner.

"I summoned him."

"Bullshit," said Alan. "She was trying to make you turn around by the power of her thoughts. Her karma or whatever you call it."

"That's pronounced *charm,*" said Becker.

Cindi grinned again. "Better," she said.

"What?" said Alan, testily. "She came over and got you, right?"

"No. Like she said, she summoned me as if from afar."

"Yeah, bullshit." Alan waved impatiently for the waitress. Becker guessed it was at least his fourth beer. Alan seemed just at that point of balance where the night could go either way. Alan clearly had decided it would go downhill.

"So you were a hotshit fed, is that the story?" Alan demanded. He was the type of blond who should not try to grow a mustache. Becker felt an urge to pluck it off his face.

"Tee talks too much."

"Tee? Who's Tee? I heard this from my mother."

"Who's your mother?"

"Mrs. Tolan. That help?"

"Not much. Should it?"

Cindi was leaning back in her chair, looking slightly amused. Becker decided she was perfectly content to let them butt heads.

Alan said, "She said you wouldn't remember her. She knew you from school."

Becker instantly reappraised Alan's age. The man had to be much younger than he looked.

Cindi laughed, without explanation.

"You're some kind of a legend among the older generation," said Alan. "What was it, you blew a lot of people away or something?"

"Cindi tells me you tried a new face today."

"No, the same one. He didn't even shave," said Cindi.

"It's not as if you were a war hero, though, is it? These were civilians you were killing, right?"

A middle-aged man in a tweed jacket approached the salesman's table. They shook hands, the man in tweed sat down, and the salesman turned the literature so his companion could read it. Seven o'clock and the man was still working. Selling was not an easy life, Becker thought. Not that that was any excuse for the man's hobby—whatever it was—but still not an easy life.

"Let it go, Alan," Cindi said. "He doesn't want to talk about it."

"That was then, though, right? You were this kind of super fed and now you're what? Nothing?"

"Now I'm nothing. You've got it."

"Alan," said Cindi. "Go away."

"Listen," said Alan. He gripped her elbow possessively and she twisted it away.

"Go on." She did not raise her voice but spoke as if she expected to be obeyed.

To Becker's relief, Alan went. He had been afraid of a scene developing that would have drawn the salesman's attention to him. He was also gratified to see that whatever bond Alan had with Cindi, it was loose enough for her to order him off.

"Kind of an asshole, isn't he?" Becker said as Alan made his way toward the bar. "I thought he was going to take me to the parking lot and bump antlers."

"He's just being protective of me," said Cindi.

"Why? Are you in danger?"

Cindi grinned. "Mom made us promise to take care of each other."

Becker winced. "Ouch."

"No harm done. He can be an asshole."

"He's your younger brother, I hope."

"Three years older."

"See you around."

She laughed. Becker liked the sound of it. She always seemed genuinely amused when she laughed, and as if she were more than prepared to stay in that mood.

"My mother was a high school teacher," she said. "Not a classmate. She taught typing."

"Oh. Mrs. *Tolan*. One of my favorites."

"You didn't have her. I'm thirty-one. You're forty-two. Does that help?"

"It clears up the arithmetic, anyway," said Becker.
"Terrible thing, arithmetic."

"It's only numbers," she said.

WHEN the man in the tweed jacket rose to exit, Becker
left. He wanted to go out the door first so that the
salesman would not look back and notice him. Only
a professional ever considered the possibility of being
tailed from the front.

"Stick around," said Becker to Cindi. "I have some
things to take care of, but I'll be back."

"Or I could meet you somewhere," she said.

"Or you could meet me," he said. "Where?"

There was nothing flirtatious about her manner as
she wrote out her address on a napkin. She seemed
more amused than anything else, as if she knew a joke
that Becker did not. He would have to come see her
to learn the punch line.

Becker went to the parking lot, sat in his car, and
waited. Before long, the salesman came out, got in his
car, and drove straight home to a neighborhood like
many others in the Clamden area and the adjoining
towns where one-family houses were perched close to
the sidewalk and children filled the narrow yards. The
only thing remarkable about this particular block was
the salesman's presence there: a single man in a neighborhood where families predominated.

Becker watched for several minutes but saw no
lights come on. The house remained in total darkness
long after the salesman had stepped inside.

Becker drove to a phone booth and called the salesman's home phone. When the man answered on the
third ring, Becker replaced the phone on the hook

and drove back to the house. The car was there, the man was there, but still not a single light had been turned on.

Sitting in the silence of his car, watching the darkened house, Becker tried to empty himself of both thought and feeling. He did not want to impose anything on the situation—there was time enough for that later. Right now he wanted to shut off his rational mind and simply react with the senses of the beast. Was there something in the house to be feared? What lurked beneath the salesman's respectable public pose?

Becker had done this before: At other times, in other places, he had relied on his instincts when the facts presented an inconclusive picture. He needed to be close enough to sense the subject's feelings; this kind of work could not be done at a desk. He looked for mannerisms, expressions, gestures, the tic of the nervous man or—Becker's own bête noire and specialty—the dead calm of the monster who took the shape of an average man but who lived to kill. Sometimes he gained that special empathy without any real effort. It was almost as if his guard's impulses sought him out. Afterwards, he could not say how it manifested itself beyond a feeling, a tingling on the back of the neck, a stirring in the bowels, a silent but overpowering sense of immediate danger.

In this case, Becker was still not sure. Either he hadn't gotten close enough or the man was not on the stalk and thus not sending out signals. They went through quiescent phases: Becker knew all about that. Their lusts and needs could be slaked for a time and they themselves forgot the awful reality of their appe-

tite and its consequences. It was the on/off nature of
their behavior that made them so very hard to find
and identify, because when they were off, they were
exactly what they pretended to be—indeed, wanted to
be: average, normal, harmless men. A sated lion was
dangerous to no one, and the species that was its prey
could stroll in front of it unmolested.

At such times the only evidence of their bloody
habits was in the refuse of their lairs. Becker decided
with reluctance that he might have to go into the
house, and as soon as he realized that, he felt the
familiar excitement building, deep and visceral, and
he knew that it came not from the salesman but from
himself.

He was grateful that Cindi was already at home,
waiting for him. He did not trust himself to be alone.

PULLING on her jeans, Cindi heard his car pull into
the driveway. She had not expected him so soon and
she was still wet from the shower. Her climbing outfit
lay on the bed where she had tossed it. Throwing the
outfit into the back of the closet, closing the closet
door, tugging the comforter up on the bed, Cindi told
herself to relax. No time for makeup, no time for
perfume or lotion. Jeans and a T-shirt and a half-
assed shower would have to do; she was fairly certain
he wouldn't mind. He did not seem like the type to
need a geisha girl.

She forced herself to slow down, to walk to the
door, to ignore the chaos and litter in the living room.
This was how she lived, take it or leave it. Her heart
was pounding as if she were halfway up the rockface
without a next move, but she determined to play this

just the way she would play the rock. Feign a virtue though you have it not, as her grandmother used to say. Act composed no matter what your stomach says. It fools almost everyone else and sometimes even yourself.

Now Becker, on the other hand, always *was* composed. Never mind faking it. Even hanging upside down, his head swinging against granite, the man had been in control. She marveled at his calm. He spoke about emotions, he admitted to fear—they had had a lengthy discussion about it after their first climb together—he claimed that he was as nervous and fearful as anyone, but she didn't believe him. The very fact that he would admit to it seemed to deny its existence. She knew Alan was afraid half the time; she could smell it on him, but he would have died before owning up to it. But then she knew Alan inside out. Bluffers and showoffs were not hard to know. Becker, she suspected, would take a great deal more knowing.

Now he was smiling at her, sitting on the sofa, brushing aside the old newspaper and putting the dried Cup o'Noodles container on the coffee table as if he didn't even notice them. Cindi fought the urge to pace and sat beside him, dropping the newspaper onto the floor behind the sofa.

"Should I offer you something to drink?" she said.

Becker put a finger to her throat where some water from the shower remained. He held the finger in front of her; a single droplet shivered on his skin.

I am not in this man's league, she thought.

"You came a little sooner than I expected," she said.

"I was eager."

She smiled, suppressing a nervous giggle. If he touched her, she was afraid she would scream. If he didn't touch her, she knew she would.

"More than eager," he continued. "I needed to come."

"I wouldn't have guessed that," said Cindi. "You don't seem like a man who lets his needs dictate to him."

"You know what spelunkers are? People who crawl into caves for fun. The deeper, the tighter, the more inaccessible the better. I've heard of spelunkers who lived in the city who had no access to caves—they explored the city sewer system instead. They needed that feeling, being underground, whatever it is, badly enough to crawl around in the city sewer."

Cindi nodded, waiting for the point, then wondering if that was the point: making her wait.

"And there are other people, I don't know what the name for them is, who will crawl into a cave with a drowsy bear and stick a thermometer in its rectum to measure its sleeping temperature."

"That would be a biologist," she said.

"That's not what I mean by biologist. It's not the hibernating habits of the bear they're after. It's the sense of crawling into a place knowing something's waiting for you there."

"Why do they do it?"

"Some people just like to crawl into small, dark places. Spelunkers of the soul. Maybe they do it because it's dangerous, or because it scares them, or because they can do their mischief there, or maybe just to be alone where no one can see what they're doing. Does it matter?"

"Why do you ask?"

"If you thought a bad man was sitting in the dark in a pitch-black house, would you go into the house?"

"Mr. Becker, you're beginning to scare the shit out of me."

"Would you even entertain the idea of going in?"

"It depends what you mean by a 'bad' man. If he was the right kind of bad, I might even invite him over to my place."

The droplet of water was still on Becker's finger. As he lifted his finger it shook and sparkled like a diamond. He put the drop on his tongue, but casually, as if he had forgotten where he got it and placed no symbolism on it. As if it were an hors d'oeuvre, Cindi thought, and maybe it is.

But he still had not touched her.

"What else do you do that you shouldn't?" he asked.

"I gamble some."

"Are you gambling now?"

She studied him for a moment. She did not think he was flirting; he seemed to have something deeper on his mind.

"Men are pretty thin on the ground around here," she said. "I take some chances."

"You can't have any trouble finding men."

"A good man is hard to find. Not an original thought but sadly true. Also, I'm thirty-one, remember."

"I'm not a good man."

"The available material thins out real fast after thirty. By this stage the question is no longer are you single, but why are you single."

"How did you get this far without getting married?"

"I didn't. Jerry played polo. Not with his own horses, of course. Other people's horses, other people's homes, other people's money."

"Other people's wives?"

"Is it that obvious? Their wives, their sisters, their daughters, their maids. The only good thing about being cheated on that much is that when you find out, you realize it's not because of you. If he'd had one big affair, maybe I would have whipped myself around, maybe I would have thought it was my fault, I didn't give him what he needed, that kind of victim-think. But when he views the whole world as parted thighs, you realize the man has a problem with his vision. Not to mention his hormones."

"It lasted what, three years? Four?"

"You're no fun."

"You finally caught him when he was sleeping with your best friend."

"His brother's wife. And it went a full five years."

"I'm not a good man."

"I heard you the first time," Cindi said.

Then a silence that Cindi thought would never end. He just stared at her with those milk-chocolate eyes. Normally she could see the humor in them and the sharp intelligence, but now she had no idea what went on behind them. They did not frighten her, but there was no comfort in them at the moment, either.

When he finally moved, it surprised both of them. She was sitting next to him with her legs drawn under her, her shoes on the floor where she had slipped them off. He took her bare foot in his hand and pressed his thumb gently into her sole. Cindi could not suppress the gasp of pleasure.

Becker spent ten minutes on each foot, holding her somewhere between tickling and massage, a pleasure that was just bearable but so intense. When he worked a finger between the toes, Cindi opened her mouth and let her head fall back and gave up.

When he drew her jeans off, he caressed her legs, running the smooth warmth of his palms along the calves, up the thighs. There was nothing professional or practiced about it; it was not a massage. It was touching for its own sake, and he seemed to feel as good doing it as she did receiving it.

They spoke some, but for long stretches the only sound was Cindi's moaning when he found a new spot or another way of touching her. She could not believe the warmth and feel of his hands.

It took two hours, the first half just touching, the second half lovemaking that seemed like just an extension of the first. Becker was as slow and patient throughout as he had been at the beginning. It was the process that intrigued him. After all, he knew the destination.

Afterwards, Becker continued to embrace her, cradling her in his arms until he knew she was asleep. He was grateful she had not felt the need for comment or witty talk. They simply held on to each other, sustaining the connection that had begun hours ago until she slipped into slumber. Even then Becker continued to hold her, grateful for the comfort she gave him, hopeful that she had not seen the desperation with which he had clung to her. He gripped her until dawn and when she rolled away in her sleep, he moved with her and put his arms around her again. Only when the sun was up did he feel his need ebb away. Like a vampire, he thought. Retreat with the sun. Only then was he sure he would not go to the darkened house and crawl into the cave.

CHAPTER 7

PULLING into the parking lot, Dyce took the only available spot and turned off the lights of his Toyota. Because the bar was popular and crowded, he left the motor running; his ignition had been erratic of late and he did not want to risk not getting the spot he needed because he couldn't move immediately when the opening came.

The red station wagon was parked behind him and to the side, but he could watch it by turning his rearview mirror. The wagon was just on the edge of the pool of light shed by the parking lot's one lamppost. Not fully lighted, but not completely dark, either. Dyce would have preferred it darker, but it would serve.

The door to the bar opened and several people came out, accompanied by a gust of music and loud voices. A couple, arms around each other, moved toward the red wagon. The woman was laughing at something the man said, and he had his arm around her waist as if afraid she might bolt. Dyce slid down on the seat and watched in the mirror as they paused behind the car on the left of the wagon. The man slipped both arms around her and tugged her into him. They stood, pressed together at the waist, leaning back with their trunks so they could look at each other as they talked. She pointed in one direction, he in the other and she laughed again. Deciding which car to take, Dyce thought.

The man whispered something into her ear and she pulled her head back even farther to look at him, startled by his suggestion. He pulled her to him again, and for a moment they leaned against the back of the wagon itself. Behind them Dyce could see the shadows of the man's landscaping tools, hafts and handles sticking up like a dead, stunted forest.

Finally the couple moved to the car on the right of the station wagon and drove off together, the woman behind the wheel. She was talking as they swung directly past Dyce's car and for a moment she reminded him of Helen. That inability to do anything in silence. Dyce wondered if the man next to her bothered to listen to her, either. It wasn't conversation. There was no exchange of views and ideas; it was noise, generated from a fear of what she might hear if she were quiet.

There was an opening next to the wagon now, but it was on the wrong side and in the full glare of the light. Dyce could not take a chance, so he settled in to wait and let himself think of Helen. It was now just past nine o'clock. She would call him around eleven before she went to bed to say goodnight. She had already called him at six to discuss her day. She had inquired about his activities as well, but Dyce didn't have those kinds of days. Things did not happen to him as they did to her. He met no strangers, he encountered no minidramas in the shopping aisles, no shoplifters tried to run away with steaks under their shirts in his world. Dyce did his work, ate his lunch, was overlooked by his superior. There was a beauty and a comfort in the numbers, of course; an elegance in the predictions formed from raw data, as simple but complex as the patterns of the ocean's waves— but he had long since given up trying to explain it all to Helen. She did not understand and after a half-hearted attempt, did not even try. Dyce kept it to himself, another private pleasure.

He did not know what to do about Helen. She was smothering him, that much was clear, but how he might stop it was as murky as the shadows in the back of the station wagon. They had had one fight, a silly squabble about nothing at all as far as Dyce could remember. At the time, he had even suspected she started it just to get a rise out of him. Dyce was not accustomed to fighting and did not understand there were rules. At first he took her petulance as some sort of game, but eventually it dawned on him that she was accusing him of not being jealous. Somewhere in her ramblings she had told him about another man who made a pass at her at work, and Dyce had not responded with the fury she hoped for. In truth, he had not even been listening and the incident was lost on him, although it would not have occurred to him to be angry even if he knew the details. What she did during the day was her business, as far as he was concerned, just as what he did when he was alone was entirely his concern.

The argument had grown and swirled about Dyce as he watched in bafflement, wondering how she could wring so many variations of woe out of the same theme without Dyce contributing anything. Finally she had begun to cry, and it was then that Dyce realized how hard it would be to stop seeing her. When she wept, she touched him and Dyce would do whatever he could to ease her pain.

He comforted her as best he could even though he wasn't sure what ailed her, and to his amazement he heard himself apologizing. When he admitted his guilt in the matter, her spirits improved immensely. She forgave him and kissed him. The crisis was past, although she continued to pout occasionally about his alleged lack of attention.

He knew she would cry if he told her he didn't want to see her anymore, or even not so often. He was afraid, in fact, that she would do much worse than cry. She had told him more than once that she would kill herself if he ever left her, and Dyce believed she was capable of it. In a way, the notion of being that important to her was rather flattering, although something of a responsibility. Dyce did not want to be the cause of anyone's death, or even their unhappiness.

POURING him a third white wine spritzer, the bartender considered what he was going to have to do with Eric Brandauer. Ginny had already complained twice. The first time, while giving him Eric's order, she had simply said, "What a prick."

He liked that about Ginny; she was a no-nonsense person. Older women made better waitresses. They didn't look so hot, maybe, and nobody tipped them big just because they were cute, but they got the orders straight and they knew a prick when they saw one. Ginny had two kids in high school and a husband who drank it up as fast as Ginny could pay for it, so she didn't have any illusions that waitressing in a place like this was a stepping-stone to somewhere else. This was it.

The second time she said, "Harold," using his proper name, which was what he preferred, not Harry, which he hated and the younger women insisted on. "Harold, you're going to have to shut that prick off."

"Eric?"

"The asshole." Eric was slouched in his chair, his left leg stretched out so it nearly tripped anyone who passed, his right leg draped over another chair. "The one sitting in two chairs."

"Eric Brandauer," said the bartender. "This is only his third drink."

"His third *here,*" said Ginny. "He's been swilling something stronger than white wine spritzers somewhere. Either that or he's just naturally as pleasant as a molting snake."

"Eric's always had a mean streak," said the bartender, hoping he wouldn't be called on to do anything. Eric not only had a reputation for being mean, he was awfully quick to use his hands. And his boots. Tending bar was not the same as bouncing, and Harold had no desire to take up a new career at this stage in his life.

"If he gives you any more trouble, let me know."

"I'm letting you know *now,* Harold. If he touches me again, or even looks at me like that, I'm through serving him."

"I'll keep an eye on him," said Harold, placing the wine spritzer on Ginny's serving tray. She added a napkin.

"I'll keep an eye on him," she said. "You keep an eye on me."

The bartender watched as Ginny put the wine on the table in front of Brandauer. He affected a hat, not quite a Stetson, but something semi-Western, that he wore very low over his eyes. Thinks he's Clint Eastwood, Harold thought. Or no, someone else, some other actor. Who was it he looked like, not quite a star but well known, a character actor, foreign. Harold remembered him from a Redford movie where he had been a CIA killer, and then he had seen him only the other night in an old movie where he played Jesus or John the Baptist with a Swedish accent. The planes of his face were the same, the high cheekbones, the long, slightly horsey look. Funny that the Swedish women all looked good enough to eat, and the men had these thin, long faces with the big jaws. Max Von Sydow, that was it. He looked like a young Max Von Sydow. Or like Max Von Sydow pretending he was Billy the Kid.

Knowing just how far to push it and when to stop, Eric Brandauer let Ginny pass without incident, but his eyes under the brim of the hat looked at her with the kind of malevolent interest that Harold usually saw on television only when the punk was about to do something rash. Harold prayed that Eric would save

his rashness for the parking lot where Harold
wouldn't have to know about it until he read the
police report in the local paper.

DYCE waited until ten thirty. His favorite classical
music station was playing one of the Beethoven sym-
phonies—he wasn't certain which, he had missed the
announcement, but he thought it was the Seventh—
and he was nearly as comfortable in the car as he
would have been at home. When the driver of the car
to the left of the station wagon finally left, Dyce
pulled into the spot, carefully leaving just enough
room so that he could open the passenger door all the
way. He would wait for fifteen more minutes.

At a quarter of eleven, Dyce gave up and drove
home. He wanted to be there before Helen called.
Explaining his absence at that hour of the night
would simply take too much effort. Seeing that he
wasn't jealous, Helen had decided to assume the role
herself and she acted as if Dyce were this wild-eyed
ladies man who couldn't be trusted out of her sight
for so much as an hour. He didn't know what he was
going to do about her.

As he pulled out of the parking lot, he saw Brandauer come out of the bar. For a moment he considered pulling back in, taking a chance, improvising
something. He could take the man and still get home
in time for the call—but then the man was in his own
car and it was too late.

Dyce drove home to await Helen's call. There
would be other nights, as many as he needed, and
things would be all the better for waiting.

•   •   •

"IT's happening again," said Becker.

"What's happening again?"

Becker was at the window once more, peering out through the Levolors.

"You need a new view."

"You could try looking at me for a change," Gold said.

"You think that's an improvement?"

"What's happening again?" But Becker had clearly changed his mind about discussing it, whatever it was.

"I was with this girl, this woman, the other night. We were talking about crawling into lions' dens . . . She has thirty-seven freckles on her cheeks and across her nose."

Gold drew a vertical line down the margin of his notepad. He did not note the number thirty-seven. He was not a numerologist.

"Bearding the lion in his den. Where did that expression come from? Lions don't have dens. They live on the open savannah. The expression conjures up this picture of the lion in a cave with the bones of all its prey scattered all over. They don't live that way. Bears don't have bones in their caves, either. They don't eat and they don't excrete all winter long and the rest of the year they live outdoors. Why do we think of the beast hunkered down with the bones of its victims around it, waiting for us?"

"Is that what we think?"

"Carnivores don't live that way. At least not mammals."

"Dragons do," said Gold. "As long as we're dealing in symbols. Dragons are surrounded by skeletons and treasure."

"Did you have to go to school for this?" Becker asked.

"Why do you have such contempt for the psychiatric profession?"

"I see you don't take it personally. Why is that?"

"What happened after you shot Sal?"

"He died."

Gold began the serpentine line that intersected the vertical one.

"Sorry," said Becker. "I've got to learn to let the easy ones pass . . . I had a reaction."

"That's normal."

"I saw a shrink for a while."

"There's no record of that in your file."

"I didn't use a Bureau man."

"You went to a private therapist for help? Why is that?"

Becker was silent.

"Why not use a Bureau therapist? . . . They're experienced in that kind of trauma . . . They're free."

"Spiders do that," said Becker. "They keep the corpses around them. They paralyze them, suck them dry, and leave the husks hanging there."

"What were you afraid the Bureau would find out about you?"

Becker returned to the window. Gold started to fill in the parabolas on his notepad.

"I don't respect you because you can't really fix anything. You can drug the violent ones or put diapers on the bed wetters or talk the mild cases into giving up out of boredom, but when they're really wrong, you can't make them right, can you?"

"What do you mean by really wrong?"

"Some people are wired differently. They like to hear people scream or make them bleed or make them die—and you can't do anything about those people, can you? You can't change the wiring."

"What do you think should be done with such people?"

Becker laughed. "Oh, doctor," he said. "Now really."

ERIC Brandauer felt like killing somebody. The bitch whose lawn he had just finished mowing had paid him with her nose cocked as if he smelled. He wanted to thrust her head into his crotch; he'd show her what smelled.

The damned weed trimmer had given out on him and he'd had to use a hand sickle that he hadn't needed in years, and he took a gouge out of his knee while working around the bitch's flower beds. She told him he should have it looked at but didn't offer to look at it herself, didn't come up with iodine or bandages or invite him in. He had a good mind to put on his ski mask and come back there after dark to pork the shit out of the bitch and smash things up a little. Just to teach her a lesson. Just for old times' sake. He wondered if he could even find the ski mask anymore.

Christ, he felt mean. At least the old life had offered some compensations; he'd been able to let off some steam now and then. Profit wasn't the only motive for burglarizing the bastards. It did the rich fucks good to have someone trash their houses. Let them know how the other half lives in shit most of the time. It taught the men humility to feel their teeth crack. All those perfect teeth, all those smiles they bought from the braces man. Let them go out and buy some more. They could afford it, and it did Eric a world of good to paste one of them now and then. Sometimes he would wrap his hands before going out on a job, just like a boxer. A good stiff wrapping with elastic, a pair of work gloves to protect the skin, a roll of nickels clenched in the fist—oh, it did their humility a lot of good. Plus it made Eric feel terrific. He was doing a service for them and himself. Now that was his definition of a good deed.

Landscaping, on the other hand, not only didn't offer any compensations but it didn't pay worth a damn, either. Here it was Wednesday and he was out of money again. He would have to go to the bank again if he wanted to eat or drink tonight. And he sure as hell wanted to drink. The only good thing to be said about landscaping was that it kept him out of jail. At least he no longer had the cops rousting him out of bed every time somebody lost a VCR. In Shereford there just weren't any junkies to blame, so all the thefts got pinned on him. And Eric hadn't stuck a needle in his vein in his whole life. He *hated* needles. Stick one in himself? He'd have to be crazy. He'd smoked some, popped a pill or two, but nothing serious. Nothing to put him in the same league with the hard-core addicts you had to live with in jail. He didn't belong there. He might not belong in landscaping, either, but he belonged in jail even less. Which was the only good reason he could think of not to grab the first son of a bitch who looked at him cross-eyed and do a number on his head.

On a whim, Eric decided not to go to his regular

bank but to drive to Guileford instead. It would be dark when he got there and there was an automatic teller machine at the train station where the light didn't work. Or could be made not to work. He wasn't promising himself anything, but if everything worked out just right, if some wimp decided to get some money and it was between trains and no one was around and Eric felt froggish, well, he just might jump. He didn't *have* to, that was the beauty of it. He would just see how things worked out and how he felt. And if nobody showed, he could always just draw twenty-five out of his own account and go back to Shereford and hassle the waitress at the Peacock Lounge. "Lounge," he liked that, the place was a saloon—hassle the middle-aged bitch until the bartender was forced to try to make him stop. Now that he wanted to see. That might be even better than whipping ass at the Guileford station. He didn't see how he could lose.

Not once in the thirty-five-minute drive to Guileford did Eric look in his rearview mirror. He hadn't done anything yet; there was no reason to worry about cops who, as far as he knew, hadn't gotten around to reading minds yet, and so there was no reason to notice the gray Toyota that followed him all the way to the train station.

ERIC drove past the automatic teller machine and turned the corner, parking in front of the office supplies company so that his car was not visible from the machine. That way all he had to do was saunter around the corner, get in the wagon and drive off without worrying whether the victim—if there was a victim, he still had not decided—could identify his car.

A woman was walking away from the teller machine as Eric rounded the corner, putting money in her purse. Let her go, too far away. Eric was not about to chase anybody down the street. What he wanted was a nice, plump businessman, somebody with enough meat that he wouldn't fall at the first blow. Eric liked it when they stood there, not quite believing him, not even having enough sense to cover up so that he could get in three or four good licks before they really understood what was happening. And men would not scream right away, the way women did. Most of them had just enough ego to convince themselves it was some sort of contest—see how many punches you can take before you fall. None of them took very many.

The street was empty when the woman left. A car drove slowly by and Eric waited until it turned the corner before crossing to the machine. He decided to give it a few minutes. It was a whim, after all, not a job. He could take it or leave it.

The machine was mounted on a concrete wall that had been installed just to house it. On the other side of the wall, between the concrete and the depot, was a small recess, out of sight and in the dark. Stepping into the recess, Eric glanced at his watch before pulling his work gloves up snugly on either hand. Ten minutes, that's all he would wait, ten minutes, fifteen tops. He was already getting thirsty.

THE situation was ideal. Dyce pulled his car into the spot just to the left of the station wagon. He leaned across the seat and opened the passenger door to check. It opened and came to a rest against the driver's door on the wagon. Dyce had removed the fuses for the overhead light and the door buzzer so he could work in silence and darkness. Perfect.

Removing the plastic cap from the syringe needle, Dyce pressed the plunger until a drop of liquid oozed from the tip. Perfect. He kept the syringe in his right hand, resting out of sight on the seat.

The station was empty. There were no trains due for another forty-five minutes. There was a light on in the office supply shop, but not enough to illuminate Dyce clearly to any passerby. Anyone passing in a car would see only the back of his head, if they even bothered to look. Perfect. ――

Dyce put Schubert's Trout Quintet on the tape machine and turned the volume down low. He turned slightly to one side so he could see Eric coming around the corner and have at least thirty seconds to go into action. Perfect.

He settled in to wait. Schubert was beautiful. Dyce felt certain he and the composer would have understood one another.

FIFTEEN minutes stretched to twenty, and Eric finally said fuck it. The place was a goddamned morgue. Two cars had passed and that was it. He didn't need this shit, and he was thirsty and hungry and had to piss. He started to pee in the recess, then decided to do it on the teller machine, just to let them all know what he thought of them. He peed a long time and actually managed to hit the face of the machine. Then, walking back to his car, he remembered that he had forgotten to withdraw some money for himself. He had to stand in his own puddle, cursing, to get the twenty-five dollars.

When he reached his wagon he was madder than when he cut his knee with the sickle, and now here was some dumb son of a bitch with his car door open so Eric couldn't get into his truck. The whole street to park on and he had to squeeze next to his wagon.

"I'm sorry," Dyce said, leaning across the seat to the passenger door. "Sir? Sir? I'm sorry, but I can't get my car started. Could you help me, please?"

Eric leaned down and looked at the man stretched across the seat and decided against ripping the jerk's door off and handing it to him. Heaven works in marvelous ways its wonders to perform, he thought.

"Happy to help," said Eric. He smiled broadly.

"Oh, thank you, that's most kind. If you could just hold this flap up so I could get to the wire."

"What flap is that?" Eric tugged his work gloves on tightly. He hadn't had time to wrap his knuckles, but this would do very nicely.

"Under the dashboard here. You can reach it if you get in the car. It won't take a minute."

The moron thought he could hot-wire this kind of car. Wasn't even looking in the right place.

"I'll be happy to help you out," said Eric.

He slid into the passenger seat and hit Dyce in the face. Dyce lifted his right arm, but Eric pinned it against the seat with his left forearm and hit him hard twice more in the face. He grabbed Dyce's lapels and jerked him forward, then butted him with his forehead. The second time broke Dyce's nose.

It was not until he was getting out of the car that

Eric noticed the syringe. Sliding across the seat, he knocked it to the floor. Eric looked at it curiously.

"What the fuck is this?" he demanded.

Dyce could not speak for the blood in his mouth.

"What the fuck *is* this! What are you up to? The fuck you doing?"

He shook Dyce, slapped him once, not paying much attention to the man, still studying the syringe. Dyce shook his head in denial, tried to spit, dribbled blood onto Eric's glove.

"This for *me?*" Then Eric got really mad.

CHAPTER 8

"I T was good of you to see me so late."

"Not at all. This is a service industry. I'm just glad we could work out a mutual time and place."

The salesman was still in coat and tie at this time of night, no doubt maintaining his image for a customer.

"Come in, come in," said the salesman. He backed away from the door, arm extended like a courtier. "Wife's not feeling well? I'm sorry about that."

"Sorry to impose, but I just thought it was better to meet at your home while she was under the weather. You know how women are."

"Tell me about it," he said, nodding knowingly. "Although I've never had the pleasure to be married myself."

"A lot of us who've been married haven't had the pleasure, either."

The salesman laughed, with a quick, easy flash of teeth and a throaty chuckle, useful for most occasions.

"I would have come by your office but I get off work so late."

"No, listen, no problem. A man needs insurance, I'm eager to accommodate."

The windows were covered with heavy drapes. The porch light had been on because a customer was coming, but the living room and entrance hall were illuminated only by a glow emanating from the adjoining room.

"Not all my customers are so eager to see me. But you may have heard the jokes about insurance salesmen."

"I've heard a few."

"I'll bet you have. Well, listen, it comes with the job. At least I'm not a proctologist, you know?"

"I hear you."

"Let's go in the den; my stuff's in there. Insurance is actually the best investment you'll ever make and, let's face it, we're all going to need it someday."

"Absolutely."

The den was dim and shadowed. What little light came from the single sixty-watt bulb seemed to be soaked up and swallowed by the wood of the bookshelves, the dark leather of the furniture. The lamp itself was turned so that the light hit the wall first and reflected back weakly.

"Have a seat, Mr. Beck," he said, waving at a recliner in front of the coffee table that was already spread with insurance materials.

"Becker."

"Becker, I'm sorry. I misheard you on the phone."

Becker leaned forward and looked into the man's eyes.

"I hope this is bright enough for you, Mr. Becker. I can turn on another light if you want, but I keep it this way for myself. Too much hurts my eyes. Photophobic. Most people find it restful once they get used to it, but just say the word."

"It's fine, Mr. Scott."

"Call me Doug," said the salesman. "Everyone does."

The man held Becker's gaze, grinning slightly, forthright, foursquare, bored already with the sound of his own voice but also eager to make the sale.

"Tell me, Mr. Becker, what can I do you for?"

I've made a mistake, thought Becker. This is not my man.

"Do you sell for just one company, or what?"

"Let me tell you how that works," said Scott. "I can sell you anything. You tell me what you need, we can find the company that suits you best, and I can sell you that policy . . . but I have found that for a combination of price and service, generally the best around is Connecticut Surety and Life. Most people don't consider service when buying insurance, but, Mr. Becker, let me tell you, this is a service industry."

Becker leaned back against the leather upholstery and heard the slow hiss of air escaping his weight. He felt the tension ebb from his body and his mind, but whether the sensation was one of relief or disappointment, he could not say.

TEE was in a jovial mood. He patted the passenger seat before Becker got in.

"So." Grinning widely.

"You look like you just ate something you shouldn't," said Becker. "And it agreed with you."

"Me? You're the one's been dining out, as I hear it."

Tee pulled away from the curb in the police cruiser and swung around the circular drive that terminated Becker's dead-end road.

"Janie tells me she served you and Cindi breakfast the other day," said Tee.

"Janie speaks to you now?"

"She's thawing out. I got her on my back burner."

"A little crowded there, isn't it?"

"Changing the subject? Tell me about it."

"Cindi had eggs, I had a bagel, as I recall it. It was a grand breakfast. Janie was a charming hostess."

"I hate gentlemen," said Tee. "Fortunately, I don't meet that many. Did she mention me at all?"

"Couldn't get her to shut up about you. It seems she has a thing for married cops."

"Chief cop."

"Even better. She's contemplating a life of crime just to keep you calling on her."

"Well, if I have to, I have to. I'm a martyr to the cause."

"Ever take the wife dancing anymore, Tee?"

"I tried to call you last night. You weren't home. You weren't with Cindi, either. Unless she lied to me."

"She didn't lie to you; she doesn't respect you enough. I was buying insurance."

"Always a good investment. And?"

"We all make mistakes."

"And then sometimes we get lucky," said Tee.

He pulled onto I-86, lights flashing to clear a space for himself.

"She called me last night, but you weren't around," he continued. "Maybe just as well because we got more information since then."

"Who called, just so we each have the same conversation."

"Woman named Helen Brasque, a checkout girl at the Grand Union on Ridge Road. Seems her boyfriend is missing. Hello, says I, that has a familiar ring, tell me about it. The guy's named Roger Dyce. He lives in Clamden, over in the old military dependent area."

"Where's that?"

"Over by the Sherman access road; we just passed it. You don't know about that neighborhood? I forgot you've been away twenty years. We used to have a missile here. Did you know that? I want to say Minuteman, but that's not it. Anyway, they had a missile stored in a silo just off the electric company's area. Less than half a mile from the high school, if you can believe it. You never been past there? The chain-link fence is still up; that's about all that's left. The things went out of style or something. I'm not sure what it is; they took it away at least fifteen years ago. Anyway, the point is, the military built some housing to put up the troops who operated it, serviced it, polished it, whatever you do with a missile. About twenty houses, all told, quick-fix jobs, built them on slabs, no cellars, a regular little neighborhood tucked away there pretty much by itself. Not bad houses, actually, a family neighborhood, lots of kids—what the hell am I talking about?"

"I've been trying to figure it out."

"Oh, this guy, Dyce, who was reported missing by his girlfriend. Or she says she's his girlfriend, but I'm not too sure of that. She doesn't seem to know much about him except where he lives. Their relationship is fairly recent and—uh—more physical than cerebral, well, you would know about that, wouldn't you."

"Christ."

"A man your age. A pretty young thing like Cindi. And I'm younger than you are. Where's the justice?"

"They say if you tie a string real tight around your dick, after three days it will just fall off. Your problems would be over."

"That's horseshit, John. I've got a string around my dick all the time, just to remind me to use it."

Tee turned off on the third exit and turned onto the Post Road, following the signs to the hospital.

"This Helen was frantic—she's the frantic type to begin with. Seems her boyfriend has been missing for four days. With a girl like her, I would figure he's just not answering his phone—except for what's going on around here. So I did the usual checking around and I found him. In the hospital here in Essex."

"So he's not missing."

"No, but here's the thing. I think maybe he nearly was. The EMS people found him at the train station in Guileford. He'd been mugged. Well, a good deal worse, really. Someone really did a number on his head, slammed the door on his arm, I mean kicked the shit out of him before they took his money. That's rare enough around here. This isn't the city, after all, although, by the train station, maybe some of the boys from Hartford are looking for new territory, but

I don't think so. The thing is, we found a syringe on the ground next to the car. On the passenger side."

"A drug buy that went wrong."

"I thought that, but we checked the substance in the syringe and it wasn't drugs. I mean recreational drugs. It was something called PMBL, a barbiturate, kind of out of fashion according to the drug people. You heard of it?"

"No, but that's not my line. What does it do?"

"It's an anesthetic. Actually a combination hypnotic and anesthetic, what they told me. It puts you out and keeps you out."

"You have a theory?"

"What kind of chief would I be without a theory?"

"A Clamden chief. Turn at the light for the hospital."

"I know where to turn. What if this guy Dyce went to the ATM at the station and our snatcher is waiting there. The snatcher follows Dyce to his car, tries to stick him with the needle and drag him off, but Dyce resists, fights. The snatcher loses his cool, beats the shit out of Dyce, and drops his anesthetic in the struggle so he can't cope with Dyce anyway."

"Why the ATM? Why not getting off the train?"

"The timing's bad; too many witnesses if a train just came in. Besides, we think the snatcher was hanging around the money machine. Somebody pissed all over it."

Becker laughed.

"It's not funny, John. You forget, this isn't the city. Commuters use the train here, not derelicts, not kids. People don't just drop by to take a quick pee at the train station. It's the kind of thing anybody who's weird enough to snatch people would do."

"Or any boy under the age of eighteen, or any half-drunk adult male, or any *dog,* for Christ's sake."

"If this was a dog, you'd better call Ripley's. The guy hit the computer keys."

"We're not looking for a public pisser, Tee. More likely he pees sitting down and wipes his dick afterwards."

"How do you figure?"

"This is not a man who calls attention to himself. If he did, he wouldn't have lasted this long."

Tee parked the cruiser in front of the hospital's main entrance, sliding in front of a departing Volkswagen that had just let off a pregnant woman. The driver of the Volkswagen honked angrily. Tee stepped toward the Volkswagen, whose driver thought better of it and pulled around, shaking his fist.

"I read that people in New York have stopped doing that," Becker said. "They don't even yell at cab drivers for fear they'll get shot."

"We need a little more random violence around here," said Tee. "Teach these people respect for the police."

The woman at the information desk seemed annoyed that they wanted a patient's room number. She made them wait until she finished her phone call.

"I asked this Helen if she knew Dyce's mother's maiden name. She didn't, of course. Then I ran the usual checks on him myself, just to see if he had a record, and so forth."

The woman at the desk finally checked her computer and told them the room number.

"They're volunteers." Tee led the way to the elevators. "You can't fire them, so they act like that. Ever notice how many of them are fat? Why is that?"

"Got a theory for that, too?"

"A man's got to speculate, John. That's why you've got an imagination . . . The MVD came up with something interesting. Mr. Dyce is a safe driver—but he hasn't always been Mr. Dyce. Four years ago he changed his name."

Tee punched the floor button, suddenly silent.

"And I say, 'From what?' " said Becker.

"Dysen. Scandahoovian, wouldn't you say? I may not know anything about the urinary habits of the perpetrator, but I do believe Mr. Dyce/Dysen was a very lucky man who just missed being victim number nine."

Becker did not respond.

As they approached Dyce's hospital room, Tee said, "I knew a kid in high school who wiped his dick. Weird. Shook, then wiped. Barely had any to mention in the first place."

"Good thing you were there to notice," said Becker.

"Guy became a golf pro, not a player, a teacher. How's that for symbolism? Spend your life with this four-foot-long club swinging between your legs. A classic case of compensation."

Becker said, "Unlike our good selves."

"Well, exactly," said Tee.

DYCE dreamed his father was alive again and looking for him. He could hear his angry voice calling "Ro*ger,*" with the snarl of an animal in the tone, and his footsteps, those dreaded, off-beat clumps of a cripple, were coming toward him. The young Dyce was hiding under the bed, whimpering with fear. He did not know what he had done to bring on the wrath this time, but then he seldom knew. Sometimes he thought his very existence enraged his father, as if his presence, perhaps even his very life, were a mistake that the man was trying to eradicate with his belt and his fists.

In the dream Dyce could see directly through the covers that hung to the floor and concealed him. His father entered the bedroom and Dyce could see him yanking the belt from his pants, see him breathing heavily through his mouth as he always did when he had been drinking. His eyes were red from the alcohol, the capillaries burst from within, and a crust of something had formed in the corners of his mouth. His hair fell diagonally across his forehead, limp and straight and dirty blond.

"Ro*ger,*" he said again, this time softer, cajoling. "Come on out, Ro*ger*. Come here son, Daddy's not mad."

Dyce was not fooled by the change in tone. He had been caught that way before. There was neither sweetness nor forgiveness in the man when he had been drinking, only malice and cunning. Much as Dyce wanted to believe it was the voice of love calling, he dared not move.

He looked straight up through the bed and saw the man's eyes cloud and the lids quiver, then close. His father sat heavily on the bed above Dyce, then fell back, inert, dropped finally by the liquor. When his father's rage was gone, he collapsed inward, as if the anger was the only thing to keep him going.

Hovering over his father while somehow still under the bed, Dyce saw the drool form and dribble from his mouth. He heard the breath making its tortured way through his nose, still miraculously straight and fine despite the brawls, the spills, and the accidents of a drunkard's life.

With his heart racing in his chest, the young Dyce crawled out from under the bed and knelt with his face next to his father's. Peace had come upon the man and he looked so young lying there. If only he could always be this way, Dyce thought. He leaned forward to kiss his father and the man's eyes flew open and he bared his teeth as he said, "Roger." His hand grasped Dyce's shoulder and the young boy felt his bowels release in fear.

Dyce awoke with a start to find Helen at his side, shaking his shoulder and whispering his name. Two men stood behind her, watching him.

"These men are from the police, dear," she said. Helen never called him *dear*.

"I'm not," said Becker.

"Oh," said Helen. "I thought you were."

"I'm Chief Terhune of the Clamden Police," said Tee. "Mr. Becker has some experience in these matters, and he's here to help out."

"What matters?" asked Dyce. He rolled his tongue to moisten his dry mouth.

"The mugging," said Helen.

"I talked to the police," said Dyce.

"That's true," said Helen, looking to Tee for explanation.

"That would be the Guileford Police. You were attacked in Guileford. I'm from Clamden."

"I don't understand."

"They're here to *help*," said Helen. Dyce wished she would shut up and leave. He needed to concentrate and not worry about what stupid thing she might say next. There was something not right here, something to be careful of.

Dyce looked at the one who was so quick to point out that he wasn't with the police.

"We think this might be part of a pattern," said Tee.

The quiet man was studying Dyce. Not staring at him precisely, but sizing him up. His eyes would wander off sometimes, taking in the rest of the room, and then return suddenly, as if to catch him off guard. Dyce averted his own eyes. There was something dangerous there. It was almost as if the man were reading Dyce's mind. Or as if Dyce were reading his.

The policeman was asking about the incident. Dyce had almost convinced himself by now that it was a mugging.

"Were you able to get a look at the man who hit you?" Tee asked.

"No," said Helen.

"You must have some idea what he looks like—white, black? Dark, fair?"

"It all happened so fast," said Helen.

"Ma'am," said Tee. "It might work better if Mr. Dyce tells us himself."

Dyce lay back and closed his eyes. "Helen, could you get me some water, please?"

"Of course, dear," she said. Again, the dear. She

was showing the police her position, he supposed. Giving herself the right to be here.

"I'm sorry," Dyce said. "They've got me all drugged up. It's a little hard to concentrate."

"Sure," said Tee. "Take your time. But any kind of description would help."

Dyce kept his eyes closed and forced himself to visualize the incident as he had described it to the police before. He could feel the quiet man's eyes on him, but there was nothing to see now. Let him look, thought Dyce. He can't see into my skull, and if he does, he'll see only what I'm thinking. But remember him, he's dangerous.

"It was very fast," Dyce said. "He knocked on the window on the passenger's side of my car. I opened the door and he reached in and hit me in the face. I was stunned. He hit me again, several times, but I didn't really seem to feel it after that first time. I had my eyes closed, of course—he was hitting me in the face. He was white, though, I think I know that much. And he was wearing leather. Yes, I can see that much now. When he rapped on the window his sleeve was leather."

"What kind of leather? Suede?"

"Black, heavy, like a motorcycle jacket."

"Did you see the syringe, Mr. Dyce?" It was the other voice, the dangerous man named Becker.

Dyce paused and rubbed his throat. The other police had not mentioned the syringe, had not seen a connection.

"Helen," he said. "I'm so dry."

Helen put the glass of water in his hand and helped him to sit upright as he sipped on the straw. Dyce allowed himself a look at Becker. The man smiled as their eyes met, politely. He seemed almost bored. So quickly? Dyce wondered. Could he lose interest that fast, or is he hiding something? He slipped back onto the pillows and closed his eyes again.

"No one said anything about a syringe," said Dyce. "What do you mean?"

Tee said, "Did you see one?"

"No."

"Do you use drugs, Mr. Dyce?" Becker's voice again.

"Heavens, no!" said Helen. "I can swear to that."

There was a weight on the bed. Someone was sitting next to him.

"I don't usually even take aspirin. That's why I'm reacting so much to the pain killers here, I guess."

There was a hand on his arm; he knew it wasn't Helen's. Dyce opened his eyes and saw Becker sitting on the bed next to him. His face was close and he was smiling, not just politely this time, but with warmth. Dyce recognized the smile. It was the same one his father would use sometimes to make him calm down before he hit him.

I know you, Dyce thought. I'm ready for you.

"What's your mother's maiden name?" Becker asked.

Dyce smiled back.

"I never knew her."

The two looked at each other for a long time. Their smiles widened as if they were sharing a private joke. Tee thought it was creepy.

"What's your mother's name?" Dyce asked finally.

"Larssen," Becker said.

When Becker rose from the bed, it seemed to Tee that he released Dyce's arm with reluctance.

"WHAT the hell was that all about?" Tee asked as they waited for the elevator to take them to the lobby. "I thought you two were going to kiss or something, staring at each other like that. What the hell were you doing?"

"Communicating."

"That what they teach you in the Bureau?"

"I'm not in the Bureau now, I'm not a cop, either. I can use whatever methods I need to."

"You trying to seduce him or something? What kind of witness do you think he'll make if the defense attorney learns you questioned him by making goo-goo eyes at him?"

"I was just establishing trust," said Becker, laughing. "Letting him know I was on his side. Besides, I don't think you're going to be able to use him as a witness."

"No, he doesn't seem to know much, does he? He doesn't even fit the pattern."

Becker looked at Tee from under his brows.

"Were we in the same room?" he asked.

CHAPTER 9

THE weed trimmer came back from the shop, thirty-five-dollar repair fee, and conked out after three minutes. Removing his work gloves, Eric tinkered ineffectually with the machine for a moment, but his right hand was so swollen it was as useless as the weed trimmer. He had dislocated a knuckle, or possibly broken it, while pounding the jerk-off's face, and the area around the joint was now an ugly purple. The son of a bitch, thought Eric. A syringe full of drugs, and he was going to stick *me*. I should have killed him. What kind of perverted thing was that? To lure someone into your car and then shoot them up with drugs? Jesus. He didn't want to get high by himself, or what? The world was full of weirdos and getting stranger every day, but the jerk-off had chosen the wrong guy when he decided to play with Eric. I should have killed him.

Eric squatted in the backyard, the weed trimmer dead and useless at his feet, while the lady of the

house and her teenage daughter played at their pool.
The daughter was a little young yet, not much meat
on her and not enough breasts that she needed to
walk around all the time with her arms crossed over
her chest the way she did. She did it even when she
was alone; he knew, because he had watched from
secrecy. Did she think she had such prizes there that
people were staring at her all the time? A bitch who
was modest even when alone? Not the kind of person
Eric had in mind. The mother, on the other hand, was
more his idea of something to do. A little too much
flesh, maybe, but it was arranged properly, and she
wasn't ashamed of it. The bitch liked to flaunt it: Eric
had noticed the way she talked to him, one hip cocked
to the side like that, arms akimbo with just a trace of
toughness, like she was daring him. That little terry
cloth jacket always open and not hiding much. She
was asking for it, no doubt about that. Husband was
this dried-up executive type, big wallet, no balls. Eric
could tell just from the types of jobs the man didn't do
around the yard, things he left to Eric because he
didn't know how to hook up a hose.

The daughter saw Eric staring and pulled on her
robe as she said something to her mother. The mother
was reclining in one of those come-and-hop-me chairs
and she turned her head to look at Eric, then spoke to
her daughter and laughed.

Go over there and slap her across the chops, not
too hard, just enough to get her attention, then pull
off those bikini briefs and show her something her
dried-up husband hadn't used in years except to yank
on. That would stop her laughing; start her moaning
for more, which he had, more than she could handle.

Do it in front of the kid, let her see how it's done, then give her a turn while her mother watched. He'd get her over her modesty quick enough.

And he'd do it, too, if it weren't for his goddamned hand. With his right hand like this he couldn't screw the cat, much less two haughty rich bitches. That jerk-off with the needle was really beginning to cost him.

Should have killed him. Should have just kept pounding since he'd screwed up the hand anyway. A missed opportunity, just like the one with the women by the pool.

But what really burned him was the real chance he'd missed with the guy. Roger Dyce, that was his name on the driver's license. Name, address, photo— although he didn't look much like it now that Eric had rearranged his nose. Why hadn't he taken his keys? Because it had been too long and Eric was out of practice. Because he was having too much fun? No, bullshit. The truth was he panicked. He hated needles, they scared the shit out of him, and he had just overreacted. Christ, he was in the guy's pockets anyway. He took the fifty-five dollars, he might as well have taken his keys. Drive over to his address in Clamden while the creep was still lying on his front seat, clean out the place. The son of a bitch deserved it.

The women walked into the house. He loved the way the mother's ass jiggled. Not too taut, had some cellulite, but not bad, either. She still had a few good years left in her. The daughter didn't jiggle at all. Juiceless, that was her problem.

They'd be going upstairs now, into their separate

Spanish-tiled bathrooms, take a shower, get the chlorine off. Christ, he could slip up there, do them each in the shower, the other'd never know. Give them both some juice.

He tossed the weed trimmer into the back of the wagon and felt a twinge of pain in his hand. That jerk-off. He didn't need a key. Call the hospital tonight, ask about the condition of Mr. Dyce. If he was still there, zip over to his house and clean it out. And if he'd checked out, well, that might be even better. Ask him what he planned to do with that syringe before kicking the shit out of him again. Maybe stick a needle in the bastard's ass—or maybe that's what he wanted. Either way. Make the call right after this job. No, now. Make the call now, here, use the phone.

Eric rang the front doorbell. Hell yes, do the wife in the kitchen while calling the hospital. The girl hears the moaning, starts downstairs, wrapped in a towel, Eric does her on the carpeted stairs. Make the call, fuck the bitches, then clean out Dyce's house. That would be a pretty good day for a one-handed man.

HELEN had taken the keys from his trousers while he slept. She wasn't sure he would have given them if she'd asked; he seemed very secretive about his house. Helen had not been there since that first time, not that she wanted to go particularly; she didn't like the place, but still it was odd that he'd never suggested it. But then Roger was odd in a number of ways.

She had brought all the cleaning equipment she owned with her except a vacuum cleaner. Everyone had a vacuum cleaner, whether they used it or not.

Other than that, she had come prepared; there was no telling what supplies he had on hand.

The smell was so bad she could detect it on the porch. Why had she not noticed it from outside that first night? She was surprised the neighbors didn't complain. Inside, it was even stronger.

A mouse had died under her refrigerator once and Helen had not been able to move the appliance to get the corpse. This house smelled like that, sickeningly sweet. Disgusting. No one should live like this. In a way, Helen thought, it reflected badly on her. She was not doing much of a job domesticating Roger if she allowed him to come home to this kind of thing.

She put her cleaning supplies in the kitchen and looked around. It was as good a place to start as any. Oddly, the sink was clean. The huge restaurant pot that she had last seen covered with cooking scum was scrubbed spotless.

She turned on the tap and the drain belched once, emitting a blast of putrid air before the water backed up and filled the sink. Helen had dealt with clogged drains before; one learned things living alone or else paid an arm and a leg to every repairman in town. She found his tools in a bottom drawer, including a plumber's wrench. Surprisingly, the wrench was not rusted shut. It had been oiled and maintained, and the bolt on the sink trap had marks on it as if it had been opened frequently. He must have had trouble with the sink before. It surprised her that Dyce had dealt with the problem himself, however. He didn't seem the handy type.

Helen turned off the water, placed her bucket under the trap to catch the spill, and began to work. Dyce had stored nothing in the cabinet under the sink except a heavy cleaver. Helen removed the cleaver and felt the flooring give spongily. She tapped it. It sounded hollow. There was obviously a space under the bottom of the cabinet. The kind of place a small animal could get trapped and die, perhaps.

The linoleum covering came off in one piece. The flooring seemed solid, but when Helen touched it, the boards moved slightly, as if they were not nailed down. One of them had a recess where a knot had been. Helen put her finger in the recess and pulled up on the board. It came out easily and underneath it she saw the first bone.

STEADYING himself against the bed, Dyce drew on his pants and slipped his feet into his shoes. He stuck the socks into his pocket to be put on when he had more time to do it one-handed. His blood on the shirt had dried to an orange-brown. He buttoned it as quickly as he could, the unpracticed left hand fumbling and skipping some buttons. Shrugging on the jacket, Dyce stood and waited for the dizziness to pass.

A nurse glanced at him on the way down in the elevator, took in his bloody shirt, his stubbled cheeks with four-days' growth of beard, his bruised face, and thought whatever she thought but said nothing. Dyce could not worry what people thought of him now; he could only get away from this place as quickly as he could manage.

A security guard glanced at him and then away; the fat lady behind the information counter didn't even deign to look at him.

The sun surprised him and left him blinking. For

some reason he had thought it was raining and cold. There were no keys in his pocket, no money in his wallet, and he didn't know where his car was. It didn't matter; he couldn't use the car in any event since they would soon be looking for it. As soon as the calm one, Becker, began to think. There was only one reason to ask his mother's maiden name. They knew something: They had sensed his pattern, perhaps not all, but some, and some was too much. In days, or minutes, Becker would be back. Or perhaps not. Perhaps they weren't going to put it together, perhaps Dyce was safe, but it was a chance he couldn't take.

He turned and walked away from the hospital, going down a long hill to the main road below. He didn't know where he was going, but then neither did anyone else. The main thing now was not his destination, but his escape.

"YOU'LL replace this?" Tee asked, detaching the police seal from the front door. "I mean, of course you will. How long you going to be?"

Becker had never seen him so agitated.

"I'm not going to hurt anything, you know that."

"I know that."

"If you don't feel comfortable about this, Tee, you don't have to let me in."

"I know you won't hurt anything. I know you know what you're doing. I know when the state boys show up in the morning, they'll never know I let you in." He paused. "Right?"

"Tee, the house is sealed by the order of the state police, but it's in your jurisdiction, too. You can break the seal if you want to."

"I know this." Tee remembered Captain Drooden, who had slapped the seal on the door only hours before. Hard-nosed bastard. Threatened to remove Tee's gonads if he so much as breathed on the house before Drooden's full forensic team could arrive from a murder scene in Greenwich.

"But you still have a problem with this?"

"I don't have a problem with it. Quit saying I have a problem. I'm not afraid of Drooden, if that's what you're thinking."

"I wasn't thinking that. You fear no man."

"It's those damned brown uniforms the states wear. Makes them act mean. Drooden doesn't scare me . . . What are you going to do in there?"

"Nothing."

Tee eased the door open but stayed on the porch. He had no desire to go in again; once had been enough. Even now the house was virtually untouched since he and Becker had responded to Helen's panicked telephone call. Just what damage she had done, he couldn't say, but he and Becker had touched nothing, even though Becker had prowled like a dog on the scent. The smell of the place was too much for Tee, but Becker had not been bothered and had squatted beneath the sink for fifteen minutes, just staring at the skeletons as if he expected them to stir and speak at any moment. When Becker finally rose, it was to tell Tee to call the forensic people in Hartford, taking the case immediately out of Tee's hands. Tee had not even considered arguing.

"If you're not going to do anything, why go in? Or is that a silly question?"

"After Drooden's men get finished, the place will

be sterile. They will have lifted all the fingerprints and sought out all the hairs and fibers, and that's great, they need to do that, but there won't be any *spirit* left. A crime scene feels like a museum after the forensic snails get through with it. It looks the same, but it's a re-creation."

"*Spirit?* Jesus Christ, what are you talking about? You're not into that kind of thing, are you, John? You're not talking psychic shit here, are you?"

"I'd prefer not to be talking at all, Tee, if you'd just step aside and then get out of here."

"Okay, you're the expert—but what are you going to do?"

"Just sit there for a couple hours."

Tee shivered. "A couple hours?"

"More or less. It's nothing mystical, Tee. It's just an exercise in imagination, but it helps me to be on the scene."

"What are you imagining?"

"We don't have to do it. Drooden will probably find out all you need with his microscopes and tweezers."

"Okay, okay. Go. Enjoy yourself." Tee stood aside as Becker switched on his flashlight and stepped into the house. "And you'll remember to put the seal back?"

"Go find Dyce."

"We're looking. He's walking wounded, how far can he get? We'll have him in no time."

But Becker was already concentrating on the house. He didn't seem to notice as Tee closed the door.

Thank God, Tee thought, that I'm just a Clamden

cop. An exercise in imagination? Sitting in a house for a couple hours where we've found God knows how many bodies under the floorboards? What kind of imaginings could that inspire?

Tee looked up and down the block as he walked to his car. Lights were on, televisions playing. The excitement of the afternoon with cop cars and flashing sirens was over, and the good citizens had already stopped thinking about the commotion in the Dyce house, whatever it was. He wished he could do the same. Traffic violations and the occasional breaking and entering were all he aspired to. He didn't want any part of communing with goddamned spirits, and the spirit of a mass murderer at that.

Thinking of Dyce lying on his hospital bed twelve hours ago, Tee still could not picture the innocuous, defeated little guy killing anyone, much less eight or more. It had almost seemed to Tee that they were after the wrong man, that the skeletons had been inherited or had crawled in there on their own to die. Any explanation seemed more likely than thinking it was the man with his face punched in on the hospital bed, the guy with the girlfriend who thought she was his mother—crime in Clamden had not prepared him for this. Everybody cheated a little bit, everybody drove too fast and lied on his taxes, and the sons of the privileged were just as apt to get into drugs as the children of the poor—maybe more likely depending on the price of the drug—but when it came to actual *crime,* in Tee's experience that was still done by criminals. The kind who started out bad and stayed bad, and they were easy to recognize. Tee knew who they were and where they worked and where they lived. He wanted his monsters to wear horns and spit fire and felt no remorse about not recognizing the man for what he was, but Becker was furious, berating himself during the whole frantic search of the hospital and the neighborhood and the town.

"I *knew*," Becker had said. "I knew but I didn't say so."

"Knew? How could you know?"

"I knew."

"Did you have any proof? Did you even know his crime? What could you have done even if you did know?"

"I knew, and he realized it, and I didn't act and he did, and that's why he's gone."

"We'll get him," Tee had said, wondering how. This was not an isolated town in Nebraska. He could not throw up roadblocks and seal off the city. Given a car and a fifteen minute head start, Dyce could be in any of three adjoining towns or a few miles from Hartford. Given an hour of lead time, he could have vanished as completely as a rat down a sewer. As far as they knew, he had had at least three hours' head start.

The mess would only get worse, he realized. Tomorrow there would be the press and the Hartford television people, and after that probably the national television as well. Mass murder was good for a minute or two on the evening news. But the actual police-work was already in other hands. Drooden was a bastard and deserved all the trouble he could get. Wherever Dyce was now, Tee was glad it was no longer Clamden.

As he drove off he realized that he could see no
light coming from the Dyce house.

STANDING in the bedroom, Becker played the beam of
the flashlight slowly over the heavy oaken furniture,
the thick drapes, the simple, almost monastic bed.
Clearly not a room where Dyce spent any time; there
were no comforts, no books by the bedside, no television. Becker held the beam on the silver-backed hair
brushes atop the dresser. Old, like the furniture. None
of it was rare enough to be antique; it was just old.
Either he had a taste for it, or he had inherited it, but
in either case, it was a link to the past. And what
keeps you in the past, Becker wondered. What happened then? Or is still happening? Whatever it was, it
would not be in the bedroom.

Becker went cursorily through the kitchen again,
but that was simply a workplace, a room in which to
butcher and boil and bury, a place of grisly utility, but
not the place to catch the spirit of the man.

Dyce dwelt in the living room: Becker could feel it.
It was the only room in the house where anyone had
actually lived. Was it the room in which they had
died? Like all the windows, these were covered and
sealed with soundproofing material. That meant there
was noise, that meant they were alive when he
brought them here. Anesthetic in the syringe, the syringe in the car. So he drugged them when he took
them, brought them into the house drugged. The garage was at the back of the house. Becker returned to
the kitchen and looked into the backyard, playing the
light on the garage and then the driveway. If he
parked in the right spot, it was no more than four

steps to the kitchen door. The house shielded him from the view of the neighbors on one side, the car on the other. Four steps in the dark of night and into the house with a body, drugged and helpless, into the house, into the kitchen. If he killed them then, while they were still unconscious, there was no need for soundproofing.

But he wouldn't do it then, Becker knew. There was no sense to it. More to the point, there was no joy to it. Drug them in the car, drag them into the house, and chop them up? Why? What would he get out of it? He was getting something out of it. He'd killed many times; he wouldn't take the risk if it offered him nothing in return.

So he kept them alive for a while. That's why he needed the soundproofing, that's why there was anesthetic in the syringe and not poison.

Becker returned to the living room. And he kept them alive in here. Where he lived.

Switching on the lights for a moment, squinting against the sudden brightness, Becker studied the room. There was only one place where Dyce would have sat. He turned off the lights and sat in the over-stuffed chair. It was easier in the dark.

He had told Tee that it was an exercise in imagination, but that was not how Becker thought of it. He had to study his quarry's lair the way an anthropologist would study the cave paintings of early man. Those paintings went a long way toward explaining the man behind them. Becker hoped to learn as much about Dyce by sitting in his living room and absorbing his presence. He sat in the dark in Dyce's chair and breathed the air Dyce had breathed. He let the

atmosphere sink in. He unleashed his mind and set it
free to wander the room, the house, to seek out Dyce
and inhabit his soul.

Sitting in the chair, looking straight ahead, Becker
turned on the flashlight. It did not hit the screen of the
television set. Why would he align the chair so he
could not watch the television without twisting his
head—unless he didn't watch TV. When he sat here
and relished what he did, dreamed what ghoulish fantasies he needed, what did he look at? The light fell on
nothing but space from the chair clear across the
room to the wall.

With the lights on, Becker studied the room again.
A sawhorse sat under the bookshelf. People used sawhorses for table legs sometimes, but one sawhorse in
a room full of heavy oaken furniture? Why a piece of
makeshift furniture in a room already overcrowded,
and why just one? What good was one sawhorse?
Probing with the beam of his flashlight, Becker
looked for another support. The sofa arm was the
only other surface of the same height in the room.

There were marks on the floor where the sawhorse
had been placed with weight on it. The scratches in
the wood were small and only in one spot. Becker put
the sawhorse on the scratches and judged the distance
to the sofa arm. At eye level, on the wall above the
sawhorse, was a mark on the wallpaper, a black horizontal line where something had dug into the wallpaper, the deep, regular mark of something heavy
pressing over a period of time. The only structure in
the room of the right length was the bookshelf. Removing the books, Becker placed the bottom shelf
against the mark on the wall. The shelf leaned against

the wall at an angle of about ten degrees off the vertical, not quite upright, but close. Easing the shelf hori-
zontally, it fit neatly across the sawhorse and the arm
of the sofa.

Becker returned to the chair and looked straight
away, then directed the beam the way his gaze fell.
The beam hit the bookshelf about a foot away from
the sofa arm. Where the head would be, thought
Becker. He saw Dyce sitting in his chair, watching his
victims. You sat and watched them. How long? How
did they die? Were you watching the death? Is that
what you needed? You liked to see them die, didn't
you? And in what manner did they die? Slowly? Of
course, slowly. That's why you brought them home.
To watch them die. The forensic people would figure
out how. Probably. But how was not what really
interested Becker. He wanted to know why. He
wanted to know what Dyce saw when he saw men
dying slowly. He wanted to know what pleasure it
gave him, what he thought it meant. There was a wire
crossed there, some permanent glitch in the circuitry
of the brain. Becker wanted—no, not wanted.
Needed. Becker needed to see with Dyce's eyes and
feel with Dyce's heart—without becoming Dyce. Tee
had called it psychic shit. A psychologist might call it
extreme empathy. Becker did not have a name for it;
he just did it. He did not think of it as anything
mystical. It was more a matter of reasoning by analogy. I line my faulty wiring up next to his, Becker
thought, and see if any current jumps the gap.

ERIC circled the house twice, sizing it up. There were
no lights on as he had anticipated. He had called the

hospital from the rich bitch's house and had been told
that Mr. Dyce was not scheduled for release for several days. Eric had pretended he was Dyce's brother,
just in case they had trouble giving out the information; he was prepared to be snooty with them if they
got that way with him, but there had been no problem. Mr. Dyce, they had said, was still under observa-
tion.

So Eric had come to observe Mr. Dyce's house for
him. He parked his station wagon three blocks away,
up against the curb, nowhere near a hydrant, as safe
and legal as could be. No reason for anyone to notice
his car, no excuse for any cruising cop to ticket it. In
his early days he had been caught that way when
some property-owning asshole had thought Eric's car
was blocking his driveway and called a cop. Eric had
come tiptoeing back to the car with a pillowcase full
of goodies on his back and a portable TV under his
arm just as the police cruiser pulled up to write out a
citation.

But that was years ago and time had taught Eric the
virtues of caution. He walked the route once, just
strolling casually, to check out the presence of any
dogs. There was a barker about a block from the car,
but he could easily avoid it on the way back. The
block that held Dyce's house was as clean of canines
as a cat convention.

He went in the back way, cutting across a neighbor's garden and through a hedge. The night had
turned cloudy and the entrance through the hedge
took a little finding, but then Eric was in Dyce's backyard and it was clear sailing. The garage shielded him
on one side. Eric pulled on the ski mask and his work

gloves. The only skin showing was around his eyes. In
this light, if anyone was going to see him, they'd have
to be pointing a flashlight right at him.

There was some kind of material blocking the window—what was this, some kind of anti-burglar device? God, the shit people tried. They just didn't have
a clue, but it gave easily enough on the second shove
and Eric hoisted himself into a bedroom. Hauling
himself in put strain on the knuckle and made him
wince.

The room was a disappointment. No jewels, no
cash, no hidden stash, not even a lousy TV. The guy
lived like a monk except for the fancy hairbrushes
that might be worth something. He stripped a pillowcase from the bed and tossed the hairbrushes in it.
Some wardrobe; the guy must have bought his suits at
Sears. Nothing in the pockets, nothing in the linings,
no little secrets tucked in the toes of the shoes.

Eric paused at the bedroom door as he became
aware for the first time of the odor. Christ, it smelled
like a backed-up septic tank. He began to question
the wisdom of his decision. Why was he putting his
balls on the line to rip off the house of some geek who
didn't own anything and lived with a dead cat? He
hadn't fucked the bitch and her daughter, either. He
could still imagine taking the kid on the stairs. He
should have, get her dripping from the shower, yank
off the towel, make her happy. It got him hot just
thinking about it now. Why didn't he? All these goddamned lost opportunities. Instead, he was in this
dingy house, afraid to breathe the air, with two old-
fashioned hairbrushes in the bag. For a moment he
contemplated giving it up and going home; it wasn't

worth the chance. Then he realized, hell, he was here
anyway, what did he have to lose? Might as well see
what's on the other side of the bedroom door.

Eric was down before he knew it. There was a knee
on his chest, another knee on his balls, *on* his balls, for
Christ's sake, and pushing down, a hand on his throat
and something very hard pressing against his forehead. Both arms were underneath him and felt as if
they might break but that was the least of his problems. It was the hard thing pressing into his head that
scared him the most. He knew what that was, he had
felt that before.

The ski mask had moved in the fall and Eric's eyes
were covered.

"Don't shoot," he croaked. "Please, God, don't
shoot."

All he could hear was breathing, and most of it was
his. If the guy pushed the gun any harder it would go
right through the bone.

"I'm not fighting. You got me, don't shoot. Christ,
don't shoot."

The hand at his throat ripped away the ski mask
and Eric blinked and blinked as the beam of a flashlight hit him in the eyes.

The man moved the pistol and pressed it just above
the bridge of Eric's nose. He could smell the oil on the
metal.

Eric tried to speak but could only whimper. The
look on the man's face scared him worse than the .38.

He's going to do it, Eric thought. He's going to pull
that trigger. He wants to.

The man's eyes were wide, his lips pulled back from
his teeth. The gun began to dance a little tattoo on the

bone of Eric's forehead, as if the man had the shakes.

Eric squeezed his eyes shut. Please, God, he thought. Don't let this son of a bitch kill me just because he can't control his muscles. But he knew that wouldn't be the reason. The man was fighting with himself *not* to do it. The desire in his eyes was terrifying. He wants to blow me away, Eric thought. He doesn't even know me and he wants to put a bullet in my skull.

CHAPTER 10

ERIC had never seen so many cops in one room before. He felt like he'd been put in a closet with the entire police academy, and every one of them wanted a piece of him. They were breathing in his face, pushing and shoving each other just to get a look at him. Even his first FBI man was here, or maybe his second, depending on what the guy who nearly killed him was. The cops acted as if he was FBI, too, but the other FBI man, the one who had identified himself as Hatcher and flashed his badge as if he were showing off, acted funny toward him. Eric couldn't quite figure out the relationship, but it sure wasn't a happy one.

Eric knew Tee, of course, even kind of liked him in a strange way. Tee had kicked him around a few times during questioning, nothing serious, nothing Eric couldn't take and laugh at. There was never anything mean about Tee's rough stuff. Eric understood that it was just to get his attention—or out of frustration when Eric was too smart for him.

Drooden, the brown-shirted state cop who acted as if he was in charge of the questioning, was a different kind of rough. One look at him and Eric could tell the bastard was just plain mean. He looked like the kind of man who believed law enforcement was a sacred duty and he was one of God's chosen enforcers. The kind of man who would lecture you as he beat you and then add a few more licks, not because he wanted to, but because God would like it that way.

The FBI man, Hatcher, looked like a bookkeeper: constipated, prissy almost. One good dump might make him a new man, Eric thought. But he was certainly proud of that badge.

There were a couple of other brownshirts in the room and one or two local cops around the edges, but the only one who bothered Eric was the one who had played a drumroll on his forehead with the .38 barrel. They called him Becker and he stood in the back of the room, watching everything but saving his best looks for Eric.

"Deep shit, boy, you understand?" It was Drooden. "You are in it up to your eyeballs and sinking."

"For what? B and E? I've been clean for five years, I'll probably get probation."

"I thought you gave it up," said Tee.

Eric shrugged and grinned at Tee. "You give up chasing pussy, Tee?"

Oh, they hated it when he grinned at them. Drooden looked like he was going to swallow his tongue.

"Homicide, boy, murder one!" Drooden was leaning in close, spitting in Eric's face as he talked. "There are eight skeletons in that house. You seem awfully familiar with the place. How do we know you didn't put them there?"

"Is that what this is all about? You guys don't just love me for my own sake?"

"We're fond of you, Eric." Tee grinned back at him. "Don't underestimate your appeal. Captain Drooden is so happy to see you he might decide to keep you."

"Like a pet, you mean?"

"Like a love slave. Chain you down and have his wicked way with you for about five years."

"Ooooeee, sounds fun."

"Terhune," said Drooden, aghast. He looked at Tee as if the chief had just cut a horrible fart.

The cops were getting in each other's way, which was all to the good, as Eric saw it. Let them fight with each other; they might have less juice when they concentrated on him.

"What made you choose that particular house tonight, Mr. Brandauer?" This was Hatcher, the fed.

"What house is that?"

"The one you broke into."

"I don't think we agreed I broke into any house. I was talking theoretically about B and E."

"Why that particular house, Mr. Brandauer?"

Becker was moving forward from the back of the room. Eric watched him closely. He stopped just behind Hatcher and studied Eric from over Hatcher's shoulder.

"No reason. I didn't see any lights. Did my man really do eight people?"

"We think you may have done eight people, wise guy." Drooden was back in his face.

"If we really think that, then we better call my lawyer, shouldn't we?"

"How did he get you into the car?" Becker asked.

This time Hatcher was annoyed by the interference, but he didn't say anything.

"What car? Who?" Eric looked to Tee; he didn't want to face Becker directly. "How many people do I have to talk to all at once? I'd like to help you people. I understand you got a problem here. You know me, Tee. I've never been a hard ass. Get me clean and I plead and fair's fair. Now all of a sudden I got to face the nation here. Give me someone to talk to, you know what I mean, we can work something out."

"Oh, now he's shy," said Drooden.

"It's not really up to you to set the conditions of this interview, Mr. Brandauer," said Hatcher.

"Better get used to gang bangs, Eric." Tee's grin was fading around the edges.

"He's right," said Becker. "Why not let me talk to him in private for ten minutes?"

Eric felt his stomach sink. Becker was the last man in the world he wanted to be alone with. But they were considering it; he saw the glances run from Drooden to Hatcher and back. Tee was not consulted.

"This guy tried to kill me! You can't leave me alone with him! That's not what I meant. He tried to kill me."

Hatcher leaned close to Eric and patted his shoulder. The lesser cops were already drifting out the door.

"You're wrong, Mr. Brandauer. If he had tried to kill you, you would be dead."

"We are taking a coffee break. We'll leave you alone for a few minutes to sit calmly by yourself and consider your story and its consequences, son," said Drooden.

Becker pulled a chair to face Eric. When he sat, their knees touched.

"Tee, this guy's a maniac!"

"What guy?"

"Don't leave me with him."

"We're leaving you alone in a locked room," said Tee.

Hatcher paused by the door.

"Becker."

"I know," said Becker. He didn't look at Hatcher.

"I mean it."

"Take a look at him," said Becker. He lifted Eric's hand. "A pre-existing condition." He pointed at the purplish, swollen knuckle. "Otherwise not a mark on him."

"I want him back that way."

"I said so," said Becker.

Hatcher pulled the door closed behind him. Becker scooted his chair closer so that his legs slipped between Eric's. He continued to hold Eric's hand in his.

"What are you going to do?" said Eric.

"What are *you* going to do?"

Eric tried to retrieve his hand, but Becker held on, gently but firmly.

"You wanted to kill me before, didn't you?"

"How did he get you into the car?"

"I could see the look in your eyes. You wanted to pull the trigger."

"Did you recognize the look?"

"What do you mean?"

"He got you into the car some way. He tried to stick you with the syringe, but you saw it and hit him. You beat him badly. He might have died."

"He didn't. I checked."

"You checked before you came over to rob his house. That was good, that was smart. It's not your fault the guy's got bodies under the floorboards."

"Is that for real?"

"He didn't seem the type, did he?"

Eric shook his head. The man had been a weakling; he'd taken his beating like he deserved it.

"They never do," said Becker.

"Is that why you wanted to kill me? You thought I was him?"

"I knew you weren't him. Did he offer you money? Did he say anything about your mother?"

"My mother?"

"What was your mother's maiden name?"

"What's that got to do with anything?"

"Any reason not to tell me?"

"Margaret."

"Her *last* name."

"Evinrude."

"Did you ever see him before?"

"See who?"

Becker spoke evenly, reasonably. "I'm tired of your horseshit, Eric. Did you know him? Had you ever seen him before? Tell me how he got you into the car."

"Are you trying to get me on some kind of accessory-to-murder rap? Because honest to God, I don't know a thing."

"How did he get you into the car?"

"I never got into any car. I don't know anything about a mugging."

"The mugging's a freebie, Eric. We don't want you for it. He's not going to testify about it. Just tell me."

"Sure, just tell you. How about if I tell my attorney now?"

"You don't need an attorney to talk to me. I'm a private citizen."

"You're not a fed? Why am I talking to you in the first place?"

"You're not. I'm not here. You heard Tee. You're alone in a locked room."

Becker placed his thumb atop Eric's knuckle and slowly squeezed. Eric was not prepared for the pain and gasped. Becker released the pressure but held on to the hand. His voice was still sweet and reasonable.

"Did you ever talk to anybody about insurance, Eric?"

"I suppose so. They call me up. Don't they call everybody?"

"Did you ever meet anybody to talk about it?"

"Ever? Maybe, sometime. I don't know."

"Did you ever see him before you beat him up?" Becker touched the knuckle again and watched Eric's eyes widen.

"Never. Are they going to let you do this to me?"

"Do what, Eric?"

"You're torturing me, man. I'm going to scream brutality to the papers."

"There's not a mark on you—except the one you put there yourself." Becker tapped the knuckle again.

Eric moaned. "You got no idea what that feels like."

"Of course I do. Listen to me, Eric. Nobody wants you here, you're not important in this one. We want him, the guy you mugged, the guy whose house you broke into. We want him very, very badly and we don't have time to waste with you, so just answer the questions and get it over with."

"And cop to all kinds of shit? How do I know what I'm involved in here? I want my lawyer."

"That's what we don't have time for. We can't wait a week to cut a deal before you answer a few simple questions. You are not going to incriminate yourself with me. Do you believe me?"

Becker pressed the knuckle and held it. Eric moaned.

"Do you believe me?"

"I believe you!"

Becker released the knuckle but continued to hold Eric's hand in his.

"How did he get you into the car?"

"He was parked right next to my wagon. He had the passenger door open so I couldn't get past him. He said he needed my help in starting the car without his key. Some bullshit. I don't think he knew how to hot-wire."

"The syringe?"

"He must have had it down on the seat. It fell on

the floor when I dragged him across the seat. I didn't know about it till then."

"You were too busy hitting him."

"Yeah."

"That's the busted knuckle. Ironic, don't you think? You use it on him, I use it on you, it gets you coming and going."

Becker released Eric's hand.

"You did want to kill me in that house, didn't you?"

Becker smiled at him.

"I still do."

THE snails were doing their usual thorough job. After five hours of labor, there was not a square inch of Dyce's house that Drooden's forensic team hadn't scrutinized, dusted, scraped, probed, or photographed. Becker could read their trails everywhere, like the rivulets of slime left behind by garden slugs. As Becker had known it would, the house had given up its ghosts, and they had been replaced by tape measures, grid lines marked with string, smudges of fingerprint powder. The house was no longer a place where a man had dreamed his nightmares and made them come true—it was now an archaeological dig. All that remained undisturbed were the bones.

"I thought it might be helpful for you to see this in situ before we take the bones for analysis," Hatcher said.

Drooden leaned against the refrigerator, watching like a protective parent. He had resented the Bureau involvement from the beginning and was barely able to tolerate Becker's unorthodox presence. A member

of his forensic team stood in the doorway, tapping the
ashes from his cigarette into an evidence bag.

"If he didn't see it last night," said Drooden.

Hatcher ignored the state cop. He had seldom met
one who liked being outranked.

"I was struck by the stones," said Hatcher. He
pointed with the toe of his shoe as Becker squatted
next to the makeshift graveyard. The state police had
removed enough floorboards to reveal all of the skeletons, which lay atop each other like the tossed shafts
of a game of pick-up-sticks. Only the skulls were kept
separate. They were sitting side by side in a row eight
long. Next to each skull, like a hyphen separating it
from its neighbor, was a small stone.

The snails had covered the area with a grid of string
bisected into three-foot squares and then photographed it from several angles so that exact measure-
ments could be reproduced later. A twelve-inch ruler
included in the photos to give perspective still lay
between a pair of thigh bones.

"I assume he kept the skulls separate as some sort
of burial notion. Given the cramped circumstances, it
was probably the best he could do." Hatcher stepped
back and watched Becker.

"You call that a burial?" Drooden asked.

"Well, he didn't just throw the skulls in there with
the rest. What would you call it?"

"You cut somebody up in your bathtub, flush his
hair down the drain, and boil his bones—I doubt that
you care enough about him to give him a burial," said
Drooden.

Becker spoke for the first time. "He cared about
these men very much. They were very important to

him." Becker looked at the forensic man, who was watching his smoke rise to the ceiling.

"They were all men?"

The forensic man nodded. "Pelvic bones look like it. We'll know for sure later."

"He cared enough about them to keep them alive for a while," said Becker. "He might very well care enough to give them the best kind of burial he could manage."

"Kept them alive while he did what to them?"

"Watched them, for one thing."

"How do you know that?" Drooden demanded.

Becker moved a hand toward one of the stones. "May I?"

The forensic man removed a pair of disposable plastic gloves from his pocket and handed them to Becker.

"Wait a minute," said Drooden. He rounded on the forensic man. "Did I say anything could be disturbed yet?"

"No, sir."

"You wait until I do, damn it."

The forensic man was standing at attention in the doorway, trying to figure how to get rid of the cigarette without leaving and without giving Drooden another chance to yell at him.

"What have you found out about him from the neighbors?" Hatcher asked evenly. He moved slightly to screen Becker who was already holding one of the stones between his gloved fingers.

"They liked him," said Drooden. "Nice man, quiet, minded his own business. He distributed fruit cakes at Christmas, attended the annual Fourth of July barbecue one of them gives in his backyard. On Halloween the kids said he usually gave candy and acted like he was scared by every ghost and ballerina that showed up. The first year here he gave them fruit, but apparently someone set him straight and after that it was always candy. The kids think he's fine. The adults don't pretend to know him, but think he's fine, too. Can you imagine Halloween at this house?"

"Did they say anything about his girl?" Becker asked, straightening. He had replaced the stone.

"No one knew about her. If she came here, they never saw her."

Hatcher looked at Becker, who nodded. The two men walked toward the door.

"Finished, are we?" Drooden asked. He turned on the forensic man, who was snuffing out the cigarette between moistened fingers. "Clean it," he said. "And Wilkins . . ."

"Yes, sir."

"You people better find out something we don't already know."

HATCHER walked Becker to his car. Some of the neighbor-children were still gathered on a lawn outside the barricade, making a picnic of watching the police come and go.

"What about the stones? Anything?" Hatcher asked.

"Just gravel, I think. But fresh; it still had a dusting of pumice on it. Either it came right out of the rock crusher or else he got it somewhere before it got rained on and was washed clean. You might check on the local source for gravel, see where they've delivered in the last four years, cross-check that with precipitation reports, find out when and where he might have got it before it got wet."

"Are you kidding?"

"I think the stones were markers. Tombstones. His way of paying his respects. He might come back for more."

"More?"

"You don't think he's through killing people, do you? He's just warming up."

"But he must know we're on to him by now. That's why he walked out of the hospital."

"He's not a criminal, Hatcher. He can't just decide to lie low for a while. He doesn't kill for profit."

"Why does he do it? Do you have any theories yet?"

Becker hesitated.

"Why not ask an alcoholic why he drinks? Because by the time he knows he has a problem, the problem is already most of his life. It would be easier if you find him and we'll ask."

"We'll find him. He's got no credit cards, no money, thanks to our friend Eric. Who's he going to turn to for help? We're covering his girlfriend, the people he worked with. If he has any family, we'll find them, too. We should have him in custody within forty-eight hours."

"Save that for the press release. This guy is not stupid. He only got caught this time because of the girl. He won't make that mistake again."

"What tipped him off that we were on to him?"

"Have you been to his office?"

"The insurance company in Hartford? Not personally. Milch has talked to his employer."

"And?"

"Good worker, low profile, not much snap to him, but he does his work on time and accurately. He was passed up for a promotion recently and they assume there was a natural resentment, but he didn't show much."

"I want to go there. Can you arrange it?"

"You can't stay on this as a civilian. You know that, don't you? Drooden snarls every time you show up as it is. It took me the better part of an hour just to talk him out of arresting you for entering the scene of a police investigation last night."

"So I won't stay on it. How's that?"

"Who are you kidding? You're already ·on it; you've swallowed the hook. You couldn't leave now without ripping out your guts."

"Shall we see?"

"Why else were you in there last night? For your own entertainment?"

"I was helping Tee. Now he's got you."

"I can get you back on temporary assignment. They'd love to have you."

"How about you, Hatcher? Would you love to have me?"

"You're good at it. I can live with you."

"Get me in to see the actuaries at Dyce's insurance company."

"I'll have to go with you unless you take temporary assignment."

Becker watched Drooden exit the house and speak into the radio in his car. The electric crackle of the response could be heard, loud but unintelligible, across the road.

"We'd need a clear understanding," Becker said.

"Name it."

"I'll work on it from this end, but I won't go near him. I don't want to be within miles of him."

"Fine by me."

"I mean it, Hatcher. I will not go down the hole for this one. You'll have to find another ferret."

"*I* didn't send you in after Bahoud. It just happened."

"I'm not going to debate history with you. All I do on this one is think, or I don't have any part of it."

"Agreed. We love you for your mind alone."

"And try to stay away from me as much as you can, too."

"Finding Bahoud was little short of a miracle, I've told you that. I admired your work greatly. Nobody expected you to take him on yourself."

"I was made certain promises then, too."

"We tried to keep them. It just happened."

"Well it won't happen this time. You find another ferret. Because I'll make you a promise, Hatcher. If I have to go down the hole, I'll tie your arms and send you in in front of me."

"Or we could try something novel for one of your cases," Hatcher said. "We could make an actual arrest and bring him back alive to stand trial."

Becker breathed with exaggerated calm and Hatcher feared he had gone too far. Hatcher did not fear most men, but he was afraid of Becker—he had seen him work.

"What have you found out from the girl?" Becker said at last.

"Very little of real use. We went at her nonstop for a couple of hours, but didn't get much. The report's being typed up now. She's a weird one."

"I'm going to see her."

"What do you hope to learn we haven't already got?" That was one of the qualities Hatcher disliked most about the man: He had no respect for the work of others but seemed to have to do everything himself, and in his own way. "She really doesn't know much of anything about him. We will know more about him than she does by tomorrow."

"We'll know more facts," Becker said.

"As opposed to what, guesses?"

"Feelings, intuitions."

"Feelings? She thinks he's a creep."

"She thinks so now. What else could she say after she discovered the bodies? It makes her look like a fool to have had anything to do with him. I want to know what she felt about him then, before, when she was sleeping with him."

"Good God, Becker. You want to know what he was like in bed? Is that it?"

"Something like that."

"You can't learn anything by that. I mean, you can't judge a person by his bedroom skill, if that's what you want to call it."

"You stick to fingerprints and blood samples," Becker said. "We've got all we're going to get out of that. We know who he is already. I need to know why he is."

"We have psychologists to give us a personality profile."

Hatcher hated it when Becker grinned at him; he always felt he was being mocked.

"I supply them with their raw data," Becker said.

Becker put the car in gear and drove away. Hatcher watched him go, knowing how close he had come to losing him. Hatcher hoped he still had the nerves for it.

HELEN knew all about this man before he even spoke to her.

"It's in your eyes," she told Becker. "You have very kind eyes."

"Do I?"

"They're the mirror to your soul, you know."

"Window," said Becker. "The eyes are the window to the soul. I think that's how it goes."

"You know what I'm talking about, then," Helen said. "I knew you would."

"It's not a theory I put much store in," Becker said. "Soulful looks are pretty easy to fake."

"But you're not faking, are you? No. You see. I knew that. As soon as I opened my door and saw you standing there, I knew. I'm very good at that. I can take one look at someone and tell what they're really like. It's just a power I have."

Becker restrained himself from asking her where her power was when she sized up Dyce. It seemed an unnecessary cruelty.

"What else do you see?" he asked. Becker wondered at the lack of information Hatcher had gotten out of Helen. She was primed and ready to talk, indeed he could see she was desperate to do so, the kind of woman who probably collared strangers in her need to unload her feelings. Hatcher would not have the skill or sense to play along with her and let her get there in her own time. She didn't need a list of questions to get her going; all she needed was an ear and a stillness that could pass for compassion.

"Strength," said Helen. "You're strong, aren't you, very strong, but sensitive, too. Women must just love you."

Becker grinned boyishly.

"But you're shy, too, aren't you?" she continued. "I can see that, yes you are, you're shy. Do you know how I know? Because I'm shy, too, although you wouldn't think so to hear me rattling on sometimes."

"Dyce was shy, too, wasn't he?" Becker asked.

"Oh, my, yes. Shy—and private? My goodness. I never knew anything about him, really, not really. Only what I knew by my intuition, you see. He never *told* me anything."

"That must have been very hard for you. You cared for him so much, but he just wouldn't open up."

"Did I say I cared for him so much? We were friends."

"I know you cared for him," said Becker, smiling. "You're not the kind of woman who would sleep with a man she didn't truly care for."

"Well, no, I'm not, I certainly am not, you're right."

"Although sometimes your emotions just get the best of you. I know what that's like."

"Do you?" Helen stopped pacing and sat next to

Becker on the love seat. Her knee touched his thigh as she turned toward him. "I thought you would."

"I'm not made of ice." Becker looked her squarely in the eyes, holding her gaze. "Neither are you."

Helen exhaled quickly, as if she'd been punched. She was melting. She hoped he couldn't see it, but he was so perfect, so much the man she needed right now, someone strong, someone who could understand.

"Sometimes these things are too strong," she said, casting her eyes down. "Sometimes they just overwhelm you."

"And no one's to blame for that," said Becker.

"But I didn't say I slept with Roger."

"You didn't say you didn't," said Becker.

She laughed and wagged a finger at him, allowing her knee to press firmly against his leg. She was being flirtatious, she knew that, perhaps even naughty, but sometimes a woman had to take a chance. He was *so* right for her.

"Oh, I have to watch you," she said. "You're the sneaky kind." She laid her arm on the back of the sofa so that it nearly made contact with his back. She wondered if he noticed. Some men would notice immediately, and others, like Roger, would be oblivious. It was hard to tell with this one. He was so *contained*. But so cute—and she knew he liked her. The other agents had not seemed to like her; she didn't know why. They had acted as if her relationship with Roger was something dirty, something she should be *blamed* for, for heaven's sake. She certainly hadn't told *them* anything they didn't need to know.

"You're a very attractive young woman," Becker said.

She swatted his shoulder lightly, remonstrating with him for such a bold remark.

"You know that," Becker said, tilting his head. "You probably hear it all the time."

"*You,*" she said, pushing his shoulder with one finger this time. She left the finger there.

"It's only natural that if a pretty woman and a healthy man get together . . ." He let it trail off, grinning at her. There was nothing lewd about the grin, she decided. He just liked to tease. She liked it, too.

Helen smiled back at him, then demurely looked away. She wondered if he could feel her finger on his shoulder.

"And Dyce was young and virile. Only natural."

"You mustn't judge every man by yourself," she said.

"Oooo-oooh," said Becker. "Something a little unnatural? Tell me."

"I can't tell you *that*. What are you thinking of?" But she wanted to tell him very much. She had wanted to tell someone ever since it happened, but she could hardly bare her soul to the people at work. She would never hear the last of it.

"Did he dress up?" Becker asked. He was chuckling, enjoying the idea. He wasn't censorious at all; he could understand, even savor the oddness. It was kind of fun if you had some distance on it.

"Worse than that," she said.

"Whips and chains? Boots?"

"You'll never guess."

"I'll bet I can. I've heard of everything."

"You haven't heard of this one," said Helen. "I don't think this has ever been done before."

"In the bathroom. In a tree. Hanging from the rafters."

"From the *rafters?*"

"It's been done," he said. "You'd be surprised."

"I'd certainly be surprised by that."

"He bent over the sink and had you throw oranges at him."

Helen laughed and put her hand on his thigh for a moment before removing it.

"People don't do that," she said.

"I swear to you. I'll bet Roger didn't come up with anything new. Fun, maybe, but not new."

"I don't know about fun," she said.

"Well, fun for him, anyway."

"Fun is not a word I'd use for Roger," she said. "He didn't seem to enjoy it so much as—oh, I can't tell you."

"Not fun exactly. I'll bet it was more of a serious thing with him."

"How did you know that?"

She leaned forward again as if amazed at his brilliance and touched his thigh once more. Helen did not know what was making her so bold, except that if he left now she didn't think she would ever see him again.

"I didn't know Roger, but from what I've heard, I'd have to guess it wasn't as if he really liked sex for its own sake. More like it was a kind of ritual. Something like that."

This time she really was amazed. It was as if he

could see right into her mind. Could he see into her heart as well?

"That's true," she said. "I never thought of it quite that way, but that's true, it was like a ritual. Or a ceremony."

"I'll bet he wore something special," Becker said.

"Talcum powder," she said, surprised at herself.

"Talcum powder?"

"And I mean that's *all.*"

With a giggle she got to her feet and waggled her fingers in front of him. Becker took her hand and she led him to the bathroom.

"Come on, I'll show you," she said, clasping his palm tightly. When she described Dyce's appearance, nude and covered in white powder, she clung to Becker's hand the whole time, squeezing for emphasis and finally, when speaking of her fear and astonishment, putting both of their still-clasped hands on her chest.

"I just didn't know what to do," she said, collapsing her head helplessly against him, leaning there for a second, then turning her head up to his, like a cat waiting to be stroked. She was pressing the back of his hand firmly into her breast.

"What should I have done?" she asked.

"Sometimes you just have to go along with things," Becker said.

"I knew you would understand."

"Did he do it again, or just that once?"

"It was the only way he really could do it," she said. "Is it wicked of me to tell you that?"

Becker looked into her eyes and brushed his free

hand against her cheek. For a moment he thought she was going to swoon.

"You should tell me everything you need to," said Becker.

"I thought there was something wrong with me. Wasn't I attractive enough by myself? Do you think there's anything wrong with me?"

She moved his hand up and down so that it rubbed against her nipple, which was hard under the blouse. This was not the recommended investigation technique, he thought, suppressing a laugh.

She had her head tilted back, her mouth partly open, her eyes half closed. Becker wondered if she had learned her methods from 1940's movies.

"If there's anything wrong with you, I haven't found it yet," he said.

"There's one other thing I could tell you, but you'll hate me if I do."

"Nothing you could say would make me do that," said Becker.

"Oh, I shouldn't."

Becker tipped her chin up with his finger and looked in her eyes. I've seen the same movies, he thought.

"Yes, you should," he said.

"When I saw him standing here, all covered in white like a ghost he was—you know."

"What?"

"You know." She rolled her eyes to avoid contact with his, acutely embarrassed—or her feigned version of embarrassment, Becker thought.

"I don't know. You have to tell me, Helen. What was he?"

She closed her eyes. "He was as hard as I've ever seen a man," she said.

Becker felt her hand slipping between his legs.

"Until now," she added.

Becker carefully bent his knees and lifted her into his arms, hoping his back wouldn't go out on him and then realizing it would be a good way out of this, if it did.

She sighed as he carried her to her bedroom and gasped with false surprise as he eased her down on the bed. But then he pulled away from her and stood.

"I can't," he said.

She stopped brushing a profusion of pillows off the bed and looked at him in confusion.

"I'm on a case. You know what that means." He bit his lip in a display of sorrowful regret, then sighed. "Much as I'd like to."

Helen thought of saying that it wouldn't take long, but feared he might misinterpret the remark. She could see he was already upset and it would be cruel of her to make it any more difficult for him.

"Oh. A case. Of course."

"Regulations," he said.

He clenched his fists and shuddered in frustration, then shrugged, his face a study in sorrow and resignation.

Helen could not help but admire his dedication.

"You wouldn't want me if it meant betraying my duty," he said.

"I understand," she said.

Becker kissed her forehead and eased toward the door.

"Will I see you again?" she asked.

"Call me," Becker said. "Anytime. Anytime." He grinned at her. "I think we need to investigate this matter further."

"Oh, Agent . . . ?"

"Hatcher," he said. "Agent Neal Hatcher. Just call."

Helen knew the agent would be back. She had sensed his longing and the urgency with which he had wanted her. It had been very hard for him to leave, and in a way she respected his sense of integrity. Yes, she did, she admired him for it . . . but she knew he would have to come back, and when she heard his tentative knock on the door she could not resist smiling triumphantly. He had had just time enough to walk to his car, think about the heaven that was waiting for him with her, and return. There were some powers that transcended duty, and she had sensed correctly that Agent Hatcher was more susceptible to them than most men, despite his protestations of obligation.

She waited for him to knock again, not wishing to appear too eager. It came quietly, almost as a scratch. Timid, like a schoolboy, not certain of the reception he would get. It made her feel even more powerful. She would not toy with him any longer. She would welcome him with all her warmth, and his timidity would melt and he would be as strong and vigorous a lover as she knew he could be.

Helen opened the door with just a hint of a knowing smile on her lips. Dyce grabbed her by the throat and propelled her backward, squeezing hard on her neck so she could not cry out. She hit her legs against the bed and tumbled down and Dyce was on her, his weight pinning her down, his fingers pressing into the flesh of her windpipe.

With his free hand Dyce scrambled across the floor, wincing with the pain in his injured arm, searching for one of the pillows that Helen had not yet replaced in anticipation of the agent's return. He came up with the red and white checked cat with the whiskers and stuffed it into Helen's mouth.

He sat on her chest, holding her down, and pressed his knees against her arms. She tried to roll her head from side to side, desperately seeking relief from the suffocation on her throat and in her mouth, but he put his free hand on her forehead and pushed her head down onto the bed.

He was saying something, but Helen could not hear it over the pounding of blood in her ears, the strangled sounds entrapped in the back of her throat.

"Calm down, Helen," Dyce said. "I don't want to hurt you, I just want you to be quiet."

He eased the pressure on her throat and Helen gasped, then sucked greedily for air through her nose.

"Just hold still," he said. He held his finger to his lips, shushing her. "Everything's all right, you're all right. I just wanted to keep you from yelling. You understand that, don't you? Of course you do. You understand. There now, there now, just calm down. I'm going to remove the pillow, all right? I'm going to let you talk, but you mustn't raise your voice, do you understand? Of course you do, of course you do. There now, calm down, Helen. That's a girl, that's a good girl."

He smiled at her; his voice was oddly soothing and Helen felt herself relaxing. Again shushing her, he removed the pillow from her mouth, but held it close to her face. His eyebrows arched up in question, waiting for her reaction.

Helen wanted to speak but could only cough at first.

"I hope I didn't scare you," he said. "You know I'd never hurt you, Helen."

She wanted to tell him that he was hurting her now, sitting on her chest, but something in his face told her he would do much worse if she complained.

"Are we all right now?" he asked. "Are we settled down? No need to talk yet. Just nod. That's right, we're fine. Now when you do talk, I want you to do it quietly, and when I tell you to do something, I want you to do it immediately and without question. Do you understand? Just nod. Good, Helen."

Dyce leaned his weight back slightly and eased the pressure of his knees on her arms.

"Now tell me, why are there policemen at my house? Why was that man just here? I know that man. He knows me. Why was he visiting you, Helen?"

Dyce looked at her calmly, quizzically, a slight smile of encouragement on his lips. Helen stared at the blood stains on his shirt, trying to think what to say.

"I don't know," she said at last.

Dyce looked at her sadly. "That's no good, Helen. That's not a good answer. Do you know why?"

Helen shook her head no.

"Because it assumes I'm an idiot." He smiled broadly, as if appreciating the joke. "We both know I'm not an idiot, don't we?"

Helen nodded agreement.

Dyce moved his hand and Helen winced, but he reached past her and switched on the lamp on her night table.

"Now, I want to try this again. I'll ask you why the police are at my house, and you'll tell me the truth this time, all right? But I want you to think about something else first."

Dyce unscrewed the shade from the lamp and dropped it onto the floor. He held the naked bulb next to her cheek. She could feel the heat. From several inches it was no more than a comforting warmth.

"Have you ever burned your fingers on a light bulb? Of course you have. Do you remember how much that hurt? And that was when you could pull your fingers away immediately. Now suppose you couldn't pull away and that pain just grew and grew and spread all over your face. Just think about that for a moment, Helen, and then tell me what's going on."

Dyce moved the lighted bulb closer to her face.

"I . . ."

"Shhh. Not yet. Just think about this first."

He moved the bulb closer still. She could hear a faint humming sound from the electrical element in the bulb.

When she began to tremble and tears welled in her eyes, Dyce spoke again in the same soothing tone.

"Tell me now, Helen. We'll start with the police. Why are they at my house?"

After she told him everything she knew, he led her to the kitchen and selected her best knife. Dyce was disappointed in the selection.

"A good knife is an absolute essential for a good

cook," he said. He had placed her on a stool in the corner of the kitchen so she could not leave without passing him. As he rummaged through the knife drawer, Helen glanced out the window. If necessary she would throw the stool through the window to get attention, but there was nobody out there.

"What do you cut things with, for heaven's sake? Do you do all your work with a paring knife?" He held one up contemptuously, then tossed it back in the drawer. "You couldn't bone a chicken with that," he said.

He settled at last on an old and long-neglected carving knife with a handle formed of antler. The blade was dull and specked with corrosion.

"You don't even have a proper whetstone," he complained.

"Please," said Helen in a voice so low she could barely hear it herself.

"This is not the way to live. You've got to have more pride in yourself. This lack of self-esteem . . ." He waved his arm to encompass the whole room. "Well, it's pretty sadly reflected in this kitchen."

"Please, don't," she said, louder this time.

Dyce was sharpening the knife on an emery wheel that was part of the electric can opener, shaking his head at the neglect of good steel. The grinding drowned Helen's voice.

"If you ever lived on a farm you'd learn something about keeping your tools in good shape," he said, testing the knife edge with his thumb.

"I'll do anything, anything," Helen said.

"Get me a paper towel," he said. He put the can

opener back in its place, handling it with some difficulty because of his injured arm.

She looked at him, not comprehending.

"A paper towel, Helen."

She tore one from the roll and held it toward him. With startling suddenness and violence, Dyce slashed at it with the knife. The lower half of the towel drifted to the floor.

"Now that's good steel," he said.

Helen held both hands over her face, and the upper half of the paper towel protruded as if she were a toddler grasping her favorite blanket.

"Please, *what?*" he asked, annoyed.

"Don't kill me."

He seemed genuinely surprised. "I'm not going to kill you, Helen. Why on earth would I do that? I thought we'd take a ride to Bridgeport together."

"Why?"

"Because we're going to take your car and because I would have trouble driving with my arm like this."

Helen nodded, understanding nothing.

"And Bridgeport because I understand there are people there who can provide me with documents. It's awfully hard to get by in America without documents. Bridgeport has neighborhoods where people are not very particular. Do you see?"

Helen nodded again. "I see."

"Shall we go?"

Helen moved slowly past him until he caught her arm. He held it gently, almost courtly as they walked onto the street. He did not explain the knife and Helen did not ask. She knew she would not like the answer.

He sat with the knife resting on the front seat by his left hand while she drove. Whenever they slowed down for traffic, he grasped the knife and held it close to her ribs, though when he spoke there was nothing in his voice to indicate the slightest concern, or, indeed, any change in their relationship. If anything, he was more talkative and friendlier than he had been before Helen discovered the skulls under his floorboards.

When they reached the thruway and headed toward Bridgeport, Dyce fell silent for a long while. Helen tried to think of nothing but the traffic and after a time the flow of the road lulled her into a form of forgetfulness. When he spoke again he startled her.

"You mustn't be afraid of me," he said. "You must obey me, but don't be afraid."

"All right," said Helen, trying to control her breathing, which had started out of control at the sound of his voice.

"I didn't put those bones under the floor," he said, as if an afterthought. "You know that, don't you?"

Helen swallowed. She did not know how to speak to him.

"I didn't know," she said.

"Oh, no," he said. A huge transport truck roared past them on the left, causing their car to shudder in its wake. "Someone else did that. The previous owner, probably."

He glanced at Helen to see how the statement was taken. She nodded, fighting back tears. He returned to his study of the traffic in front of them. Dyce regarded the role of passenger as one of codriver.

"What did he say when you told him about the

talcum powder?" Dyce asked. "I wonder what he thinks of me."

He turned to face her on the seat, like a girlfriend settling in for a cozy chat.

"Did he think that was strange?"

CHAPTER 11

"I ALWAYS knew there was something wrong with Dyce," Chaney said with considerable pride.

"What did you think was wrong with him?"

"An excess of ordinary. There's such a thing as too common, you know. Or maybe you don't know; you're not an actuary. That's one thing we look for, something that occurs too often. You might think that if sixty-three percent of the workers in a certain industry retire at age sixty-five, the national average, and die at the age of seventy-five point seven years of heart failure, also the national average, then that sets your average for that industry, but me, I look at that and say, hold it, what's going on here, that's way *too* average. Who are these people, clones? You see what I mean?"

"No," said Becker who understood but wanted to encourage the man to speak.

Chaney took an impatient breath. Laymen were slow, no two ways about it. He was leading Becker down a lengthy corridor toward the actuary pool.

"People are different," said Chaney. "We aren't paramecium, we aren't lab mice or fruit flies all grown from the same egg fertilized in a petri dish. We have to expect the random in all of us. An average is just what you get when you cut off the heads of the tallest and put the shortest on stools. It's an *arithmetic* construct. You follow? No one is really average. Just as no one could really be as bland as Dyce seemed to be. No matter how vanilla pudding he was on the outside, I knew there had to be something going on inside, some quirk to make him human. What did he do, exactly?"

Becker looked down on Chaney's shaven head. The stubble on the sides of his skull where he still had hair was growing dark. A five-o'clock-shadow on the head, Becker thought. The ridge atop the skull was pronounced, almost pointed.

"This is just a routine investigation, for background purposes primarily."

"Sure," said Chaney. "That's why the boss is all over himself to get me to cooperate. Come on, you can tell me. What did the little bastard do?"

"We're not sure he did anything," said Becker. "That's why we're investigating."

Chaney tilted his head and gave Becker a knowing smirk as they paused outside the actuarial office. Becker wondered if everyone else had the same urge to rap the man's parietal bone with his knuckles.

"He hated me, of course," said Chaney. "Might as well get that on the record in case he talks about me."

"Why is that?"

"Jealousy. You probably don't know this, but actuaries are actually a pretty unorthodox bunch. We're the artists of the insurance business, you might say. Perhaps you didn't know that, if you get your information from herd movies and the like, but we're all rebels."

"I'd heard that about actuaries."

"You're joking, of course, officer, but it's true. Insurance people as a whole are not very colorful; that's a demand of the business. People want to think they're being insured by someone as sober and conservative as a U.S. President. Not overly bright, but foursquare, you know? But actuaries are a different breed."

He plucked at the gray cardigan sweater he wore. It looked to Becker as if it had earned its grayness from incessant wear, but Chaney was clearly proud of it. It was an emblem of his independence.

"You don't see executives in any other department out of suit and tie."

"And this is why Dyce was jealous of you?"

"Not the sweater, the attitude. A little dash, a little style. He *always* wore a suit and tie. He was senior to me, you know. Oh, yeah. I went right over his head and he hated me for it, I'm sure. Not that he ever let on. He never let on to *anything.*"

Chaney pushed open the door as if it were the gates of a castle.

"Here's the guts of the industry," he said. "Or a better analogy would be the brains. Without us, the insurance industry would be working blind."

"That would make you the eyes," said Becker, but Chaney appeared not to hear.

The actuarial pool was a large room crowded with people at computer screens. Accordion piles of computer printouts sat by each desk, and everyone seemed to be either reading the printouts or tapping buttons on the consoles. At first glance there was nothing to distinguish it from the work warrens of many other industries, nor anything to verify Chaney's claim of a wild and crazy breed of workers. Becker noted that it appeared to be a singularly male calling. There were only three women among the more than thirty employees.

"Dyce worked here," said Chaney, switching on the computer at the empty desk. "He was doing some of the basic research on the Steinkraus file. Under my direction, of course."

Becker went carefully through the desk drawers, searching without expectation. He was not disappointed to find nothing beyond the essentials of office work.

"You know Steinkraus Industries, of course. The holding company? It's my baby."

Chaney nodded toward the screen where columns of figures meaningless to Becker vibrated ever so slightly as if waiting their turn to dance.

"Quite a job," said Becker. Chaney grinned proudly and nodded. "Was Dyce working on anything else?"

"Not at the moment. Not officially at any rate."

"And unofficially?"

"I could look at his files," Chaney said, pushing a key and summoning up the contents of Dyce's computer.

"Treat me as a computer illiterate," Becker said.

"Well . . . he was working on a lot of things, or had been in the past. It would take awhile to figure out just what. Some of it is here, and some of it—see that symbol there?—that means he was accessing other computers to get more data. It will take a little doing to find out what exactly is in there."

"But you could do it?"

"Of course I could *do* it."

"Sounds pretty complicated."

"Oh, please. I could get this done in a couple of days."

"How about by tonight?"

Chaney hesitated, his eyes scanning the busy room as if counting up the hours he would need.

"I can bring some agency experts in to help," said Becker innocently.

"I doubt they'd really understand it all, don't you? No offense."

"You don't offend me," said Becker. *"I* don't understand any of it. Computers are a complete mystery to me, not to mention actuarial science. That's why I rely on someone with your expertise. I suppose there is someone else around here I could ask if you're too busy."

"No one who can do it the way I can."

"By tonight?"

Chaney sniffed and squared his shoulders under the cardigan.

"Check back by eight," he said. "I'll be able to tell you what Dyce ate for breakfast."

"I know what he ate," said Becker. "I want you to tell me why."

THEY pulled off the thruway exit ramp as the sun was setting behind the snaggle-toothed silhouette of the

Bridgeport skyline. Dyce talked calmly but incessantly as he directed Helen toward the water, seeking by instinct the poor and then poorer sections of the battered city. When he had her pull into the empty lot of a warehouse, the sun was creeping into the greasy waters of Long Island Sound.

Helen seemed to have slipped into a kind of trance induced by terror and Dyce's chatter, and he continued to drone on to sustain it.

"That's very good, Helen, very good. This is not a bad place, is it? A little paint, a little elbow grease, but you know what neighborhoods like this are like. It's hard to find anyone who cares anymore; people will live just anywhere. Now, Helen, I have a plan. What we're going to do is protect you from the police."

He gripped her right arm and she jerked involuntarily, then calmed. Through the windshield she could count the windows on the warehouse. They were cast high up under the eaves, serving for light and ventilation, not vision. Helen counted the windows, then the number of panes in each window, then the number of panes on the whole building, then the number of broken panes. On the highway she had done it with cars, cars passed, cars passing. It seemed to stretch the time; with each car counted, she was alive that much longer.

Dyce ran his fingers up and down the underside of her exposed arm. "This is not my idea," he said. "They're making me do it. That man who was at your house, it's his idea. I mean, he's responsible for this. I want you to know this; this is definitely not my idea." He sounded disgusted.

A pigeon fluttered through one of the broken panes

and entered the warehouse, safely home for the evening. Helen wondered if the birds ever cut their wings on the broken glass. She felt the cold of Dyce's knife against her arm; but she didn't feel it. She saw him holding it there; but she didn't see him. She heard him but only the tone, which was soft, almost a lullaby— the words made no sense. She clung to his voice, which had been nonstop for the last half hour. As long as she heard him, she was still alive.

"You might have certain legal problems, aiding and abetting, that sort of thing, I'm not sure what your legal position is, so this will help you. This will make it look as if you drove me here unwillingly, this will make it look as if I forced you to help me, it will look as if I tried to hurt you, but you know I would never hurt you. You know how I feel about you. I would never hurt you. This is just to help you, this will give you an alibi."

He was pinching her arm slightly, gently, moving his fingers up and down the inside of her arm and pinching. It didn't hurt, she didn't mind it. She was alive after each pinch.

"It's just a little sharpness, just momentary. You won't even notice it. Do you see the sunset? Isn't it beautiful, just look at that, Helen, so much beauty in such an ugly place."

Helen felt the knife point as it entered her flesh, but the pinching had worked. It didn't seem much worse than another squeeze, just another little stitch in the skin, and she didn't feel the blade at all as it traveled down her arm from inside her elbow to her hand.

It was quite a good knife after all, Dyce thought. A bit unwieldy, but it took an edge like a fine razor. The blood welled up and oozed out of her arm. He held her hand down between the seats, slightly back so she couldn't see it from the corner of her eye and pulled back on the skin so it would not close on itself.

"This part will be over in a second or two, Helen. Don't even think about it, it will stop of its own accord. It's not at all dangerous, but it will look good when they question you. You can tell them anything you want and they'll believe you now. Do you see the swallows? That's what they are. I love to watch them swooping along, don't you? They're so graceful and they only come out in the evening like this, did you know that?"

Helen watched the swallows darting after insects and remembered a score of a movie that set the motions of birds to music. The music sounded sweetly in her mind.

Dyce had trouble controlling his breath. He had not anticipated how good this would feel. He had never killed before, not really, not for its own sake. The death of the men had been necessary to achieve the desired effect, merely a consequence of their preparation. This was different. This was exciting in itself. She looked so pretty now. He had never thought of her as pretty before, but now she was absolutely beautiful. Beautiful in death. Dyce thought maybe he loved her after all. Her fingers in his hand were growing cold, but he wished now that they wouldn't go too fast; he wanted her dying to last.

His voice sounded harsh for the first time. "No, don't move the arm, Helen, just let it hang down. If you move it now you'll spoil everything." She had only wanted to wipe away the tears that were running into the corner of her mouth. He gripped her fingers tightly and held her arm down and behind her. She heard the sound of something dripping into the back of the car. She knew what it was; she didn't know what it was. As long as she heard the drips she was alive.

"That's better, Helen. Now just relax. We've had a long drive, you're probably feeling a little tired. If you feel drowsy, just shut your eyes. Go on, shut your eyes, Helen. Take a little nap if you want. Why don't you take a little nap. I'll be right here to watch over you. You know nothing can happen as long as I'm here. I'll take good care of you."

Her eyelids fluttered closed and she sighed as if grateful to give in to sleep at last.

"When we've finished here, I tell you what let's do. Let's find a nice hotel. I want to be with you, Helen. I want to spend the night with you. I want to make love with you. Do you remember that first night we were together? Do you have any money with you? I'll have to borrow your money. You look so lovely now, Helen." He wished she would turn toward him so she could see how he was smiling at her, how happy he was. She would want to know she had given him such happiness. She deserved to know that. She was his first. So much more important than sex; she had introduced him to a pleasure that touched his soul.

At the end, when Dyce thought she was gone and finally released her hand, she tried to fight, startling him with the suddenness and ferocity of her attack, flailing her arms, clawing at his face and hitting again and again at the knife that he held up to protect himself. She had little real strength left, of course, but he was surprised that she had managed any at all. Even in the ferocity of her struggle she didn't cry out, as if she wanted to keep the matter between the two of them right to the end.

Ultimately she fell back, sobbing silently, covering her eyes with hands deeply gashed by their foolish onslaughts against the knife. She died that way, her face covered, the last of her blood accelerated out of her body by her own flailing efforts.

Dyce could not help getting some of the blood on his clothing as he tossed her into the trunk. The car would be stolen by morning, he reasoned, and whoever did it would not be quick to notify the police about a body found with the spare tire. He wished she hadn't fought at the end. It ruined the glow he was feeling.

After cleaning himself as best he could, Dyce walked toward the lights of the city. He was grateful for the falling darkness as it would help disguise his clothes and general condition—not that anyone would care very much in the sections he was heading for. But he was also glad he had the knife tucked into his belt. There were many scary people in this part of town.

"I UNDERSTAND you've joined up again," said Gold. He was playing with a three-colored pen, switching the nib from red to green to blue.

"Temporarily," said Becker.

"That's a start."

"That's all there is. It's a convenience; the badge opens doors."

"Uh-huh."

"I hate when you do that," Becker said.

"Do what?"

"Grunt knowingly. It sounds like a parody of a shrink. You might as well say, I zee, very interessting."

"You're in a good mood."

"I was supposed to have a date tonight," said Becker. "I came to see you instead. She's going to be pissed and all I have is you for consolation."

"How is that going? That relationship."

"I don't know. I haven't seen her enough to find out."

"Evasive."

"It's none of your business. Sex is not my problem."

"Did I mention sex? I asked about your relationship. Does that just mean sex to you?"

"I want to ask you some questions today."

"That's not the way it works."

"Nothing personal."

"That's the only kind of question worth asking. How is the relationship?"

"Yours and mine? Fragile, I'd say."

"The girl." Gold glanced at his notes. "Cindi."

"I remember her name. It's fine. She's too young for me. She probably has an Oedipal attraction to me, I probably have a dirty-old-man attraction to her. That sounds unhealthy but binding, wouldn't you say?" Becker paused. "I like her," he said.

"And how does that make you feel?"

"It scares me a little," said Becker.

"Do you want to talk about it?"

"Maybe later. I have other questions first."

"What kind of questions?"

"About sexual perversion."

"Um."

"I thought you'd like that. Don't worry, it's official business."

"We don't call it perversion anymore. It's paraphilia now. Whose paraphilia are we interested in?"

"My man. His name is Dyce."

"Your man?"

"The man I'm after. Yeah, he's my man. Or he will be. I almost have him already, and if you give me the right information, he'll be all mine."

Gold placed the pen on his desk and looked squarely at Becker. There was an intensity in Becker's tone he had not heard before. Gone, for the moment at least, was the caustic, bantering note that let Gold know he was being tolerated even when Becker was cooperating. Usually Gold felt as if he were a priest debating religion with an atheist who went along with the discussion purely for the sake of an argument. Gold was himself a doubting priest at best. The miracle of psychotherapy had long since been replaced by a form of utilitarian respect for the rituals. Now, however, he sensed an opening into Becker's carefully constructed armament.

"You'll have him in what sense? You mean you'll catch him?"

Becker paused. He picked up the pen from Gold's desk and stared at it blankly for a moment.

"I mean I'll have his secrets. No. I mean his secrets will be my secrets."

"Is that what it feels like? As if you're sharing secrets with someone you're after?"

"Not sharing. We both possess them." Becker jabbed at the pen, changing the color back and forth as Gold had done.

"You empathize with him," Gold prompted.

Becker dropped the pen on the desk.

"No," he said impatiently. "I become him."

Gold held his breath. He was afraid to speak at all for fear he would say the wrong thing. He stifled the urge to grunt and slowly nodded his head.

"I feel what he feels and think what he thinks. And that's how I find him. It's as simple as that." Becker laughed at himself, a brief snort. "As simple as that."

"How can you do that?"

"I start with a lot in common."

Gold felt the goose flesh on his arms.

"Will you help me?"

"I want to," said Gold.

"I mean with Dyce. I need to know about paraphilia."

"I'll help you. Will you help me to understand you?"

"They may be the same thing," said Becker.

CHANEY glanced impatiently at his watch as Becker entered the actuarial room. The agent was half an hour late and Chaney had thought several times of leaving, just to show his independence, but his pride in his accomplishments had kept him there.

"Sorry I'm late," Becker said. "I know how important your time is. I had to see a shrink."

"You're in analysis?"

"Group therapy," Becker said. "Dyce and I are taking it together."

"If you have Dyce . . ."

"Joke," said Becker. "Inside joke. How did it go? Did you find out anything for me?"

"Certainly. I've printed it out for you, but you might want to take a look on the screen here. This is Dyce's private log. He had it pretty well camouflaged with codes and countercodes, but I got it out."

"Didn't take you long."

"Well, it wasn't easy, but I didn't have any great trouble with it."

"That's why I asked an expert," said Becker, smiling.

"Well, it was only Dyce's mind I was up against," said Chaney. He ran a hand down the back of his shaven skull. "He was devious, but not terribly clever, if you follow."

"I'm trying to," said Becker. "What is it, exactly?"

"Names. He got them from the raw solicitations of field agents. These aren't necessarily customers, you understand, just people who have filled out questionnaires, or that agents filled them out for."

Becker looked at the screen. Some of the names he recognized immediately. Nordholm, Dahl, Hedstrom, Nilsson.

"Is there a pattern?" he asked innocently.

"Of course. Don't you see it?" Chaney paused to punctuate his moment of superiority. "It's fairly obvious. They all have mothers with Scandinavian names."

"Why would that be?"

"Who knows?"

"Is there anything unique about Scandinavians as a group? Anything that sets them apart?" Becker asked.

"From an actuarial point of view, do you mean?"

"From any point of view. I need any ideas I can get."

"Well, actually, I did think about that, I assumed you would want to know. There is one interesting thing—from an insurance perspective." Again Chaney paused to feel his advantage. "Scandinavians tend to live longer than other ethnic groups. That's mostly climate related, both in Scandinavia and here."

"How do you mean?"

"People in Minnesota live the longest, on the average, of any state in the Union. Did you know that? Minnesota not only has the highest concentration of Scandinavians in the nation, it also has one of the coldest climates."

"That's important?"

"It seems to be. The same is true of Scandinavia, too, of course. Part of that might be the high level of social services in both countries, too. But people in cold climates tend to live longer anyway."

"I would think Alaskans would live the longest in that case."

Chaney shook his head dismissively. *"Too* cold. Too many people living high-risk lives. Too many indigenous peoples with a low standard of living, too many transients. No, your best bet, if you want to live a long time, is to have Norwegian parents and live in a cold state with good health care close by. Minnesota. We ought to charge less for a general life policy in the state, but it's against federal regulations. Can't discriminate." Chaney said it as if it were an insult to the precision of his craft. "That pushes your premiums up, you know."

"Why mine?"

"You're a white Anglo-Saxon male. You're going to live longer—on the average—than an Afro-American male. That's just a statistical fact, not my opinion, but we can't charge the Afro-American more for the same coverage just on the basis of his race. Or, put the other way around, we can't charge you less. To the government, either way we do it, it's discrimination. So we charge you the same as the other guy and you get cheated." Chaney shrugged. "That's democracy. Politicians aren't interested in statistics."

"Except voting patterns. How do you know I'm Anglo-Saxon?"

"Your name's Becker? That's English—or German. Northern European in any event. Basically the same stock. By the time you get to this country, the life expectancy is virtually the same. You've got a good year and a half better expectancy than somebody with Mediterranean heritage."

"How do you know my mother's not a Greek?"

Chaney laughed. "Looking at you. Your hair, your features, your skin color, your height, your body type. You look like your ancestors were roaming northern Europe since the last Ice Age . . . She's not Greek, is she?"

"No."

"What was her maiden name?"

"Kriek."

"German. I knew it. Don't misunderstand me.

We're all mongrels in this country. Do a few case
studies, go back more than two generations on anybody in America, and you won't find very many who
aren't as mixed genetically as an alleycat. All the gene
pools bleed into each other here. I've got a grandmother from Turkey—although you'd never know it.
Still, certain types hold true. Give me your genealogy
and I can come up with a pretty accurate picture most
of the time."

"And most of the time is good enough for an actuary, right?"

Chaney paused, wondering if his profession were
being insulted.

"We deal in large numbers, if that's what you
mean. We're not *supposed* to be an exact science."

"That's what I meant."

"So, is there anything else you need?"

"This information, Dyce's list. Is there any way
anyone else could have compiled it? I mean anyone
with a computer and a modem?"

"Well—if he knew the codes. You can tap into the
White House bathroom these days if you know the
code."

"But it would be difficult?"

"Sure it would—unless you were from another insurance company."

"Insurance companies exchange information?"

"All the time. We have to cross-check to fight
fraud, for one thing. If somebody insures his wife for
fifty thousand and she dies, that's not a big event, but
if he took out a fifty-thousand-dollar policy with ten
other companies—hello. Suddenly you're looking at
a significant event. But the main reason we exchange

information is that actuaries need the largest database possible to do the best job. We transfer information every day."

"To the same people. Or the same computers?"

"The same computers, basically, yes. Why?"

"Could you tell if another computer tried to get at this information?"

"The database or this list?"

"The list, I would think."

"That would be easier than protecting the whole database. Yes, I could set up an alarm that would tell me if someone tried to get into Dyce's file."

"Good. Please do that and notify me immediately."

"Want to tell me why?"

"Mr. Dyce is going to want to come back for his list. Maybe not right away, but sooner or later, he's going to have to."

"He'd be stupid if he does."

"Not stupid. Not stupid at all. Helpless."

Tee noticed certain things. One was the remarkable resilience of a town like Clamden. In the week following the news of Dyce's crimes and his subsequent escape, the townspeople had reacted with the predictable outcry of disgust, horror, and outrage—much of the latter directed at the police in general and Tee in particular for not somehow magically foreseeing Dyce's plans and providing adequate protection to the citizenry. There was talk of getting a new chief, discussion of citizen patrols, an increased sale of locks and safety devices, demands for a curfew to safeguard the children, all the expected flurry of alarm of a

people who had suddenly been made to feel insecure
in their own homes. What surprised Tee was how
quickly things returned to normal. After two weeks,
people still asked him about the case and the so-called
manhunt, but by then only with the casual interest of
someone massaging an old wound. It took longer for
the macabre jokes to die down than for the concern to
subside. The citizens ultimately reacted to Dyce's
murders with the statistical optimism of someone
who has been struck by lightning and emerged to tell
about it. The incident was over and so unlikely to ever
happen again that its occurrence imparted a sort of
immunity from future occurrence.

Another thing that Tee noticed was that not everything returned to normal. His friend Becker was
changed in ways both obvious and subtle. He seemed
distracted much of the time, which was understand-
able. He was conducting the real manhunt, after all,
but there was something more fundamental: Becker
had lost much of the air of unruffled calm that had
always distinguished him. Minor irritants annoyed
him openly, his posture and demeanor suggested a
different person, a frailer, warier person than the man
Tee had known since youth. It occasionally seemed to
Tee as if his friend were not the hunter but the man
being hunted.

Becker's visits to Cindi's house also became more
frequent. That, at least, Tee could understand. His
friend's car was parked on Cindi's street most nights,
but the hours were getting later and later so that Tee
wondered if Becker was having trouble sleeping.

"Is it any of your business?" Becker asked. They

sat in the coffee shop, once again ignored by Janie, the waitress.

"What did I say? All I said was, how's it going with Cindi?"

"And I asked if it was your business."

"It was polite conversation. You're losing your sense of humor lately."

Becker stared at Tee. There was no malice in his look, but an implacable, searching quality that demanded an answer and always made Tee uneasy.

"It's my job," Tee continued. "Especially now. What kind of cop would I be if I didn't notice your car when I saw it?"

"What kind?"

"Especially now. It's not that I'm keeping tabs on you. I cruise, that's what I'm supposed to do. I cruise neighborhoods, I test shop doors at night, I investigate cars that are parked where they don't belong, and cars that are abandoned. It's what I do. Especially now."

"Especially now."

"Now more than ever. People like to see the police going through the motions; it makes them feel comfortable."

"Little do they know," said Becker.

Tee wasn't sure whether to laugh.

"Or maybe you haven't lost your sense of humor exactly," Tee said. "Maybe it's just got too subtle for me."

"Didn't mean to disparage your fine police work."

"If I could just point out, I was the one who noticed something funny going on in the first place."

"And I'm the first to give you credit," said Becker.

"I stress your finely developed sense of paranoia in my report."

"You might try to spread the word a little broader. People in town think we're a bunch of half-wits."

"We?"

"Like we should have known some insurance salesman was inviting the boys in for a while and then boiling them up?"

"Notice a certain lack of local respect, do you, Tee? A chief is not without honor except in his own community. They all see what a fine job you're doing now, though. Cruising and noting my comings and goings. That should make them feel better."

"I just asked how you were getting along . . . Look, are you pissed at me about something?"

"Pissed at you? Why would I be? You're the one who gave me my current occupation."

"You didn't have to do it. How did I know what it would turn into?"

"You are the one who presented me with your nephew's wife and baby, aren't you?"

"Present you? What's that? She happened to be around, I thought she could be helpful. Who twisted your arm to get into it? Did anybody pressure you in any way . . ."

"Forget it, Tee, it's not your fault. I'm not in a very good mood, that's all. I haven't been sleeping much."

"Because of this thing?"

"My dreams keep me awake."

"You can't dream if you're not asleep in the first place."

Becker gave him that questioning look again, almost as if he were hopeful of discovering a new truth.

"Are you sure of that?"

"Look . . . you don't have to stay on it. If it's getting to you, just quit. It's not your job anymore, you gave it up once already."

"Just give it up?" Becker grinned.

Tee shrugged. "Let Dyce go. They'll find him or they won't. In any case, he won't come back here."

"Won't he?"

"Why would he?"

" 'Cause this is where he gets his kicks?"

"Come on, John. He can buy a cauldron anywhere. All this guy needs is a house and a stove."

"Not quite. He needs his tranquilizer, PMBL. We don't know what his source is, but it's certainly not over the counter."

"His source doesn't have to be around here, does it? It could be any pharmacy outlet in the country."

"Could be. Could be he drives halfway across the country to get his supply. Could be he gets it through the mail, but I doubt it. He's been very careful. But even supposing he does get it from somewhere else, there's still something else he needs from here."

"I'll bite. What does he need from here he can't get anywhere else?"

"His victims. He's got them selected already. He's gone to a lot of trouble and time to locate them, and he's used a lot of expensive hardware to do it."

"Your famous list."

"His list, not mine."

"You know what I mean."

"I don't have a list."

"Christ, I get the point. It's just a manner of speaking." Tee waved for Janie, then sighed.

"Why can't he just make up a new list. All right, not *just*. I suppose it's complicated, but still, why not do it the safe way? Why come back here? They sell insurance in Utah, don't they?"

"He could make up another list. Maybe he's doing it now, in which case we won't catch him, not now, maybe not ever. But I don't think he is. He doesn't have the time."

"Time? He's got all the time in the world. What's he got to do in such a hurry?"

"Kill."

"Come on, John. What is he, Dracula? He's got to hurry up to kill? If I was doing it, I'd take all the time I needed and set it up right."

"That's because you'd be doing it logically—but then you're not doing it in the first place. And why aren't you?"

"Why aren't I what? Boiling bones?"

"It's a real question."

"Because why should I?"

"That's the point. You've got no reason to. You have no need to. And I don't mean killing, exactly. I think that's incidental. That's probably just a way of dealing with the disposal problem. When I say kill I mean a whole complex of emotional reactions involved with whatever it is he does to these men before he gets rid of them. Whatever that compulsion is, I don't think it can wait. It has to be fed, and it has to be fed a very special diet. It happens the diet he knows about is around here. Which is why I think he'll be back."

Tee felt an inward shudder at the off-hand phrase "disposal problem." There was something eerily detached, yet at the same time intensely personal about Becker's manner when he discussed Dyce that made Tee increasingly uneasy.

The two men sat in silence for a while, Becker lost in his thoughts and Tee studying his friend with concern.

Becker finally broke the silence.

"We're getting along fine," he said.

"None of my business," said Tee.

"She's a nice woman . . . Too young for me."

"I wasn't prying . . ."

"She keeps me from dreaming."

"Look, John . . ."

"Or at least from sleeping." Becker smiled humorlessly before raising his hand slightly above his shoulder. Janie, the waitress, came to the table with a pot of coffee in hand.

"So what is it with you and Janie?" Becker asked after the waitress had withdrawn. "She ignores you because you made a pass at her, or because you didn't make a pass at her?"

"I remind you I'm a married man."

"Oh. Pardon me."

"Also a gentleman. Naturally I cannot discuss these things. My lips are sealed."

"In other words, you made a pass at her, she refused you, you made an ass of yourself, and she hasn't spoken to you since."

"Not quite. She wanted to play with my gun."

Becker laughed. "A consummation devoutly to be wished, I would have thought."

Tee leaned forward and spoke in a whisper. "I'm serious. She wanted to fondle the goddamn .38."

"Confusing symbol with substance."

"Whatever that means. Stop grinning. She wanted to stroke it. Weird."

Becker laughed, glancing at Janie.

"Don't look at her, for Christ's sake. And stop laughing. I'm not sure it's funny. You shouldn't laugh at her."

"I'm laughing at you," said Becker. "The horny chief finally gets the girl in his cruiser and all she wants is his hardware."

"She's looking at us," Tee hissed. "Stop it. Act natural."

Becker tossed his head back and laughed aloud.

"Ah, Tee," he said. "If I could act natural . . . If I knew what the hell that was." Becker stuffed a napkin in his mouth and shook with laughter. At least it sounded like laughter, but Tee thought his eyes looked enormously sad.

BECKER found Cindi in her basement, hanging from the ceiling like a three-toed sloth pondering its next move.

"Comfortable?" he asked.

She was dangling from a horizontal I beam running across the ceiling joists, clinging to the half-inch flange of the beam with the heels of each boot and the first knuckle of her fingers. Becker had seen her work out on the beam before, and also on the exposed pipes which she had reinforced with U-bolts and wire, converting her cellar to a kind of adult jungle gym.

She tipped her head all the way backward to see him as he came down the stairs, making her look a bit like a slain deer being carted away on shoulder poles.

"Hello, Becker," she said coolly.

Becker removed his jacket and sat on one of the old packing mats that Cindi had lifted somehow from a moving van. They were not there for padding in case she ever fell—as far as he could tell, she never fell—but for insulation against the cold cement of the floor when she did her loosening exercises. The basement was totally unfinished; except for the beam and the pipe reinforcements, it was unimproved in any way.

"There's something oriental about this room," Becker said. "You know, spare and clean, but somehow evocative of—of—what would you call the essence of this room? Indoor plumbing?"

Cindi released the beam with her feet and swung down to hang by her fingertips. Her feet were a foot off the floor. She walked hand over hand to one end of the beam, then worked her way backwards. After repeating this procession three times, she swung one foot onto the beam again and let go with one hand so she hung by one heel and the opposite hand. She let the free arm and leg dangle as she stared at Becker.

He had removed his shoes and was slowly stretching his thigh muscles on the mats.

"Keep your clothes on," she said.

Becker looked up at her and grinned. "That sounds like a promising invitation."

"You've got the wrong day," she said. Cindi switched arms and heels and let the others dangle, still staring at Becker.

"It's like having a conversation with a gibbon," he said. " 'Course, I've always liked doing that."

"You're thinking it's Thursday," she said. "You're

confused. It's Saturday. Our date was for last Thursday."

"I was in Washington. Talking to my shrink again."

"What about?"

"Partly about why I wasn't with you."

"I hope he offered a better explanation than you have."

"He doesn't explain things. He asks questions."

"Did he ask you why you didn't call me to tell me you weren't going to show up? Did he ask you why you've been avoiding me generally?"

"He didn't have to."

"I don't want to be an imposition on you, Becker. I don't want to make you do anything you don't want to do. But I don't like being used like a port of convenience, either."

"I UNDERSTAND."

"If you don't want to come around, don't come around. But don't come around at all."

Becker looked at his feet. Cindi began a series of pull-ups on her heels and the fingers of one hand. She's stronger than I am, Becker thought. And wiser.

"You going to say anything?" she asked finally. Becker wished that she would give some sign of exertion, at least. She didn't appear to be even breathing hard.

"I've never been any good talking to angry women," he said.

"If you always act the way you do with me, you must have had lots of practice."

"I told you I was no good for you."

"No, you didn't."

"I didn't?"

"Of course not," she said. "You wanted to sleep with me."

"I still do."

"Look, Becker, I like you, you're an interesting man, but basically I don't like the way you want to treat me. I've got better things to do. So do you, apparently."

Becker sighed. "I don't have anything better to do than you."

"Well, you're right about that," she said. She dropped to the floor and began doing push-ups on her fingertips, her spine rigid as a plank. Becker watched the muscles in her shoulders work under the spandex. He resisted an urge to grab her buttocks.

"I mean to say I'm worth something, you understand?" she continued. "You've got nothing better going in your life than me. You just happen to be too stupid to appreciate it."

"I do appreciate it," Becker said. "I already said so. You're the best thing I've got going."

"I'm young and I'm smart and I've got a good heart."

She rolled onto her back and lifted first one leg and then the other and hooked them behind her neck. Sweat finally broke forth, bursting like a sudden freshet on her skin.

"In fact, I've got a great heart," she said. "I'm a damned nice person. Better than you are."

"A lot better," Becker agreed.

"A lot better," she said. Her voice finally showed some sign of her exertions. "Plus you're too old for me."

"I warned you about that, too," he said.

"No, you didn't. I didn't need you to tell me. All I have to do is look at you. You're too old for me, Becker. And you're not nice enough, and generally you're not worthy."

"I wish you'd call me John," he said.

"What I'm saying is, I think you'd better take a hike."

"The reason I go to the shrink is—I'm a mess."

"I could have told you that."

"You might have saved me a few trips to Washington."

"You're closed up like a tin can. I can't get close to you, I doubt if anybody ever has. I don't know if you're worth the effort. You may be hollow for all I can tell."

"I'm not hollow," he said.

"How would you know?"

"Because if I were hollow, I wouldn't hurt."

For the first time she stopped exercising and looked directly at him. Becker felt suddenly overcome by shyness and could not hold her gaze.

"Why do you hurt, John?" she said finally.

Becker pulled his knees up to his chest. "I don't know," he said in a small voice. "But I don't want to take a hike," he said.

"No."

"I want to move in," he said.

Cindi paused for a long moment, looking at him. She lifted his face so he could not avoid her eyes. Becker tried to grin but could not sustain it.

"Well, okay," she said finally.

CHAPTER 12

HATCHER shook a small bag and the stones clunked together dully.

"The only source of gravel within thirty-five miles is a quarry in Clamden. They made one hundred thirty-five deliveries of grade-C gravel—this is grade C, it goes by size—within a fifty-mile radius of Clamden in the six weeks before we found Dyce's—uh—operation."

Hatcher laid a computer printout in front of Becker before he continued.

"These were still covered with dust—a fine rock powder, actually—that's the residue of the crushing machine. Did you know they actually *make* gravel by crushing rock? I didn't know that. I thought they just dug it out of a gravel pit, but they have to break up the big rocks into smaller ones, then run them through this machine—anyway, these still had the powder on them, which meant it hadn't rained on them between the time they were crushed until Dyce

acquired them—you realize this doesn't tell us anything about when he actually got hold of them. They
could have been sitting in his rock collection for ten
years. Maybe he got a wheelbarrowful at a time and
was just keeping them handy."

"You know anybody who bothers to store gravel
indoors?"

"So he got a fistful, put them in a flower pot."

"And never watered the plant? Besides, he didn't
plan these things. He didn't sit down and decide to
kill eight men."

"How do you know?"

"That's not the way it happens."

"Statements like that worry me, Becker."

Becker studied the printout. "How do you think
they make me feel? Look, Hatcher, you're right. We
don't know when or where or how Dyce got the
gravel. My bet is he didn't take it until he needed it,
and he didn't need it until he'd already acted, but I
don't *know* that. I don't *know* anything about Dyce.
I'm just hoping to get lucky. You cross-checked with
the weather bureau, right?"

"Right. Assuming Dyce got the gravel to use as
a . . ."

"Headstone."

"So you say. Assuming he got it on or within a day
of the time he murdered Mick, and eliminating all
deliveries from the quarry that happened before the
last rainfall, which was fourteen days earlier, we have
seven places the gravel was unloaded. They are
marked with asterisks on your printout."

Becker put his finger on one of the names.

"I know," said Hatcher. "I thought that would

appeal to you. They were using it for the pathways."

"Riverside Cemetery," said Becker.

"I know, I know." Hatcher shrugged. "It's ironic. It doesn't mean anything."

"I agree," said Becker.

"You agree?"

"Probably just an ironic coincidence."

"Then why are you smiling? I really wish you wouldn't do that, Becker."

"Smile?"

"Smile if you have to. Just not at me."

"Why?"

"Humor me. I don't like it."

"Did you interview the people who work at the cemetery?"

"Certainly. No one recognizes his photo or description. Did you expect them to?"

"I don't hope to be that lucky. Who's buried there?"

"In the cemetery?"

"Yes."

"In the whole goddamned cemetery?"

"He's there to visit someone's grave, isn't he? Isn't that why people go to cemeteries?"

"Most people don't go at all," said Hatcher, "except to bury somebody. People don't 'visit' graves anymore, do they?"

"He was there for some reason."

"We don't know he was there at all. And even if he was, I thought you thought he was there to get a 'headstone.'"

"He could get a stone anywhere, pick one up out of the street. If they were using these for pathways

. . . it's not as if they're consecrated rocks. I think he was there—if he was there—for some other reason and happened to see the stones at a time when he needed one. Which means either that he goes there regularly—if he goes at all—and his visit happened to coincide with a time when he needed a gravestone. What's wrong with that theory?"

"Is this a quiz, Becker?"

"Just checking my thinking."

"It probably wasn't that he just happened to be there at a convenient time, because three of the stones still had dust on them, which means—since you don't think he got them in advance—that he goes there when he's killing somebody—or because he's killing somebody—something along those lines?"

"Now you're getting the hang of it."

"It's not hard," said Hatcher. "Just toss logic and probability out the window and we can all be geniuses."

Becker studied Hatcher a moment. "There's no point in being envious of me, Hatcher."

"Envious, Christ . . ."

"Because it's no fun."

"That doesn't stop you from doing it."

Becker paused. "Can't argue with you."

Breathing deeply to let the moment pass, Hatcher continued. "So you figure he goes there to commune with the spirit of someone when he's in the act of—whatever?"

"I think it's possible. I think doing this thing to men stirs him to the depths. Let's find out who's in the cemetery. Do a genealogy on Dyce."

"We have. All his relatives are dead."

"That's fine. We're looking for a dead one if Dyce visits him in the cemetery. While you're doing the paperwork, I'll go visit the cemetery. You were there, weren't you? What's it like?"

"What's a cemetery like?" Hatcher could think of nothing appropriate to say about a cemetery. "Very nice," he said.

THE man behind the car-rental counter had the right look to him from the back. Dyce noted the pale hair, neatly trimmed, the long expanse of neck, the ears that pushed out from the head. When in a good mood, Dyce's father had sometimes made fun of his own ears. "I'm just waiting for a good wind," he would say, "then I'm going to take off and fly." And he would wiggle his ears, his eyebrows moving up and down at the same time. Dyce would laugh, delighted by this inexplicable display of whimsey. His father looked so unguarded, so harmless.

"A regular Norwegian squarehead," Dysen would say. "My mother used to cut our hair, practically scalp us, and those were the days when everyone's hair was short. Everybody had big ears; look at the old pictures. But I was worse than most, practically a Dumbo, and don't think the kids didn't give me shit for it."

And then his mood would turn darker as he recalled the slights of his youth. "I'd get back at them, though, don't worry. They could laugh and fart around during class, but I'd be waiting for them after school. Your old man knew how to take care of himself, don't you worry about that, old Rodger-Dodger." He would sometimes try to return to the lighter mood, but the moment was past and Dyce had been reminded of the paranoia and anger lurking always just a fraction of an inch from the surface. He would no longer laugh with his father and that seemed to make the older man angrier.

The man behind the counter turned and the resemblance vanished. He had a round, vacuous face, a countenance without contrast of bone or flesh. His name tag read Tad.

Dyce lay his new driver's license on the counter. "I'd like a compact car," he said.

"Certainly, Mr. . . . Cohen. Do you have a major credit card, please."

Dyce produced a Visa card, as freshly minted as the driver's license, also issued to Roger Cohen. This was the first test of the license since he had bought it for one hundred dollars two days earlier. He had already used the Visa card to get a cash advance against a nonexistent credit line of five thousand, some of which he used to pay for the license and credit card.

Dyce watched closely for any sign of suspicion as Tad went through the paperwork to release the car. If he had any doubts about the authenticity of the documents, none showed on his placid face.

He smiled routinely as he handed the cards back and gave Dyce the keys to his rented vehicle. Dyce carefully replaced the cards in his wallet, an item as new as the cards themselves. Everything about Dyce was new now, from the clothes he wore to the papers in his pockets, all of it financed with the several new cards in his wallet. The bruises on his face had nearly vanished, and the moustache, enhanced with mascara for the driver's-license photo, was coming in nicely.

Once in the car and on his way out of Bridgeport, Dyce finally relaxed. The ease and simplicity of it all scared him more than anything. To think that an underworld of minor thugs and petty hoods could elude the system so efficiently. He could imagine how his grandfather would have inveighed against them, and how his father would have given them grudging admiration.

It was not until he reached New Haven and turned north on Interstate 91 that Dyce realized he had been automatically assessing Tad, the car-rental clerk. I must be crazy, he thought, thinking about that now. There was no time for it; he was being pursued. It was insane to even think about it and besides, he had vowed to put all of that behind him. It was not as if he *had* to do it. Surely he was enough in control of his emotions to deny himself such a dangerous pleasure. Especially in view of the disruption it had just caused. He promised himself to give it up, to give up even thinking about it. This was the perfect opportunity to start fresh in every way. The past was behind him now and he would keep it there; he was certain he could do it. He would shed the old skin and put on a new one as easily as he had slipped out of the hospital and created a new identity.

There is no way they will ever find me if I behave myself, Dyce thought. Criminals are creatures of habit; that's how they are caught, everyone knows that. I am not a criminal, in the first place, and in the second I am too bright to let myself do anything stupid. He remembered the man in his hospital room, the one whose eyes seemed to cleave through Dyce's skull. That man was the danger, Dyce thought. The others do not frighten me. I could walk past them as if invisible—but the one with the searching eyes . . . He tried not to think about it.

After an hour Dyce stopped in the town of Waverly. Within five minutes he had located an independent insurance agent working out of a real-estate office, and asked to be taken on part-time as a salesman. The real-estate agent, happily surprised to find a man who was willing to canvass clients as well as do administrative work, hired him immediately.

"Do you know how to work one of these?" the agent asked, patting the personal computer terminal on his desk.

"Some," said Dyce. "I'm sure I could learn what I need to."

"I'm sure you could, too," said the agent. "You seem like a bright guy to me."

Dyce ran a hand over the terminal as if he were stroking an animal.

"Nice machine," he said.

His father's grave was marked by a simple marble stone whose original reddish-brown hue had aged into a darkish pink that seemed inappropriate to Becker. He remembered helping his mother pick out the headstone at a time when she was scarcely capable of making the least decision and the proper headstone struck her as a very important one. Ultimately she had opted for the slight reddish tint over the plain gray because she felt it would reflect some of the softer side of the man.

Becker was not aware there was a softer side. He

was eighteen and remembered his father as a stern, unyielding maker and enforcer of family law.

"There was much more to your father than you knew," his mother told him, echoing a sentiment she had expressed to the rebellious boy throughout his teenage years. "He had a very sensitive side, too."

Even now, many years later, Becker found his mother's statement hard to believe except as an abstraction: Men can show more sensitivity to their wives than to their adolescent sons. But in reality he could not see how that could apply to *his* father. In his memories, Becker could never conjure up his father's face. The man was always a looming presence, something large and dark and forbidding just at the edge of Becker's awareness. He pictured the presence behind him, watching, and somehow in the frame of a doorway, as if just entering. Or just catching the young Becker in the act of something. "Authority," Becker said to himself now, laughing inwardly as he heard the word coming in Gold's voice. That looming presence you feel as your father is why you have such difficulty with authority today.

Typical of Gold, Becker thought. Quick and easy and clichéd—but possibly right nonetheless.

A bird landed on the tombstone next to his father's and cocked an eye at Becker briefly before taking to the air again, the white underside of its tail flashing intermittently like a burst of Morse code.

His mother's stone was a plain gray. Becker had selected it himself ten years after the first one. She had possessed a softer side, too, no doubt, but it was obscured by his father's shadow. And unlike his father, his mother had no advocate to sing her praises or hold forth for her better aspects. The only thing Becker could recall his father ever said about his wife was in praise of her industry, not her feminine sensitivity.

"Your mother works hard enough without your adding to it," he had said, referring to some mess or other of the young Becker's. Indeed, everything Becker did seemed to be resented by one or the other of them as adding to their burdens in life. Becker himself felt like the biggest burden of all, one borne out of duty rather than love or pleasure.

Some people should not have children, Becker thought, including himself in the proscription. They haven't the gift or the patience for it and they do a bad job. Without knowing they're botching it, probably. With reasonably good will and decent intentions.

Becker had been squatting on his haunches before the graves. He stood now and looked down at them, two grassy plots marked off at head and foot by stone but bordered laterally only in the mind, part of the broad sweep of tended grass, indistinguishable. Part of the lawn now, Becker thought. Surviving only in my memory, and there only infrequently. But alive in the way an artist lives on in his work; their handicraft walks above them now in the twisted framework of my psyche.

The bird returned, flying close enough to Becker to make him flinch, then flapping off, disoriented.

They weren't that bad, Becker thought now, granting his parents a half-hearted absolution. They weren't bad enough to make me the way I am. The rest of it has to come from me, some element uniquely my own.

Then, without thinking or knowing why he did it, Becker stepped forward and stood directly atop his father's grave. He stomped one foot on the soil, hard enough to leave a mark, then, in a confusion of feelings, he looked around to see if he had been observed before returning to the gravel pathway.

Gold will love it, he thought. His neck and ears were warm with the flush of embarrassment. Gold will have a field day . . . If I tell him. There is so much I haven't told him, why start now?

It was not until he had walked for several minutes through the cemetery that Becker realized he had been practically running, trying to escape the shame of his action.

The bird seemed to be following Becker, swooping in erratic, confused figures around him wherever he went. Drunk, thought Becker. It must have eaten some rotting fruit. Drunk—or dying. The symbolism of that was a little too pat and he laughed at himself. I am regressing, he thought. I came here to find Dyce, some piece of Dyce, some part of the fiend that I can identify as part of me, and instead I am turning into a sentimental, angry child stomping on my father's grave, seeking portents like a superstitious mystic.

The bird landed on another headstone, then flew off again, but Becker's attention was suddenly alerted. Atop the grave marker was a single stone, identical to those on the pathway. The name on the stone was Rosen, a woman who had died five years earlier. Looking about, Becker saw three more stones resting atop monuments, two of them also in the Rosen family, another several yards away in a plot belonging to a Martin Aaron who had died four months ago. Within five minutes Becker had located another ten headstones adorned with rocks from the path.

The caretaker looked at him in puzzlement, trying to figure out what Becker was so excited about. He was an old man, past retirement age, who still spoke with the accent of his native Italy.

"Jews," he said with a shrug.

"What do you mean?" Becker asked.

"You ask who puts the stones on the graves? I tell you. The Jews."

"I know the graves are Jewish, but how do you know the people who put the stones on the monuments are Jews?"

"Who else?"

"Have you seen them? Do you know if it's a man? A woman? More than one?"

"Seen them? What do you mean, have I seen them? Sometimes I see them if I happen to be there. Most times, I don't see them, but it's Jews. That's what they do."

"What they do?"

The caretaker wondered if it was his English that was the problem. What he was describing was an everyday occurrence for him.

"They visit the grave, they put a stone, a pebble, a little rock on the headstone as a sign that they visit. It's like a mark, hello, I been here. Somebody else comes by, he sees the stone, he knows Uncle Seymour's been looked after."

"Only Jews do this? Leave these stones for markers?"

"Only ones I know about, but hey, there's no law. Anybody wants to can do it."

"But it's a Jewish tradition?"

"Tradition? I don't know. I'm a good Catholic. They do it, that's all I know. Every month or so, I go by, I take the stones off. You let them pile up, it looks sloppy, people think nobody's taking care."

THE car skittered along the shoulder, the wheels spinning over stones and sand, until it veered back onto the road. Dyce's father put the pint of rye whiskey between his legs and wiped his lips with the back of his sleeve.

"Burns like a bugger going down," he said, turning his half-crazed eyes toward Dyce and grinning. A blast of horn from a startled motorist in the oncoming lane made Dyce's father swerve back from the center line.

"Assholes on the road," said Dysen. "But you got to expect that. We're in asshole territory now. That's why your grandpa lives here. They named the place for him." Dysen paused, waiting to be asked. As usual his son disappointed him. "Assholeville. Named after your grandpa." Dysen laughed.

The boy continued to watch the road with riveted attention, his hands gripping the dashboard, his feet pressed to the floor as if he could control the car from the passenger's seat.

"Relax. Will you relax? Sit back in your seat. I'm watching the goddamned road. That's my job, not yours."

Dyce acted as if he didn't hear his father. He stared straight ahead, trying to keep the car on the road by strength of will. Mr. Dysen looked over at the boy, ignoring him as usual, trying to thwart him, and felt his anger rising sharply.

"I said relax," *he said, and struck the boy with a straight, sharp punch on the shoulder.*

Dyce looked at his father, startled but not surprised.

"That was just to get your attention. Now relax."

The boy sat back, rubbing his shoulder.

"I am relaxed," Dyce said.

"You're about as relaxed as your grandpa's ass muscle. Boy, that came down in a straight line, didn't it? From old Nate through your mother straight to you. Ass muscles tight as a fist. A fart couldn't get out of any one of you. Especially your mother."

Dyce turned away and looked out the side window. Christ, now he'll sulk, thought Dysen. Can't say a damned thing about his mother without him acting like that, all teared up and defiant. What the hell does he know about her? I was the poor bastard who married her. He only had to deal with her for four years before she died. What the hell does he know?

Dysen lifted the bottle to his lips again, just a sip this time. He didn't want to be drunk when he dealt with asshole Nate—but he sure as hell didn't want to be cold sober, either . . . God, it felt good. Not going down; it never stopped burning going down, but when it hit bottom and spread out like warm fingers, it was as good as coming. Get to come in your pants a dozen times or more for the price of a pint. Can't beat that.

When he looked, Dyce was trying to steer the car from the dashboard again. Dysen relented. It couldn't be easy, having no mother, and he had to admit that sometimes he was a little tough on the kid himself. It was good he'd only tapped him on the shoulder, Nate got on his high horse if he found bruises on the boy. Especially on the face—that drove him crazy. As if any normal eight-year-old boy wouldn't have bruises. He had gotten banged up worse than his son ever had, just running around, getting into fights on the playground, whatever. Still, he couldn't afford to alienate old Nate any more than normal, not as long as the old bastard still had control of his checkbook.

Dysen rumpled Dyce's hair. "Old Rodger, old Rodger-Dodger, old Rodger-Codger-Lodger-Dodger."

The boy tipped his head away from his father's hand, waited a tactful moment, then smoothed his hair.

The little son of a bitch hates me, Dysen thought, furiously. He wanted to smack him across the face, he wanted to pull the car to the side, get out, and kick his ass properly. He clung to the steering wheel until his fingers hurt, steadying himself before he took another drink, which he deserved as a reward for self-control. The warmth of the whiskey brought with it a wave of sentiment and suddenly Dysen was close to tears. My son hates me, he thought. I love the little shit and he hates me. I took care of him all his life, and he can't stand to have me touch him. But he loves his goddamned grandfather. That old fart could paw the boy all he wanted, pet him like he was a fucking dog, stroke him until it looked unhealthy to Dysen. The little shit never pulled away from that. Stroking and cuddling and kissing like two women. It didn't look right for men to carry on like that. And whispering to him about Jesus. Christ, that old fart and his Jesus.

"Never trust a religious man," he said aloud.

Dyce was silent. The car had to negotiate a series of blind curves, weaving its way through the last of wood-

land and then they would see the sign that said, "Min-not, Town Limits." Then through the town with its white, three-story houses and green lawns, through the three stoplights, and out into the country again, but this time startlingly different as the land flattened out and a shallow basin of green corn and yellow wheat replaced the forested hills. Dyce urged the car forward, through the dangerous turns, through the town, and to his grandfather's huge stone house—and safety.

"Especially if he gives up his religion and finds God," Dysen said.

"Grandfather has a personal relationship with Christ," said the boy.

"Which is pretty interesting, considering 'grandfa-ther' is a Jew."

"Jesus was a Jew," said Dyce.

Dysen clenched his jaw. "You don't have to believe all the shit the old man tells you. You could try some common sense for a change."

"And I'm a Jew and a friend of Jesus, too."

"Goddamn it, stop that shit!" Dyce recoiled to avoid the blow, but Dysen merely turned down the windshield visor in front of the boy to reveal the mirror.

"Look at yourself. You're a Dysen, you look like me. That means you're a Norwegian; you go back to the goddamned Vikings. You're not a Jew, that's ridicu-lous."

"My mother was a Jew."

"Your mother is dead. Look at your face, look at yourself. Look!" Dysen squeezed his son's head in steely fingers and made him stare at his reflection in the mirror.

"See what you see? Those are Dysen bones, that's a

Dysen nose and ears and eyes and mouth. Look at your chin, boy. Look at my chin. Jewish, my ass. You're a Norwegian, and proud of it, or you better be, or I'll kick some pride into you.''

When Dysen released his grip they were through the curves and into the town. Dysen was still muttering.

"Jew, my ass. The old bastard is just trying to steal my own son away from me.''

Yes, please, thought Dyce. Please, please, grandfather.

"It'll take more than a goddamned check every blue moon to get my own flesh and blood off of me. He can't buy you, Rodger-Dodger, he can't buy my boy.''

Dysen was close to tears again, swept up with love for his son—until the boy tipped his head, eluding another affectionate ruffle of the hair.

Dysen took one last sip at the final stoplight in town, and to hell with anyone who happened to be watching.

The cultivated basin beyond the town came upon Dyce with all the welcome warmth of an embrace. He could smell his grandfather in the scent of overturned earth, he could see his beard moving with the wheat, sprouting from the ears of corn. When they reached the turnoff for the long drive through fields to his grandfather's house, Dyce was holding his breath. His heart still raced from the mention of his going to live with grandfather. It was the first time he had heard anyone else mention the possibility. Until now he had thought it was a secret wish held only in his own heart.

Buy me, grandfather, he yearned. Buy me away from him. Let me come to live with you. I'll pay you back no matter how long it takes or what I have to do for the money.

•   •   •

*THE house had been built over one hundred fifty years
earlier to shelter the owners of the farm against the
harshness of the Connecticut winter, and it was built to
last from stone wrenched by the plow from the New
England soil. The original builders had been clever in
the use of stone—they had had to be because the land
was covered with them like leaves from a tree after a
storm. Stones made the fences separating fields, and
stones made the wells, and stones made the houses,
rough, uncut stones that still had the shape with which
they had been yanked from the soil. The house was
stone piled on stone three stories high and laid across by
beams cut from the timbers of Connecticut's forest.
There were two chimneys on Nate Cohen's house, one
on either exterior end of the huge building and, like the
walls, they too were constructed of stone. It was not a
house that wind or storm or fire would defeat.*

*Much of the original farm was gone, split into parcels
and swallowed by the more successful neighbors, but
the house and the barn and the outbuildings remained,
still intact and maintained scrupulously, just as Nate
Cohen maintained all that over which the Lord had
given him dominion. Because he was a good husband to
the Lord and that which was His, and because he de-
spised all that which was slothful and decayed and
fallen to ruin—including his son-in-law.*

*He waited for them now on the porch of the old
farmhouse, having spied them when they turned onto
the access road and watching their progress since by the
thin trail of dust that followed above and behind their
car as it drove through the fields.*

The old man was the first thing Dyce saw, before the

house, before the barn. Standing on the porch impatiently, his hands on his hips, waiting for his grandson.

He was also the first thing Dysen saw and he muttered under his breath, "king of the assholes," but Dyce didn't care now. He was safe now and protected, at least for the length of their stay.

Dyce ran from the car while his father was still slipping the bottle under the seat and chewing on a clove to hide the scent of alcohol. He ran to his grandfather, who came down the porch steps, arms extended. The boy leapt into his arms and was lifted off the earth and pressed against the old man's neck and beard. Dyce could smell skin and hair and sweat and he thought his heart would burst.

CHAPTER 13

Lying in Cindi's arms, Becker heard the low whine of car tires on pavement as the cruiser prowled by. The night was very quiet, otherwise, with the kind of hushed awareness with which nature anticipated a coming storm. The lights of the car ran quickly across the wall, then onto the ceiling before vanishing.

Cindi stirred and rolled away from him, which told him she was ready for sleep in earnest. She liked to make a show of drowsing off while clinging to Becker as if he were some enormous Teddy bear, but finally she would turn her back to him and slip into real sleep the only way she knew how, on her side, legs up, clasping a pillow to her. It never failed to touch him to see her thus, such a brave and secure young woman giving in to such vulnerability at night.

Easing himself out of bed, Becker glanced at the red numerals of the digital clock. It was 2:45. He wondered when Tee slept, if he was still cruising by at this hour. Perhaps when Becker himself did—when he

238

could no longer put it off, when it came on him with a rush and swept him away without a chance to fight or care what lay in store for him in his dreams.

Standing at the window, naked but for his shorts, Becker stared into the unusual silent stillness of the night. The normal night sounds were stifled and the sky was unyieldingly black. Becker had a sense of dark clouds roiling atop each other, gathering strength and violence, but he could not see them.

Tee's cruiser came back down the road, completing its swing of dutiful vigilance. Becker stepped back from the window. He did not want Tee to see him watching Tee watching him. There seemed no need to complicate the game. As the headlights hit the window, Becker turned to see Cindi's body glowing palely in the illumination dimly reflected from the walls and ceiling.

She was completely naked and her shape seemed to meld into the white pillowcase at her breast as fine distinctions faded in the brief and feeble light. When the headlights were gone, Cindi's image continued to shine on Becker's retina.

He waited a moment for his eyes to adjust and when they did Cindi seemed nearly to have disappeared. Becker could make out the brighter whiteness of the sheets and pillows, but Cindi's flesh, pale though it was, had all but vanished in the gloom.

Becker closed the bathroom door and turned on the light. He searched until he found a container of baby powder. Turning the ventilated lid, he sprinkled some on his hands and rubbed, feeling the silky smoothness of corn starch. The scent reminded him of Cindi, of certain hollows and depressions where the odor lingered long after application.

He smiled wryly at his reflection in the mirror. "You're going to have a fine time explaining this in the morning," he thought.

Leaving the bathroom door open a crack for the light, Becker returned to the bed and gently dusted Cindi's legs with the powder, then her buttocks and her back. She moaned happily as he rubbed it delicately on her body with his palm. But when she turned her head, half awake, for his kiss, Becker eased her back into position. He kissed her softly on the cheek, then slipped away from the bed as she smiled and settled back into sleep.

Becker closed the bathroom door entirely. A line-thin ray of light shone through over the sill and seemed to die, exhausted, a few feet into the room. Becker paced away from the bed, six steps to the corner, as far away as he could get from the bed. Dyce's chair had been twenty feet from the makeshift table or altar. With his back against the wall, Becker sat in the corner and looked at Cindi's body on the bed.

She was now as white as the sheets, a peculiar, unnatural, spectral pale in the dim light. After a few minutes, as he continued to stare at her, his eyes began to rebel against the conditions, and the body appeared to rise slightly above the bed and to float in position all on its own.

A ghost, thought Becker. The optics necessary to create a ghost. Is this what you were looking for, friend Dyce? When you covered yourself in talcum powder and looked in the mirror, what did you want to see? A spook? Something as silly as that, children in bedsheets, Halloween tricks? And when you sat and stared at your victims, did you see the same thing? In Helen's bathroom, dusting yourself in the dark, were you trying to create the same vision in yourself you sought in the men you killed? But not just ghosts; it had to be something more than that, something profound enough to kill for.

Cindi's leg jerked and she groaned in her dreaming. Becker watched as her breathing became more even again, slowly subsiding to a rhythmic rise and fall. It wasn't just optics that made her appear ghostlike, he realized. It was the slight motion caused by her breathing that gave her the sensation of hovering. Ghosts moved, they quivered, they shook.

But you didn't want them to move, did you, Dyce? The drug you gave them, PMBL, is a hypnotic; it reduces men to a comalike state. Metabolism is reduced, bodily functions slow, and that means breathing, too. They were scarcely alive. You sat and watched them. In the dark? In the gloom. That room was sealed off from sunlight like a cavern. You sat like this, watching the men who were laid out flat, men who could not twitch and toss and turn to spoil your illusion, men who barely moved. Did your eyes play tricks on you, too? Did you see these men as ghosts—or did you see them as something real? Something from your own experience, friend Dyce? All of our perversions come from something real in the beginning; they don't just arrive from nowhere. Men lying flat, barely breathing, pale as talcum powder, pale as ghosts. Pale as death. Ghosts move, dead men don't. You wanted them dead, didn't you, Dyce?

You sat in the dark and saw them dead, wished them dead, and ultimately made them dead. Like in the graveyard, you were communing with the dead, weren't you, you son of a bitch.

On the bed, Cindi rolled toward the center, tossing the pillow aside so it fell on the floor. She reached out an arm for Becker's body but her eyes did not open. Becker rose and slid into bed beside her. The light from the bathroom made the door above it appear as dark as the entrance to a cave.

LYING under the eaves, Dyce could hear the rain on the roof, which seemed just inches above his face. It was a comforting sound, one of many in the old house. Dyce loved the sounds of the insects in the country night, he loved the way the wind moved across the open flatland and made the house whistle when it blew hard. He even loved the groan of floorboards, the squeak of doors that age had tilted slightly off the square. None of the sounds frightened him, no matter how dark it was or how late—and it got so very dark in the country on a cloudy night. When his grandfather went to bed for the night, all lights in the house were off and it was as if the old man had pulled the switch on the universe. Even that did not frighten Dyce. He felt safe and protected in his grandfather's house; he knew the presence of the old man would ward off evil. If there were any spirits hovering in the dark, they were from Christ, attracted by grandfather's goodness.

Dyce tried to concentrate on the rhythm of the rain this night, to let the gentle patter lull him into sleep— but the voices kept intruding. Try as he might, he could not shut off his hearing and blank them out. They were louder tonight than usual, angrier. Although he could not make out the words, he could distinguish the voices—his father's tone, high, on a rising pitch, alternately whining and yelling, then slipping occasionally lower, as he uttered imprecations in what he thought were asides to himself but could be clearly heard by anyone in the room. And his grandfather's voice, much lower than his father's, slower and more measured—the voice of God, Dyce sometimes thought—not Jesus who he thought would speak in a gentle tenor, but God the Father, strong but compassionate. This night even grandfather's great patience was being tried and he, too, was angry.

Dyce slipped out of bed and opened his dormer window. Light from the parlor below his bedroom spilled out into the night, swallowed immediately by the rain. And the rain kept him from hearing, too. The voices were louder this way but still masked by the constant tapping on the roof. Dyce did not really need to hear them to understand. The two men had this same argument every time, and in his mind Dyce could see them as he had seen them several times before when he crept from his bedroom and stole halfway down the stairs to peek into the parlor. His father would be pacing, jabbing at the air with his fists, snarling sometimes as he faced the old man. All pretense at sobriety would be long gone by now after repeated visits to the bottle under the car seat. The bottle itself was probably gone and the knowledge that he would have nothing more to drink until midday when the Minnot liquor store opened would be enough to drive Dysen into desperation.

Nate Cohen would be seated in his highbacked chair, the arms worn shiny by use. From his angle on the

stairs, Dyce could just see part of the side and back of
his head as he leaned forward slightly. The old man sat
ramrod straight whenever he was talking to his son-in-
law, never allowing his back to ease into the chair as if
that would be a sign of weakness before the devil. Dyce
knew that grandfather thought his father was the devil.
Sometimes Dyce believed that, too. That was often the
only way to explain his behavior. He could see the wave
in grandfather's silver hair, curving as gently as a furrow in the field, over and past the ear. In the background, behind his father, was the heavy brass
candlestick with its eight candles that grandfather used
for his devotionals. Grandfather did all of his worship-
ping at home; there was no church that did it right, he
had explained to Dyce.

They would be arguing about money, Dyce knew.
His father would be demanding more, alternately cursing and wheedling, frustrated in his powerlessness.
Grandfather would be demanding changes in Dysen's
behavior, some of them about the drinking, some about
his treatment of Dyce. Sometimes he would insist that
Dysen give his son up, let him come to live here in the
old farmhouse—that was when Dyce felt his heart soar
with hope. But his father never agreed. He would continue to yell and whine and in the end he would always
return home to the city with Dyce beside him. The trip
back would be a time of peace, his father happy and
gloating over having won out over the old man again,
and Dyce would be torn between sorrow at leaving his
grandfather and yearning that this moment of satisfaction for his father could last and last. His father never
hit him on the way back to the city.

Finally, unable to blank out the voices or to hear

them clearly, and alarmed by the increase in hostility, Dyce stole to the stairs. He wore flannel pajamas that his grandfather always had laid out for him on the bed and that he always carefully folded and put back atop the covers when he left. He loved the pajamas but he never thought of taking them with him. They were part of grandfather's house, another sign of love, just like the sheets that were always fresh and crisp, the woolen blankets with the crease down the middle from being folded and stored for his return. The wooden floors were cold to his feet as he crept across his room. There was a board that creaked every time, no matter how he tried to avoid it, but he knew they were talking too loud downstairs to hear it.

Dyce settled on the stairs and watched as the familiar pattern began to change. His father was drunker than usual and he would pause sometimes in his ranting as if trying to remember what he was saying, and where he was.

"You struck him on the way here in the car," said grandfather, and there was an ominous note to his voice.

"I never." Dysen seemed insulted by the suggestion.

"You hit him on the shoulder. I saw the bruise."

"He fell down. He's a kid, he falls down."

"You hit him. The boy told me. I saw the bruise when I bathed him."

Dysen squinted at the old man knowingly. "You spend too much time giving my boy baths, how about that? He can wash himself, he's old enough to wash himself." Dysen rocked back on his heels, grinning tri-umphantly as if he had scored a telling point, then staggered as he fought to keep his balance. When he recovered, he seemed lost for a moment.

"He can wash his own damned self," he said finally.

"He has marks all over his body," said grandfather. "He tells me what you do to him."

Dysen shook his head vigorously. "He's a lying little fucker."

"I can report you," grandfather said. "I can have him taken away from you. You are a drunken sot and you mistreat the boy. I will have the authorities give him to me."

"The fuck you will," said Dysen. "You just want him for yourself, you old bastard. You just want to give that boy baths all day long, how about that?"

Nate Cohen rose to his feet. His voice was trembling with fury.

"You AntiChrist!" He lifted his arm, finger pointing at the sky, shaking.

". . . raise your hand to me, you son of a bitch," Dysen said. "I'll take your head off, you old Jew fuck!"

Dyce gasped as his father cocked a fist and stepped toward his grandfather, then lurched past him and toward the stairs. He was on Dyce before he could get to his feet. His father showed no surprise at finding him there.

"Trying to take my boy away from me," he said. He hugged Dyce to him and the alcohol on his breath enveloped them both. "Trying to steal old Rodger-Dodger."

His father swept him up in his arms and staggered down the steps, nearly falling.

"Put the boy down," grandfather demanded. But Dysen clung to his son with both arms.

"We know what the old fart's up to, don't we, Rodger?" He lurched into the parlor, still carrying Dyce.

"I want what's best for the boy."

"We know what he's up to," Dysen repeated. *"We're just a little too fucking smart for the old bastard."*

"Put the boy down, you'll hurt him."

"Never hurt my own son," Dysen said. He thrust his head forward and snarled at the old man, the snarl turned into a laugh, and he wobbled on his feet, suddenly confused again.

"Put him down, let him go to bed," grandfather said. *"He doesn't need to see this."*

Dyce sat heavily onto the sofa, pulling his son atop him, laughing as the breath left him, as if it were a good joke. Dyce looked to his grandfather, his eyes pleading for help. Dysen's cheek pressed against the boy's and the stubble of his beard scraped the skin. Suddenly he was kissing Dyce and squeezing him harder as his mood vaulted into maudlin.

"I love my boy," he said. *"Love my Rodger-Dodger. Won't let you have him. He wants to stay with his papa, don't you. Rodger, tell him, tell the old fart you want to stay with your papa."*

"No," said Dyce.

"No?" Dysen stared at him, blinking, trying to clear his vision as if the boy's remark had made it blurry. *"No?"*

"I want to stay here," Dyce said, but he was so breathless with his own audacity that he wasn't certain if the words came out.

Dysen looked at Dyce for a moment, then at grandfather, shaking his head, bewildered. A smile played at his *lips and for a second Dyce thought it would be all right, he understood.*

Dysen slapped the boy with the back of his hand, then with the open palm going the other way.

Grandfather screamed "No!" then was yanking Dysen to his feet and away from Dyce, pulling so hard the material on Dysen's shirt ripped.

In a blur, his ears still ringing from the blow, his vision misty with tears and disorientation, Dyce saw the two men struggle. Grandfather was surprisingly strong for his age, but even when drunk Dysen knew how to fight. By the time Dyce could get to his feet, his father had the old man on his knees, his hands on his throat. Dyce could hear grandfather coughing and gasping for breath. Dysen was roaring with oaths. In his anger, he seemed happy, and Dyce realized he would gladly kill his grandfather.

Dyce swung the candlestick with both hands from the waist upward. The brass base hit his father in the back of the skull where the head met the neck. Candles flew throughout the room and one hit Dysen on the ear as he turned his head toward Dyce.

His head continued to swivel as he fell, stiff legged, and his eyes caught his son's on the way to the floor. When he remembered it, Dyce thought the eyes were still glowing as they bore into his own even though reason told him his father was dead when he hit the floor.

CHANEY was glowing with satisfaction. He looked to Becker as if the buttons on his cardigan would burst with pride.

"Got him," Chaney said.

He led Becker down the hallway toward the actuarial room, nearly skipping in his excitement.

"Tell me," said Becker.

Chaney kept walking and Becker realized the man wanted to relive his triumph in his own domain, to be overheard and admired by his fellow actuaries. Becker held any further questions until they stood at Dyce's old desk.

A young woman sat at the desk until Chaney shooed her away with a gesture. It was a theatrical impulse, Becker thought. Chaney could have demonstrated his prowess at any terminal, but he wanted to do it at Dyce's.

"Got him cold," Chaney said, pointing at the computer terminal as if it were Dyce himself. His voice was elevated just enough to be easily overheard by the others in the room. Becker realized how Chaney had succeeded in rising above the others into the position of supervisor—he knew how to stage-manage his moments. Becker wondered if Dyce had disliked the man as much as Becker did.

"Why don't you tell me about it?" As if he could have prevented him.

"Well, the key to success is setting up the right trap in the first place," Chaney said, launching into a detailed, technical explanation of his prowess with the computer. The speech was aimed at his peers, not Becker, who understood just enough of it to realize it was fairly ingenious. Not brilliant, but bright. Not, most likely, much better than anyone else in the room could have done. They were actuaries, but manipulation of the computer was essential to their functioning.

When Chaney breathed, Becker cut in.

"Where?"

"What?" Chaney was annoyed at the interruption.

"Where was he when he tried to break in?"

"I'm getting to that."

"And how do you know it was Dyce?"

"How do I know?" Chaney looked taken aback and uncomfortable. "Well, I don't *know* know, but I know. I mean, who else could it be? Who else even knew his file existed? We're going on certain assumptions here, aren't we? Do you want him to sign his name? The trap was set up to alert us when someone tried to get into Dyce's file. I mean, we *assumed* it had to be Dyce, didn't we, Becker?"

"That's Special Agent Becker, actually," Becker said.

The woman who had been sitting at the desk and now stood, arms folded and watching a few feet away, suppressed a giggle. Chaney glowered at her, then glowered at Becker.

"Would you like to continue?" Becker asked politely.

"That's what I was trying to do," said Chaney.

"Where was he when he tried to break in . . . He did break in, didn't he? He was successful."

"You didn't tell me to stop him, just find out when he tried to do it."

"Did he try or did he do it?"

"He did it. He read his file. I mean he 'tried' in the sense that he didn't escape my detection."

"So, where was he?"

"I have that information," Chaney said, speaking as if his bit of gold had turned to dross.

I shouldn't do this, Becker thought. It costs me nothing but time and annoyance to let the man do his little victory dance. Why hassle him and make him look like a jerk in front of his people? Not that I'm making him look like a jerk. He is a jerk, and they probably all know it anyway, so what do I accomplish? I satisfy a small vindictive urge. Petty, petty, Becker thought. No wonder Hatcher is district agent in charge and I never rose higher than special agent. Even the 'special' was no distinction since everyone was called special agent. A hangover from Hoover's grandiosity. No ordinary agents for the Chief.

"The request for information came from an office in Waverly, Connecticut. It began as a request for rates on home owner policies; that's how he got into the system, and from there he moved into actuarial and finally into his own files. He knew all the codes, he had no trouble."

"So he wouldn't know he was being watched."

"There was no way he could detect that from his side. As far as he knows, he got away with it."

"Do you have an address for that office in Waverly?"

"Of course. He didn't just read his file, by the way, in case you want to know." Chaney had turned snippy.

Becker just stared at him.

"Well, he tried to destroy the file, too."

"Did he?"

"You can't erase a personal file from outside the system, of course; we have safeguards on that. Either Dyce forgot or thought he'd take a fling at it anyway. He didn't get away with it."

A small triumph, and not one that belonged to Chaney but to the designer of the original system, but Becker let him have it anyway.

"Well done."

"Thank you."

"What time did this happen?"

Chaney glanced at a notebook in his hand.

"Eleven thirty-six."

"It's only ten o'clock now," Becker said.

"I was going to say P.M."

"He broke in last night and you didn't tell me until now?"

Chaney smiled involuntarily, nervously.

"Actually, it was Friday night."

"This is Monday!"

"I didn't find out until this morning myself . . ."

"If you're going to build a trap, you ought to be able to tell when you've caught something," Becker said. "By now our boy has probably taken the cheese and disappeared back into the woodwork."

Becker yanked the phone from its cradle and punched Hatcher's number.

"You can have your desk back, Miss," Becker said, dismissively turning his back to Chaney.

I really have to work on my people skills, he thought briefly, waiting for Hatcher to answer.

HE brushed grandfather's hair and watched the old man's face ease into relaxation. It was one of the few times Dyce saw his beloved grandfather allow himself to relax, and it thrilled him to be the instrument of it. He used the twin brushes with alternating strokes and watched the hair straighten momentarily, then recover into the gentle waves.

"I must have an Italian in the woodpile," grandfather would say with a wink. "I still have all my hair and all my teeth. Can you believe that?"

"Yes, I can," said Dyce, who believed everything his grandfather told him.

The old man looked at his reflection in the mirror, nodding approvingly, then smiled at the boy who stood behind him. "The Lord takes care of His own in many ways," he said. "He even helps out with your vanity sometimes, although I don't believe He approves of it. But He understands. 'Cause the Lord himself is vain, Roger. Did you know that?"

"Yes, grandfather."

"You did? You did know that?"

"No, sir, I didn't."

"You certainly didn't learn it from your father."

"No."

"And I don't believe I have told you this. About the Lord being vain."

"No, sir."

"Then you don't know it." Roger shook his head, pausing for a moment with the brushes. "How many strokes is that?"

"Seventy-eight," said Dyce, moving the brushes again.

"You mustn't say you know a thing if you don't know it, Roger."

There was never a note of threat to his grandfather's tone. Dyce did not fear being corrected by him because a blow did not accompany the lesson.

"I won't."

"What you know is all you will have in this life. What you know of man and what you know of God. Now the reason I can say the Lord is vain is because of the praise He demands of us. Look at what the Bible tells us to do. Look at what the Lord commands us to do. Praise Him to the Heavens. Sing out His praises. Glory unto God. The Lord wants to hear us praising Him. Glory to God in the highest. He requires it, Roger. And, of course, He deserves it. Vanity in a man is a human failing—not a bad one, mind—but vanity in God is holy. There's the difference. You won't hear that in any church."

"One hundred," said Roger, letting the brushes fall to his sides.

"You might do a few more tonight, lamb," grandfather said. "Considering."

Dyce understood the special circumstances. Grandfather had worked hard all day preparing for the ceremony. He had built the box himself from lumber stripped from the loft in the barn, sewn the cloth, prepared the body. All the while tending to Dyce, feeding and dressing him and offering hug after hug as he explained all that he was doing. The boy understood that his grandfather was concerned about his state of mind, but Dyce was not feeling sorrow the way grandfather feared. He couldn't say he was feeling much of anything except the tingling of hope. If he knew his father was dead, if he could be absolutely certain that he would never come back and that he could stay here forever with grandfather, then he knew what he would feel. But it was too soon; his father was dead too short a time to be fully believed. Dyce had simply put his emotions in abeyance; grief was not called for and hope was too painful if it were to be undone. What he felt more than *anything was anticipation, as if the great event had not already happened but was yet to come. He could not have said what the great event was to be.*

"Let us prepare ourselves," grandfather said at last. He touched Dyce's hand holding the brush. Dyce saw the brown spots on his skin, the large veins that looked swollen, close to bursting through the flesh. Grandfather was seeking his eyes in the mirror and Dyce looked at him and smiled broadly. He hoped the old man could tell how much he loved him, how much he wanted to please him. How very grateful he was for the love the old man showed to him. Dyce would do anything for his grandfather.

"I like to brush your hair, grandfather."

"Do you, boy?"

"Yes, sir."

Grandfather's voice was oddly strained. "Why is that?"

Dyce lay his cheek against grandfather's hair and closed his eyes. "I love you," he whispered.

Grandfather didn't answer and when Dyce looked in the mirror he saw the old man's face twisted into the strangest mask. He looked as though he might cry, but there was something else there, something that Dyce had seen a few times before, but could not identify.

"We must prepare," grandfather said again, in a voice that was cracked. He moved to the window and looked out. "The sun is down," he said. "It's time."

WHEN the candles were lighted and all was ready, grandfather fetched Dyce from the bedroom, leading him into the darkened parlor by the hand. The candles provided the only light in the room and shadows danced

*on the walls and ceiling and floor. His father lay in the
coffin grandfather had made that day, his head resting
on a pillow. A black tarpaulin covered the legs of the
sawhorse on which the casket rested, making it appear
to float in the air.*

*"We will watch him for three days," grandfather
said. "We will pray and ask the Lord to return him to
us. If the Lord chooses not to do so, then we will bury
him."*

*His father's features loomed in the semidarkness of
the room, as sharp as if chiseled from New England
rock.*

*"Come," said grandfather, pulling at Dyce's hand as
he moved closer to the coffin. Dyce pulled back, drawing away.*

"I don't want to."

"He cannot hurt you now."

"I don't want to."

*Grandfather stopped tugging at his hand. He walked
to the casket alone and stood above the corpse, looking
down.*

*"Lars Dysen, you took my only child, my beloved
daughter, away from me and killed her with your abuse
and neglect. You drank and whored and blasphemed
and wasted the life the Lord gave you. You mistreated
my beloved grandson and beat him and deprived him of
the joy of his youth. You have been a canker in my life
since the day I first saw you and I have hated you, and
the Lord has turned His face from you and brought you
to this end . . . I forgive you now for all you have done
to me and mine and I pray that the Lord will forgive you
also. I pray for your return to us, and if the Lord sees*

fit to take you unto himself, I pray for your redemption."

Nate Cohen leaned into the coffin and kissed his son-in-law, then stood aside and regarded his grandson.

Dyce shook his head violently.

"You must," said grandfather. His voice was calm and understanding.

In the flickering of candlelight, Dyce thought he saw his father move. He began to cry.

Grandfather was nodding his head slowly now. "You must," he repeated. "The Lord wants you to."

Dyce whimpered. Please don't make me, he thought. Please, grandfather, I'll do anything for you, but please not this, don't make me do this.

Grandfather stood waiting. With his eyes on grandfather, not looking at his father, Dyce approached the coffin, little bursts of fear shaking his chest with sound.

Grandfather lifted the boy and held him over his father's face. Dysen's face moved, seemed to rise, to come forward toward Dyce's face. The boy could see his eyes through the pale lids, the pupils wide with anger, red streaks shooting off into the whites like furious fire. Dyce squeezed his own eyes closed, but he could still see his father's face, drunken, dangerous. Deadly. I do not want him back, Dyce thought. I want him dead, dead, dead.

"Kiss him," said grandfather.

The old man's hands trembled with the effort of holding the boy up. He put his knee against Dyce's buttocks to help support him. Dyce felt the pressure in his bottom and groin.

He opened his eyes and Dysen was even closer, pale, so ghastly pale, but all the blemishes were gone. The broken blood vessels, the veins burst in the nose, the red flushes on the cheeks that seemed to burn when he drank—all had vanished into a smooth, snowy white.

"Kiss him," grandfather said. "You must." His knee pressed harder into Dyce's bottom as he urged him forward a bit more so that the boy's face was nearly touching his father's.

Again the corpse seemed to move. Dyce squeezed his eyes closed and pursed his lips, then touched them to his father's skin. It was so cold. Grandfather had shaven the corpse in the morning, but the beard had continued to grow and a slight stubble pricked against the boy's lips.

Grandfather sat in his chair and Dyce stood beside him, holding the old man's hand.

"Now we will watch," said grandfather. "When I am gone, you must do this for me."

Dyce stared dutifully at the corpse for a while, watching it seem to sway and lift in the candlelight, choking down his terror. After several minutes he became aware of grandfather's hand clutching his own. The hand seemed so warm and the warmth just kept increasing. Dyce glanced at grandfather to see if he felt it, too. Grandfather did not return his look, but pulled slightly on Dyce's hand, drawing him around to the front of the chair.

"See how peaceful he looks," said grandfather. "How serene. Nothing troubles him now."

Dyce climbed onto grandfather's lap and lay his head back against the softness of the old man's silver beard. Grandfather put one arm around the boy's waist and with the other continued to hold his hand in his gentle, fiery grip. When he spoke, his breath tickled Dyce's ear, making it tingle.

The two of them continued to watch the corpse in silence. Dyce felt grandfather growing hard against his bottom. He shifted his weight and grandfather imperceptibly tightened his grip on Dyce's waist, pulling him more firmly into his lap. Dyce loved the warmth of grandfather, the safety and comfort of him. He would do anything for him. After a time the feel of the firmness pressing against his bottom no longer confused him.

"How serene," grandfather said.

They watched until the candles guttered out and the room was in darkness.

"WE'VE got Special Agent Hoban coming down from Boston; he's actually the closest. He should be in Waverly already. We can fly in to an airstrip in Minnot and from there it's a half-hour drive to Waverly. The plane's ready for us now at McNeil airport. Allowing for traffic, we'll be at the insurance agent's office within an hour. It's a Cessna eight seater, a little bumpy, but we can't get a jet into the Minnot field. You can handle a little airsickness, can't you, Becker?"

Becker studied the traffic in front of them as they raced toward the airport. The driver was good; he made high speed seem almost safe.

"I'm not going," said Becker.

"What do you mean? We've got the guy."

"So far you've got a computer terminal, but I'm not going with you anyway. I told you, I'm not going down any more holes for you. You go down this one."

"Hole, what hole? He's trapped in plain sight."

"A lot of people are using the word trapped, but I haven't seen anyone actually caught yet."

"We know where he is, we know who he is, he doesn't know we're coming. What do you want? You expect him to come out with his hands up before we even get there? We even know his family."

"When?"

"Records and Statistics came up with it last night."

"Everybody's taking his time about telling me things."

"I *am* in charge, you know," said Hatcher. "You want to know how we found the family?"

Becker shook his head. People asked the stupidest questions. The driver was passing on the inside lane, weaving like a fish through the rapids. He hated driving in cars with broken seat belts and the belts in the backseats of federal cars seemed never to work.

"He worked for a pharmacist once, apparently while he was still in college. Delivering prescriptions. The DEA had his prints on file for the standard security procedures because he was handling prescription drugs and controlled substances. What do you want to bet that's where he learned about PMBL? Probably stole some from the supply room. A gallon jug would last him for life. So we got his real name, his family background, and his source of supply all from the same search. Talk about serendipity."

"We didn't find any gallon jug of PMBL in his house. Where is his supply?"

"I mean we found out where he probably got it."

"If he got it ten years ago, does that mean he's been killing men for that long? Or did he take a sample of PMBL just in case he might someday want to start drugging his victims?"

"When we find him, you can ask him. We might be digging up kitchen floors for a week just to keep up with him."

"You find him. I'll ask him when he's behind bars in a straitjacket."

"What are you afraid of, Becker?"

Hatcher regretted the remark immediately. Becker turned slowly away from the traffic and looked into Hatcher's eyes. He didn't appear to be angry, Hatcher thought. His gaze was pitying, murderous, maybe, but not angry.

"Sorry," said Hatcher.

"Who's his family?"

"Well, as you know, his real name isn't Dyce, it's Dysen. Norwegian, right? The kind he's looking for, but his mother wasn't Norwegian; that's the strange thing. Her maiden name was Cohen. Jewish."

Becker nodded. "Jewish."

"Your theory on the stones and the grave markers? Okay, you may be right about that, but not in the cemetery in Clamden. He has no family there. You're wrong on that one. If he went there to commune when he picked up the stones, he wasn't communing with family. We went back to his great grandparents on both sides and none of them is in the Clamden graveyard."

Becker shrugged. "The stones were just gravel, they could have been from anywhere."

"What's wrong, Becker? You don't like your own theories anymore?"

"I guess I don't like them when they become yours, Hatcher."

"Have you lost your touch all of a sudden? Have you lost the legendary Becker feel of a case?"

"I wish," said Becker.

"Well, we didn't need it anyway, did we? We cracked this one with ordinary detective work. The kind the less gifted among us can still perform."

"More power to you." Becker leaned forward slightly and caught the driver's eye in the mirror. "Reynolds, after you drop Hatcher at the airport, you can swing me back toward Clamden."

Reynolds, reduced now to just eyes and brows in the mirror, sought out Hatcher for confirmation.

Hatcher said, "You can still be useful up there, Becker. You're the only one who knows what Dyce looks like."

"Tee saw him in the hospital, too."

"Who, the local sheriff? Come on."

"He's a good man and he knows as much about this case as anybody."

The car nosed in front of traffic and came to a halt at the terminal amid the honking of horns.

Hatcher got out and leaned toward Reynolds.

"Get a hold of Sheriff Terhune. I want him in Waverly as fast as you can arrange it." Hatcher slammed the door closed. "And take Becker wherever he wants to go."

They watched Hatcher stride quickly into the terminal. He was thick through the hips and his toes splayed out to either side like a dancer's. In a hurry, he looked like a duck. Behind his back the men called him Donald.

As the car backed into traffic then spun away from the curb, Reynolds was already on the radio.

CHAPTER 14

SPECIAL Agent Ty Hoban's full name was Tyree Zorro Hoban after the legendary masked swordsman and a character in an old John Ford Western. Being a black in Boston and somewhat beleaguered by life, Hoban's father usually sided with the Indians, but something about the character of Tyree caught his fancy as he watched the late movie on the TV in the hospital waiting room while his son was being born. Hoban was only grateful that his father hadn't been watching *Tammy* at the time—or *Gidget Goes Hawaiian.* His mother was Hispanic, so Hoban's father threw in the Zorro as a nod to the only Spanish hero he could think of. By the time Hoban's mother came out of the recovery room, the deed was done.

If anyone in the FBI other than the clerk in personnel who handled birth certificates knew Ty Hoban's full name, they had been smart enough not to let on. People generally did not tell Ty Hoban things that might annoy him, since he had inherited his father's huge, muscular frame to go with a name that was asking for trouble. Hoban was not terribly well-coordinated—a bit on the clumsy side, in fact—and had never played football or basketball, despite his height and heft, but if other people wanted to think he was an ex-linebacker and gave him the commensurate respect, he was not one to disabuse them.

The disadvantage to being a six-foot-four black man in a business suit was that it made being inconspicuous extremely difficult, not to say ludicrous, particularly in a small Connecticut town like Waverly. Keeping a low profile was not within Ty Hoban's range of abilities, although he had many others. Selecting an agent on the basis of his race or appearance was strictly forbidden within the Bureau's code of bureaucratic behavior, however, and so Hoban, the closest man at the time, was sent to the insurance agency in Waverly as the advance scout of the larger troop of agents that would be there later in the day.

A brown-haired man with a full beard looked up questioningly from his desk as Ty Hoban entered the office, temporarily filling the doorway.

"May I help you?"

"Ty Hoban," said the agent, extending his huge hand.

The man half rose to shake hands. "Roger Cohen," he said. "Pleased to meet you. What can I do for you?"

"Well, Mr. Cohen, I hope someone can sell me some insurance. I just bought a house in Waverly and the bank tells me I have to have homeowner's insurance before they give me the mortgage."

"I can certainly help you with that. It will take about ten minutes."

"Everyone else gone to lunch?" asked Hoban. "It seems awfully quiet."

"It's a quiet town," said Cohen. The owner and I are the only ones who work here and you're right, he's at lunch. Did you want to wait for him?"

"That would be Mr. Rice?"

"Rice? No, his name is Hogg. Charles Hogg."

"Really? The people at the bank told me I should see Mr. Rice. Maybe I have the name wrong? Rice? Tice? Something like that."

Hoban watched the man closely. His eyes looked vacant as he slowly shook his head.

"No, no one like that here. As I said, there's just the two of us."

"Was it Dice, maybe? I'm sure they said there was somebody around like that."

Cohen continued to shake his head.

"I guess I just misunderstood," said Ty. He leaned back in his chair, relaxed and casual, but his eyes never left Cohen's face. He fit the description only in hair color and age, but it wouldn't be the first description that was wrong. Ty had been told to A&D. Ascertain the suspect's whereabouts and deploy forces until the order to apprehend. Deploying would be a little tough since Ty was the only force at his command at the moment, but as for ascertaining, it looked to him as if someone had screwed up again. If this puny little thing was the man who collected bones under his kitchen floor, then his appetites were one hell of a lot fiercer than his appearance. Ty knew better than to judge by looks alone—how often was he himself misjudged?—but still, instinct played a part in these things, and this guy looked as if he'd have trouble dissecting a frog in biology class.

"There is another insurance agency in town," said Cohen. "I don't think they can do anything for you we can't do, but . . ."

"No, this is fine," said Ty. "I don't want to cause anybody any trouble." He'd check out Mr. Charles Hogg, too, of course, but his guess was that his man was probably at the other insurance agency, or in another town, or nowhere at all. It wouldn't be the first time he'd been given the wrong address.

"No trouble," said Cohen. He looked on his desk for something he couldn't find. "Should we look at the homeowner's policy, then?"

"You bet."

"I'll need some information before I can give you a quote, but I promise you I'll find the best deal that's around. That's the advantage of coming to an independent agent; we're not locked into any one company."

Ty put his hand atop the computer terminal. "That's what this is for?"

"That's it, that's our access to just about any company in the country." Cohen rummaged in his desk for a moment. "I'm out of forms, I'll just get one."

He was on his feet and walking toward a door in the back of the office before Ty could think of a way to stop him short of tackling the man.

"Won't be a minute," said Cohen, smiling, as he stepped through the door.

The speed of the man's withdrawal surprised Ty and set off an internal warning. Ty still didn't think he

was the bone man, but there was no real assurance
that he wasn't, either. After all, he was in the right
place, he was the right age and general size—along
with forty percent of the male population in the country. No one had said anything about a beard, but then
no one had seen him for several weeks, either, and it
definitely made Ty uncomfortable to have him disappear like that. A&D meant keeping the suspect under
surveillance until some larger cheese like Hatcher
could come waddling in, quack a few times, and get
credit for the arrest—it did not mean sitting on his ass
and watching him slip away into a rat hole.

By its location, Ty could tell that the storeroom did
not have a door leading to the outside but he couldn't
be sure there wasn't a window. Ty decided to give
"Cohen" three minutes. If he didn't return by then,
Ty would go help him search for the right form himself. If he did come right back, it was a pretty good bet
he wasn't the suspect.

Ty left the office and walked around the corner of
the building. He spotted a window that probably led
into the storeroom, but it was closed and the shade
was drawn. If "Cohen" was going to flee that way, he
would already have made his move and he couldn't
have done so through a closed window. Ty turned
and went back inside.

Once he was back in the office, Ty glanced at his
watch, then crossed to the storeroom door.

"Mr. Cohen?" he called. "You all right in there?"

There was no response. Ty tried the door. It opened
immediately. Ty paused a moment, then stepped into
the dark storeroom. As he felt for a light switch with
one hand, the other moved reflexively toward the

holster under his jacket. He felt a pinprick in his thigh and swung a huge arm in front of him to sweep the man away, but Cohen had already stepped back. Agent Hoban could see him pulling farther back into the dark behind a file cabinet.

"Freeze," said Hoban, freeing his gun. "Federal agent."

"Don't shoot. Don't shoot. I'm unarmed."

Ty reached toward the pain in his thigh and felt the syringe sticking out of his leg.

Don't panic, he told himself. You can handle this. First get the man into the light, then get to the phone.

"Come out of there. Now!"

The man, Cohen or Dyce, stepped into the office, his hands in the air. He looked entirely too calm.

Ty backed toward the phone on the desk, keeping the man at gunpoint.

"You sterilize this needle?" he asked, realizing the irrelevance of the comment as he spoke.

"Oh, yes. You won't get infected. I wouldn't do that."

Thoughtful little asshole. "What's in it?" Ty asked, pointing at his leg. He couldn't decide whether removing the syringe would make matters worse. The leg no longer hurt, which he knew was not a good sign.

"PMBL," said Dyce.

"What the hell is that?" Ty saw the phone but couldn't seem to move any closer to it. He thought of shooting the bastard's head off just because. What the hell *is* it? he demanded, only then realizing he hadn't spoken. Couldn't speak.

"I would tell you, but I don't think you'd under-

stand," said Dyce. The man was huge and the dose
was only the usual one. As the man sat heavily on the
desk, Dyce was afraid that he hadn't given him
enough. The agent continued to stare at Dyce as the
gun slowly lowered into his lap.

Shoot the motherfucker, Ty thought. He's killed
you, shoot his head off. But he couldn't lift the gun,
couldn't pull the trigger. As he pitched forward onto
the floor he could no longer see it rising up to hit his
face.

It took a considerable effort for Dyce to drag the
man to the storeroom. It would not be possible to get
him into the car without being seen, and taping his
arms and legs would buy Dyce only a few minutes
beyond the life of the drug anyway. Killing him, on
the other hand, would give Dyce enough time until
Hogg happened to go to the storeroom. That could be
minutes or it could be days. He could cut the man's
throat with the scissors from his desk. Or he could
inject an air bubble into his artery. He had heard that
that would do it, but he wasn't sure. The scissors were
more certain.

Dyce found the FBI badge and identification and
put it in his pocket, then thought about taking the
gun, too. He held it in his hand and experienced the
surprising weight of it. It was beyond imagining that
he would ever point a weapon like this at another
person and pull the trigger. Just contemplating the
violence of it made him shudder with distaste. He was
not that kind of man and had no desire to become
one.

The artery in the man's neck was easy to find. Dyce

pressed and held a finger against it and watched the artery swell.

The agent was looking at him, but there was no message to read in his eyes; he seemed to be looking on with complete disinterest. The scissors were large and bulky and dull, a clumsy instrument. Dyce remembered the surprising blade on the knife he had used with Helen. That had been so pleasant, he recalled. A moment they had shared together—a long moment. It had been ruined at the end by her outburst, but on the other hand it was her very vitality that had made the experience so good in the first place. This agent wasn't going to struggle, but Dyce wished there was some animation in him. Watching the peace come over Helen's face had been so sweet. The agent didn't look peaceful so much as arrested mid-breath. He looked as if he had been abruptly clubbed, pole-axed like a steer. Serenity would come in time as the muscles gradually relaxed, but Dyce, alas, did not have time.

"This is going to be a little on the sloppy side," he said apologetically to the agent. "I haven't really had time to prepare. If I'd known you were coming . . ." Dyce giggled. "You should always call first, didn't you know that?"

Although the dose was average, its effect was stronger than usual. Dyce regretted it, but how could he have suspected this man would be so susceptible. He'd been afraid the normal dose wouldn't be strong enough. He knew it was too late to change anything, but if only there was enough energy left in the man to respond in some way. There was beauty in doing it the old way, beauty and peace, but the time with Helen had been exciting in a brand-new way.

The artery stood out against the pressure of Dyce's finger, throbbing. Invitingly, Dyce thought. "You won't feel this, of course, but I don't think it hurts much anyway. Not that anyone has ever told me." He started to giggle again.

He opened the scissors and drew one of the blades across the artery. A white line showed against the dark skin, but no blood. Dyce tried the other blade and managed to get only a trickle from damaged capillaries. The blade was too dull to penetrate to the artery.

"I mean, really," he said in disgust. He looked into the agent's eyes, which looked back with the same impassivity. "I might as well be using a saw," he said.

Dyce turned the man's head away so that the blood, if he ever managed to get to it, would spurt away from himself. Using the tips of the scissors, he began to snip.

"My apologies," he said. "This is really clumsy . . . Under different circumstances, I think we might both have enjoyed it."

But Dyce was enjoying it now, surprising himself with the pleasure he took, even in this unaesthetic way.

The blood, when it finally came, was astounding in its volume and pressure. To think that all that pressure came from the tiny pump of the heart.

It took him several minutes to clean his hand before he closed the closet door behind him and then he had to go back in to retrieve the syringe.

Surprisingly, although the needle had snapped off in the big man's leg when he fell, the syringe itself was unbroken. He would need another needle, perhaps several, and more PMBL. There was a needle in the car hidden under the material of the visor and enough PMBL under the seat in a water bottle to suffice for one more injection. After that he would have to return to his supply.

Dyce's heart was pounding and he realized it came from excitement, not exertion. Helen had been a revelation and this agent a confirmation. There was more to dying than just being dead. The state of death was serene—but dying, dying was a dynamic act shared by two. Dyce was sorry that it had taken him so long to realize it—but grateful he had learned at last.

DYCE glanced in the plate glass window of his office and was surprised at how calm he appeared as he walked toward his Valiant. A casual observer would never know he was a man who had just had a life-altering experience. Dyce laughed inwardly at his inadvertent pun. The experience had actually altered two lives.

A clerk from the hardware store was standing in the store's doorway. He nodded and smiled politely at Dyce.

Dyce took the time to pause. "How are you today?" he asked. "Looks like a good one, doesn't it?"

The clerk glanced up at the sky. The cheekbones are perfect, Dyce thought. And the nose, sharp and raw as a chip of flint. The eyes were wrong, but they'd be closed.

"High time we had a good day," the clerk said. Even the mouth was right, with the same taut lips as his father's. Dyce felt the stirring within and wondered that it could strike him even now, even when he should be fleeing and sated. In a way the death of the agent may have been only a tease, he realized, not a resolution. He may have served only to whet Dyce's appetite. Or perhaps to combine two appetites into one larger, all-encompassing, insatiable one. He felt like a man who had lived his life on a diet of brown rice and has just had his first taste of ice cream.

"Well, have a good one," Dyce said. He felt the clerk watching him as he forced himself to walk casually toward his Valiant and slide behind the wheel.

Perhaps we'll meet again, Dyce thought to himself. He adjusted his rearview mirror and saw that the clerk was, indeed, watching him. Not with any great interest—there was little else to look at on the street—but watching him nonetheless. We may well meet again, he thought. We shouldn't, but we may.

Driving well within the speed limit, Dyce left Waverly and headed north toward Minnot.

"WE stopped calling it sexual perversion a few years ago," Gold said. "Too judgmental. Paraphilia sounds more scientific, anyway."

"As if there were science involved," said Becker.

"We have our professional image to maintain," said Gold wryly. "Otherwise, we could just call everybody loony and be done with it. Being scientists, however, we like to sort our loonies into categories and give them names."

"You've loosened your sphincter muscles a bit since we began," said Becker.

"That's the effect you have on me. You're so comforting to talk to."

Becker laughed.

"Is this a new tack? Shrink as wit and good guy? Shrink as pal?"

"Shrink as human, maybe. Since I can't impress you with my credentials or my vast learning, I might as well try my menschlichkeit."

"I'm impressed."

"Great, then let's get on with it. What do you need to know about paraphilia?"

"How does it happen?"

Gold shrugged. "I don't know how specific I can be, but which particular variety? There are an awful lot and some of them have yet to be identified, like the insects in the Amazon basin."

"Dyce's variety. I think he has to make himself look like a corpse to get aroused. And I think he likes to look at other corpses. I don't know if he does anything to them or not, but I'm pretty sure he sits there looking at them. Probably in the dark. And not just any corpse or he could get a job at a mortuary. They have to look a certain way."

"That's what the mother's maiden name is all about?"

"I think it's a start. If you like redheads with green eyes and freckles, it's not a bad idea to start with people with Irish names. He wants Scandinavians, or people who look that way. So he starts with people whose mothers were of Scandinavian descent. He's got access to thousands of names anyway and this way he's not going on a random search; he knows where they live, where they work. It's easy enough for him to get a look at them and see if they're what he's after."

"Why doesn't he find someone who looks right in the first place?"

"Because it's difficult and dangerous. If he sees somebody in a line in a supermarket, how is he going to find out enough about the guy's patterns to abduct him? Follow him home? Hope his wallet falls out of his pocket so he can get an address? Strike up a conversation and have witnesses see him? It's not as if he's just trying to pick somebody up; he's selecting a victim, and he's very careful about it."

"Why does he use the mother's name? Why not the victim's own name?"

"I'm not sure. There's always the fact that you can't be sure the father is really the father, but I suspect it's to avoid creating an obvious pattern. I think he's been at this a long time, and the only way he's gotten away with it is by making it appear that nothing at all is happening."

"Any idea why your boy likes Scandinavians?"

"His father was Norwegian is all I know. His mother was Jewish, but she died shortly after he was born anyway."

Becker paused and Gold studied the ceiling for a moment.

"Well—in general, paraphilias are caused by some sort of psychic trauma that occurs when a child is between the ages of about three and eight. That's when the pattern is set in the mind—a lovemap, some call it, but I'm not crazy about the term. It sounds too much like pop psychology, although it's meant very seriously. Anyway, something happens to the child to derail the normal erotic drive. It could be child abuse—it frequently is—or the loss of a parent or sibling. It could be as simple as severe sexual repression in a family's attitudes so that the child finds a way of expressing his desire by masking it. Spankers, mild sadists, people who can only have sex if it's seen as punishment. It could take the form of a fetish that substitutes for forbidden lust—rubber suits, leather, silk garments. Or it can be caused by very complicated circumstances and find expressions that are bizarre in the extreme. There are men who need to kill their partners after sex as a form of atonement. You probably know about those."

"Why do you say that?"

"Professionally, I mean. Does any of this help at all? Or even tell you anything you didn't already know?"

"Not really."

"Sometimes it helps just to hear it said aloud," said Gold.

"Maybe."

"And how about you?"

"What about me?" Becker asked.

"Any closer to telling me about *your* traumas? It's all for the same price, as long as you're here."

"Is there any hope for curing somebody like Dyce? If you could find out what has caused him to be this way, could you undo it?"

Gold studied Becker for a long moment.

"Truth?"

"No, lie to me."

"No, there's not much hope. We could keep him drugged, which would probably prevent him from doing it again, whatever it is he does. But to change him fundamentally? He's a very, very sick puppy. This isn't neurosis we're talking about. My profession isn't too bad with neurosis; we can cure it, or help it, or mask it. But psychosis? No. He's probably that way for life."

"The wiring is twisted."

"In the brain, you mean? Yes. Things are hooked up wrong. Some conditions are just because of chemical imbalance, we think. Bipolar manic depression, definitely. Schizophrenia, probably. In time we should be able to control those conditions completely with a pill. I don't mean drug them; I mean treat them specifically as we can do with hypertension or diabetes. But psychosis is different. You're right—it's in the permanent wiring by the time they're adults, and we're just not able to tinker with the wiring in the brain. Not yet."

"So there's no hope."

"For Dyce. There's hope for you."

"I'm not talking about me," said Becker.

"That's all you've talked about since I've met you," said Gold.

They sat in silence for a long time.

"Tell me about people who enjoy killing," Becker said at last.

THE flight to Minnot was like a half-hour roller-coaster ride—a good twenty-nine minutes longer than

necessary for anyone but a teenager. Or perhaps
someone who's had his stomach surgically removed,
Tee thought. It was certainly more than he needed; he
got the point on the first dip and didn't need any
further reminder of the frailty of the aircraft, the
whimsical nature of air currents, or the delicacy of his
own inner ear.

"It's summer," the pilot yelled over the sound of
the engine after the plane had regained altitude only
to be sucked downward abruptly once more. "The
sun heats up the ground, the air rises, and you get
these wind shear kind of things."

Wind shear was a word Tee associated with airline
disasters. He reached forward to brace himself, but
there was nothing to hold onto in the tiny aircraft.
Agent Reynolds had shooed him onto the plane with
assurances that it was perfectly safe—and also the
only thing immediately available. The pilot/
meteorologist appeared to Tee to be sixteen and wild-
eyed. He likes being bucketed up, down and sideways,
Tee moaned to himself. The kid is up here for the
sport.

"It's nothing to worry about," said the pilot. He
grinned at Tee's discomfort, revealing a large gap
between his front teeth, a condition Tee had always
associated with stupidity. "Don't fly much, do you?"

"Only in real airplanes that give peanuts," Tee
said. He couldn't decide what to do with his eyes.
Looking out made him dizzy and if he looked at the
instrument panel, all the whirring dials and flashing
numbers alarmed him. The plane tilted sideways and
groaned loudly.

"How about you?" Tee asked. "Do you fly much?"

The pilot laughed. He thinks I'm joking, thought Tee.

"It's just the summer," the pilot said again. "It's not dangerous. Except during landing."

Tee decided his best bet was to close his eyes and pretend to be asleep. If that didn't work, he would try to throw up in the pilot's direction so he could get a little satisfaction before the adolescent killed them both.

He had tried to protest, but Reynolds had hustled him to the airport and onto the plane before he had much of a chance to think up a good excuse. Not that there was ever a very good excuse for a law officer to ignore a direct request by the FBI, but some kind of demurrer seemed in order if only to establish his independence. The fact was, he didn't have any excuse; he could be spared at any time and the department would function pretty much the same. It was actually rather exciting to be invited in on the last of the chase for Dyce—it was the feeling of being commanded that he objected to.

They circled once over a surprisingly flat area of ground that appeared suddenly amidst the surrounding wooded hills as if a giant foot had landed there while striding past. Luxuriant crops covered the area, and along one side was a green strip, distinguishable from the rest of the land only by a windsock at one end and a white streak of powdered limestone that had been laid down the center. The windsock stood straight out from its pole.

"Kind of tricky here," the pilot said before nosing the plane into a steep decline that Tee would have thought was a power dive rather than a runway approach.

The young pilot brought the plane down as if the grassy airstrip at Minnot were a diving board and he were taking a few preliminary bounces to test the spring.

"Not bad, huh?" The pilot flashed the gap between his teeth at Tee.

I knew he was a teenager, thought Tee. He wants a grade.

"Pretty good, I'd say," said the pilot. He taxied to the end of the runway and stopped. "You don't mind walking to the terminal, do you? I have to take up a glider now and it's right here."

Tee saw a goateed man and his pretty daughter standing next to an engineless aircraft a few yards away. The girl looked to be about the age of the pilot, which meant she was too young for Tee. But not too young to appreciate.

"Where is it?" Tee asked.

"Right there." The pilot pointed at the glider.

"I mean the terminal."

"Oh. Well, we call it a terminal." The pilot nodded toward a building alongside the field, equidistant between the two ends. Tee had thought it was a refreshment shack.

Tee staggered briefly as he got out of the plane and clutched at the wing for support, hoping the pretty girl had not noticed.

"Great day for it, isn't it?" asked the man with the goatee.

The girl smiled shyly. The flash of her perfect white teeth transformed her from pretty to a ravishing beauty and Tee felt his knees weaken, no longer sure if it was airsickness or the lust, longing, and bittersweet sense of loss that beset him several times a day when he saw loveliness that was forbidden him. More and more beauty was denied him every year, an unrelenting calculus that depressed him when he paused to think about it.

He had not been entirely wrong about the terminal being a refreshment shack. The proprietor, dispatcher, air-traffic controller, and owner of the field was stocking one of three candy dispensers as he explained that a car had been left at Tee's disposal along with directions to find Hatcher and he, the owner, would explain it all to Tee just as soon as he got the machine loaded and ready to go. Tee assumed the vending machines provided more of an income than the airstrip.

Standing outside the shack, waiting for his car, Tee saw Dyce drive by. The road was no more than ten yards from where Tee stood, and for perhaps a second he and Dyce looked directly into each other's eyes before the car passed. It wasn't much and the man's appearance was greatly changed by his beard, but Tee recognized the eyes of the man who had looked up at him from the hospital bed, the eyes that had locked with Becker's in that peculiar, semiseductive confrontation. He was convinced he had seen the shock of recognition in Dyce's eyes just now, which meant that there was no time to lose in pursuit.

Dyce's car did not change speed and Tee could not see him moving his head to look back in the mirror, but he knew it was Dyce. As startled as Tee, no doubt, but too cool to give himself away. It was a game that

Tee had to play, as well, and he made himself walk slowly back to the terminal as long as he was in Dyce's line of vision. He wasted no time once in the terminal, lifting the proprietor by the armpits and propelling him to the board with keys dangling from hooks.

"Call the police—no, give me the keys *first*—and have them get in touch with Hatcher of the FBI. Hatcher, he's in Waverly. Got it?"

Tee was already sprinting toward the waiting Toyota. "Tell him I'm following Dyce, going that way." He jabbed his finger in the direction Dyce had taken, then leaped into the Toyota.

WITHIN two minutes Tee caught up to the Valiant that was still driving within the speed limit. The roads through this flat section were long and straight, with few turnoffs, and if the Valiant had been trying to elude pursuit, it would have had to speed, but the car was fairly dawdling along.

Tee began to wonder if he had the right man. He had seen him for but a second, at a distance, in a moving car, wearing a beard. Hatcher would have his ass served on a platter if Tee had pulled him away from a stakeout to chase the wrong man. Surely, he won't come, Tee thought, if he really has Dyce cornered in Waverly. Pray God he'll know better than to leave the real one behind and come following me. What the hell do I know? I'm the chief of police in *Clamden,* for Christ's sake.

The road continued straight as a plumb line and the Valiant drove steadily onward at thirty-five miles per hour with Tee four hundred yards behind.

Unless I'm right, Tee thought. Then I'm a god-damned hero. Maybe Dyce had not recognized him as Tee originally thought and was just going on his merry way, oblivious to the car behind him.

The Valiant seemed to be slowing and Tee eased off the gas. He wished to hell that Becker was here. A mistake wouldn't ruin his career since he didn't have a career to ruin anymore. The difference, he knew, was that Becker wouldn't make a mistake.

It's about your self-esteem, big guy, Tee thought. You got to learn to think positively about yourself. You saw the guy, you recognized him instantly. There wasn't any doubt then; you didn't say to yourself, gee, it looks like Dyce. You *knew* it was him. So stick with that, trust yourself. You're not some local jerk, you're the goddamned chief of police.

The Valiant turned to the right and vanished for a moment in the intervening swell of corn. Tee reached reactively for his car radio, then realized he didn't have one. There was no way to let Hatcher know where he was or where he was going—in fact he didn't know himself. He would just have to play it by ear, watch Dyce come to a stop, then find a telephone. If he had turned here, at least he couldn't be going far. There was no major highway in this direction, Tee felt pretty sure, just corn and more corn and maybe a house or two.

Tee eased around the corner and saw the Valiant ahead of him, slowing still further, his blinker on. Awfully obliging, Tee thought. The man is such a law-abiding citizen he puts on his blinker on an empty road—except when he decides to boil a few bodies in the kitchen. He's not quite so law-abiding then. Well, there are laws and there are laws, aren't there, jug-head? It passed through his mind fleetingly that he himself was not the law here; he had no jurisdiction outside of Clamden, he doubted that he could make an arrest, and if he did, would it violate Dyce's rights? But then, I'm not making an arrest. I'm just following the guy.

The second turn took Tee deep into the heart of a cornfield with stands of green corn reaching above the car and closing in on either side. It was like driving through a transparent tunnel under an emerald sea. The road was only packed dirt and rutted, a farmer's access lane, narrow enough that a tractor hauling equipment would brush against the stalks.

With the corn this close, Tee could no longer see the large stone house and barn that he had noticed from the distance, but when the Valiant turned again, he realized that had to be where Dyce was heading. Tee stopped his car and thought. He couldn't follow by car any longer. If Dyce hadn't noticed him so far—and apparently he hadn't—he could hardly miss him if he pulled up into the barnyard. He wasn't sure, but the chances were good that the final turnoff led to the farmhouse or a cul-de-sac. It was too deep in the field to go much farther unless it went all the way across, and even then Dyce would hardly think it just coincidence that another car was tooling through the cornfield. If it was Dyce. Tee tried not to dwell on that possibility.

Or it could run all the way through the field; it could lead to some other access road. Hatcher would like that, too. Follow him to the middle of a cornfield, stop and wait while he drives out the other side and all the way to Canada. Tee felt a sudden intense dislike for Hatcher. The man was an absolute prick, Becker was right about that.

Wishing he could think of something better, Tee got out of the Toyota and walked into the cornfield, two rows deep. He followed the row that ran parallel to the lane and headed toward the path where the Valiant had made its last turn.

Listening first, Tee cautiously peered out from the corn to scan the lane. It ran for thirty yards, then turned left, vanishing once more into the corn. The Valiant was nowhere.

Tee crossed the lane and took to the corn once more, staying parallel to the lane, then turning with it. This is not my line of work, Tee thought. Already his heart was racing and his breath was short, although he'd done nothing but walk a few dozen yards. He felt an uncomfortable tingling on his skin as if he was about to sweat.

I'm scared, he thought. What the hell am I scared of? Being boiled in a pot, that's what the hell I'm scared of. Isn't that good enough? He felt for the revolver riding on his hip and pushed off the leather thong that held it in place. He considered drawing the revolver and carrying it at the ready, but then thought, for what? To arrest the wrong man? Ridiculous what embarrassment can do, he thought. So what if you make a mistake and look like an asshole. Don't you look stupid enough already, creeping through a cornfield? If you want to pull the gun, pull the damn thing. He left it in his holster and bent to peer cautiously once more into the lane.

Seeing just a glimpse of the dull green of the Valiant, he jerked his head back behind the sheltering corn. What now, chief? There was the car, parked at the end of the lane, a few yards away. He could hear noises from the farmhouse, music playing, the noise of a black rapper sounding ludicrously incongruous in a field of corn. Tee tried to calm himself; he could hear little besides the rapper's voice and the insistent electronic drum above his own breathing. Was the Valiant's engine still running? Was Dyce parked, or not?

Tee knelt on the soft earth, his backside brushing against the corn as he went down. Be quiet, for Christ's sake! God, he really wasn't meant for this kind of thing. Where the hell was Becker with his icewater nerves? Just establish that the car is parked, then get the hell out of here and find a phone. If the engine is still running, he's not going to stick around and you'll look like an idiot. Christ, you are an idiot. His sweat glands were working overtime now; he could feel the dampness in his armpits. This is stupid, this is so stupid. Just turn around and run if you feel so scared. No one's watching. Just hightail it out of here and worry about your dignity later. Staying as low as he could, though not certain why except for some childhood memory of doing what they did in the movies, he eased his eyes toward the edge of the curtain of corn.

I investigate burglaries and refer them to the state police, he thought. I stop suspicious-looking characters who are cruising Clamden neighborhoods. On the holidays I direct traffic so we can hold parades. I don't even do most of that anymore. I'm the chief now. I have the officers do it. Ten years ago Ralph

Smolness swung a chair at me when I answered his wife's call about domestic violence. That's it. That's what I do. I don't play Indian in the cornfield with a maniac who's going to make soup out of me if I don't quit bumping into stalks.

The engine of the Valiant was running, the car was vibrating slightly. Dyce was not in the car, at least not in sight. Tee wiped away a drop of sweat that was threatening his eye. The rapper was saying something that sounded like "fug it, fug it." Probably not, Tee thought. There were still laws, at least in Connecticut, and why in hell was he thinking about that? The music sounded over and over in his head; he couldn't get the noise out of his mind even when the record ended.

He lifted himself to his knees and heard the corn behind him rustle again. Be *quiet,* he warned himself, then realized he hadn't made the sound just as something hit him hard in the right buttock. Oh, fuck it, he thought. He tried to reach for his gun, but a foot in his back pushed his face in the dirt and another foot stood on his right arm. The lyrics "fug it, fug it" were still reverberating in his mind and the beating of his pulse in his ear matched the beat of the drums.

SOMEONE was in grandfather's house. He couldn't believe it. Someone was living there. He heard the jungle music, the unrelenting drums, the raucous squeal of guitars, the lyrics that went beyond suggestive to demanding, all of it profaning grandfather's values and his memory. No, not his memory. Nothing could touch his memory, for that lived within Dyce's soul.

There was a tractor parked by the front porch,

someone in overalls sitting on the stone steps, eating, leaning his back against the stone pillar that had once held the porch roof. Behind the man was the porch itself, or what remained, charred by fire. No one was living there. It had been repaired—could not have been without Dyce's knowledge and permission—so the man blasting the music into the rural air was only there temporarily. Dyce could deal with him, if he had to, when he replenished his supply of PMBL. The last of it had just gone into the cop in the cornfield.

Dyce dragged Tee's body two rows farther into the corn so that it could not be seen by anyone passing on the road. He walked to Tee's car and drove it deeply into the field, curving his route so that no one glancing down the entrance furrow could see anything at the end but more corn.

DYCE prepared grandfather's body as he remembered grandfather having done for his father ten years earlier. The coffin, however, was beyond his talents. Unskilled with saw or hammer, he simply laid the old man's body on a plank set up on the sawhorses covered by the black tarpaulin. For three days Dyce sat vigil in grandfather's chair in the darkened living room, and with every hour his faith in grandfather's religion drained a fraction more until finally, the vigil over, there was none left. His faith in the resurrection was nothing more than a distant hope, his credence in the hellfire and the righteous, whimsical god who fueled it with his wrath dwindled to nothing. But he never lost faith in grandfather himself. If grandfather's God was wrong, that did not mean grandfather himself was wrong.

On the morning of the fourth day Dyce carried

grandfather's withered body to his bedroom, dressed him in pajamas and laid him to rest under the blankets. The old man had become so frail in his final years it was like carrying a child. It was winter and Dyce had kept the heat off so the decomposition was slight, but the odor, as he cradled the body against his chest, was very strong. Dyce choked back his revulsion and forced himself to breathe deeply. If grandfather stank, then the stench was good and pure.

When all signs indicated that the old man had died peacefully in bed—as indeed he had—Dyce called the authorities and told them he had just returned from a weekend in upstate New York looking at the campus of the college he was to attend in thirteen days and had discovered his grandfather dead. Dyce waited a week after the official funeral before he set fire to the house. He knew he would not return and he could not bear the idea of anyone else living in the home where he and grandfather had loved one another.

The fire department responded more quickly than he had anticipated, saving most of the roof and the attic rafters and a portion of the porch where grandfather had sat and waited and watched for the arrival of his grandson.

It was good enough, Dyce decided. No one could live in the house and there was something comforting about the indestructibility of the stone walls that continued to stand, blackened by smoke but as solid as the earth from which they came. From a distance the house still looked whole and someday, when he had wrested his fortune from the world, Dyce could return to live again in his only inheritance.

• • •

THE cemetery was empty except for the men digging a fresh grave in Section Three, and they were too far away and preoccupied to pay any attention to him. With one more look around to assure his privacy, Dyce knelt on the grass beside grandfather's grave. A spider had spun a web from the plastic flowers that sat atop the funerary urn to the ground and the encased carcasses of two victims hung from the threads like roosting bats with their wings enfolded round them. Dyce removed the plastic flowers from the top of the urn, snapping the web, revealing the glass gallon container beneath. He would need all of it this time, he would have to take it with him, so Dyce pulled out the bottle. Dirt and some kind of moss encrusted the bottom of the container so it came up with resistance, and algae was slowly colonizing the imperceptible valleys of the glass surface, but inside the bottle and its plastic lid, which was still untouched by nature's slow incursions after fifteen years, the liquid PMBL was still as clear as spring water with the faintest touch of blue. Like water from a glacier, Dyce thought. Like drinking water of an earlier age before pollution. Like the water in Canada, maybe. He would find out soon enough.

Holding the bottle to his chest with both arms wrapped around it, Dyce spent a moment alone with grandfather. At first it was hard to concentrate; there were so many things on his mind. They were chasing him and they were so close. He didn't understand how they could be so close, two of them within an hour— but they were stupid, they were gullible. He had no doubt that he could outwit them. There was only one of them he feared, the companion at the hospital of the cop he had just dealt with—but he wasn't here and maybe he wasn't coming. If he did come, Dyce knew what he had to do. He could ignore the others or deal with them as they came along, but that one he would have to kill.

He struggled to put such things out of his mind and to get in touch with grandfather. Eventually the peace settled over him and he could see the old man again, and smell the scent of the plain soap he used to wash his body and his hair. He could feel the gentle prickle of grandfather's beard touching his cheek, and then the back of his neck as grandfather got behind him. He could hear the rapid panting of grandfather's breath into his ear, he could feel grandfather pressing against him from behind, pressing and pressing until the panting stopped with a shuddering sigh.

Dyce felt a moment's anger with grandfather for dying—no, not for dying, but for failing to come back. For leaving Dyce alone and without hope. But the moment passed and he left grandfather as he always did, with love and longing.

He positioned the plastic flowers atop the urn and then placed a stone atop the grave marker before leaving, clutching the bottle carefully in both hands.

This time he took a different route out of the cemetery and passed his father's grave. Dyce had not visited the grave in many years and it took him a moment to find it. Dysen had not been buried near his wife nor the plot that would become grandfather's a decade later. Grandfather had seen to it that Dysen was planted in the ground as far from the Cohens as possible. Dyce stood by the far edge of the cemetery where the weeds protected themselves from the mower while growing tall next to the border fence. Cobwebs proliferated between the fence rails, and the whine of automobile tires could be heard from the nearby road.

Although he tried, Dyce could remember little of his father. Nothing came back to him except the smell of liquor on hot breath, and a sense of fear. He could not picture his face clearly; he could not recall scenes or incidents. There was none of the vivid imagery that would come to him in his dreams—only the sense of fear. And then something else, something he had never felt before when he thought of his father. He looked up to be sure he was still alone. The grave diggers were closer now; their work was along the fence, one section away. Dyce turned his back to them to be sure they couldn't see the tears in his eyes.

I don't know why I'm crying, he said to his father's grave. But it's not for you. Not for you. For grandfather, not for you. But he stayed beside his father's grave much longer than he had planned, weeping silently at first, then sobbing as if his chest were being torn open.

You were a monster, he cried in his mind. A monster! Grandfather told me, again and again. I know what you were. A beast without control, without love, without pity. You killed my mother, you tried to kill me, you ruined our lives, grandfather had told him, like a chorus, like a litany.

I do not cry for you! I can't even remember you. There's nothing of you in me, I am my mother's child, I am grandfather's child, I am not yours!

•   •   •

WHEN he left the cemetery, Dyce was alarmed at how long he had stayed. Time had seemed to fall away and he had had no idea of the hour that passed. He had been careless; he had made a mistake and for the strangest of reasons. He did not understand what had overcome him at his father's grave, but he must not let such foolishness affect him in the future.

He headed north, leaving Minnot in the direction of I-91, which would take him through Massachusetts and Vermont and eventually to Montreal, but he got no farther than the edge of town where Main Street connected with Route 17, the feeder road to the thruway. A state police car was parked there, its lights flashing, and behind it a brown Dodge. A uniformed trooper was leaning over the driver's side of the lead car in a line of six waiting to pass. The driver's door opened and an elderly man with a beard got out in obvious puzzlement. Another trooper and a man in a business suit came slowly down the line of cars, peering into each.

Impatient drivers behind him were throwing their cars into reverse to back up and try alternate routes and Dyce joined them while the approaching trooper and suit-clad officer were still three cars away. In his mirror he saw the lead trooper wave a woman through with little more than a glance.

They are faster than I realized, Dyce thought, and the FBI man was more resistant than I would have thought possible. The important thing was not to panic and run into their net. I must hide for a time, and to do that I will need a few things.

The town center was clean of police. They will be

close to the highways, he thought, trying to keep me in, not on the inside trying to flush me into the net.

Dyce drove to a supermarket and walked quickly but without too much haste through the aisles. He wouldn't need much; it shouldn't be more than a few days and he could live on very little. There was a hardware store in the same lot so it would be one-stop shopping.

A stock boy glanced up at him as he passed and Dyce felt his breath jerk in his chest. The boy was perfect, not really a boy but a young man, and his features were everything Dyce needed. Dyce made a brief detour to the pharmaceutical aisle for an impulse purchase before checking out.

THE farmer's tractor was gone by the time Dyce returned, which was a good sign. Dyce would not have to waste any more time dealing with him and if he returned tomorrow, he would be excellent cover. Dyce needed all the time he could muster now because the police officer was large and heavy but he could no longer be allowed to stay in the corn and recover in his own good time.

The extension ladder he had purchased at the hardware store had a rope and pulley, which allowed it to be levered to its full length. The pulley helped in lifting the cop up the ladder, too, but it was still very difficult and took a long time. By the time Dyce had hidden his own car and pulled the ladder in after him, it was growing dark and beginning to sprinkle. The rain would take care of any tracks he had left behind and the night would shield him from all but the most determined and skillful of pursuers. He was safe now and could see and hear anyone approaching, and if they approached too close, there was still a little room for them to keep the cop company.

The rain brought out the smell of charcoal that still lingered after fifteen years. The sound of rain pattering overhead had always been comforting and for a moment he felt as safe and comfortable as if he were in his old room under the eaves, waiting for grandfather to come and give him his bath.

He was excited.

HATCHER dreaded making the call and he wanted to be alone when he did it. If groveling was called for, he could do it—it was for a larger cause than his own ego—but not with a witness. He had enough trouble with the men under him with this stupid duck business. He didn't know where they got it or what it referred to, but he had overheard them use the term, he had caught the quacking sounds when they thought he was out of earshot. There was no need to add any further fuel for disrespect.

At first he had planned to make the call from the radio in his car, but there was too big a chance someone else in the system would come in on his frequency. He did it finally from a pay phone, charging the call to his Bureau card.

Becker sounded annoyed to hear from him.

"We have a little problem here," Hatcher said. "I thought you might want to offer your notions."

"What." Not even a question, as if he *knew* things would get screwed up and Hatcher would be forced to ask for help. Hatcher realized he was already squeezing the telephone receiver. He tried to keep his tone light; don't give the son of a bitch too much satisfaction.

"It seems Dyce realized who Ty Hoban was and he—uh—he killed him." The silence was thunderous.

"You sent Ty Hoban in first? And alone?" Becker spoke in a choked whisper.

"Hoban was an excellent man," said Hatcher.

"I know that. He's not exactly the best man for undercover work in Waverly, Connecticut, though, is he?"

"I was following policy, it was just A and D."

"Jesus Christ, Hatcher."

"He may have handled it wrong," said Hatcher. "We'll look into that."

"And Dyce got away," said Becker.

"We don't think so."

"Good, then you have no problem."

"But we're not sure."

Becker sighed and Hatcher squeezed his eyes closed, waiting for the sarcasm. Becker said nothing at all, which Hatcher decided was worse.

"Your friend Terhune apparently spotted Dyce driving north past the Minnot airport and went in pursuit. We've sealed the area, and if he made his way to any major road, the state troopers haven't spotted him yet. My guess is he didn't get out; he would have had to do it awfully fast. And if he was in a hurry in the first place, he wouldn't have been going through Minnot on the back roads. We think he's holed up in the Minnot area someplace."

"Who's we?"

"Well—me."

Again, Becker was silent. The bastard wasn't going to help a bit.

"And Washington. I've been in contact, of course."

"Of course."

"And they confirmed my theory."

This time Becker laughed, a short, nasty bark.

"You're all right then, aren't you?" Becker asked. "Ass covered and theory confirmed. What do you want from me that Washington can't provide?"

Hatcher seriously considered hanging up. Why give the bastard the satisfaction of asking? There was only one good reason—Becker might very well know the answer.

"We were just wondering if you might have any notions—considering your closeness to the case—you know, just wondering if it might occur to you . . ."

"What."

"Well—where to look."

Once more, the damning silence.

"We're following the standard procedures, of course. I'm getting more agents from New York and Boston, and we'll go door to door starting in the morning. I mean, if he's here, we'll find him, but I, we, thought you might have some—insight—into how he might be thinking right about now."

This time Hatcher kept silent, too. He had asked him; he wasn't going to beg. The silence stretched.

"Ty Hoban is six-foot-four and black," Becker said at last. "Did you think he wouldn't be noticed?"

"He was sent in to A and D, that's all. He may have exceeded his brief; we're looking into it."

"He would have been noticed anywhere within the

town limits, you can't blame him. Why not send a man in a clown suit to a funeral?"

"I have decisions to make, and I make them."

"Yeah, and when it counts the most, they're wrong," Becker said. Hatcher breathed deeply and let it ride. "You're a fucking menace, Hatcher." Hatcher let that one ride, too, waiting. If Becker was belittling him, at least it meant he was still involved.

Another pause. Hatcher studied the woman dashing with her dirty clothes to the laundromat across the street from the public phone. I'm getting wet, Hatcher thought. Why don't they put pay phones in glass booths anymore? If Becker knows it's raining, he's probably making me stand here on purpose.

"Where did Dyce live when he was growing up?" Becker broke the silence at last.

Got him, thought Hatcher. He was too good at it to turn his back on it. Or too involved in some way that Hatcher didn't understand.

"I don't know."

"When he applied for work as an actuary he would have had to list his degree. Find out where he got it, wake some people up and see what he gave as a permanent address when he entered college. If it's in Minnot, and I think it probably was, roust the town clerk out of bed and find out who lives in the house now. Then put a man on the local cemetery where his relatives are buried."

"The cemetery?"

"Hatcher . . . An inconspicuous man, out of sight."

"I know that. Anything else?"

"Try the house where he grew up."

"He wouldn't go there if somebody else lives there now."

"Do what you want, then."

"I mean, you're probably right—but why would he go there?"

"Because something happened there. Why would he be back in Minnot in the first place? It was the first place he ran when he was in trouble. First to Waverly, which is close enough for him to drive over every day if he wanted to, then when Ty flushed him, he went straight to Minnot itself, not the highway. Something's there he wants, or needs."

"Anything else?"

"Don't fuck it up again."

"I can have a plane at the airport for you in ten minutes," Hatcher said.

"I'm not coming."

"You'll have a better feel for things if you're here on the ground."

"I go down no more holes for you, Hatcher. I told you that already. Find him or not, it's up to you now. It's no longer any affair of mine."

"I understand," said Hatcher. "There's one other thing . . . Just after your friend the chief of police had someone call us and report that he had seen Dyce and was following him . . . ?"

This time Hatcher made Becker wait.

". . . Well, after that, Chief Terhune disappeared."

The silence had a very different quality to it this time. It was broken only when Becker hung up.

THE music came first, before the sound of the tractor, the thrumming of the bass notes cutting through the air as if they were connected directly to the auditor's viscera. Dyce felt them before he actually heard them, and long before the rest of the music was audible. As it approached, the noise of the tractor obscured the sense of the music, but the steady pulse of the drums and bass came through everything.

Jungle music, Dyce thought again. At grandfather's house. It must be Birger Nordholm, although the music didn't sound like anything he would listen to.

With the noise of the tractor to cover the sound of his movements, Dyce crept to the edge and peered out as the tractor entered the yard. He glanced back once to make sure the cop was all right and saw him lying perfectly still on his back. Only the wheels of the tractor could be seen, huge and black and cleated, moving parallel to the house and across the yard—or the space that had once been yard but was now so overgrown with weeds and gouged and flattened by continual passings of the tractor that it was hard to give it a name. Traveling in a blare of racket, the tractor moved out of sight, heading toward the south field, which had once been scrubland where Dyce and grandfather had taken walks through stands of supple sumac, the weed of trees. Grandfather had cut and split the trunks and shaped them into arrows for the bow Dyce had fashioned from a fallen branch of the apple tree by the house. They had spent a summer shooting wayward shafts at a target painted on the barn, but never at a living thing. Grandfather did not approve of hunting, and Dyce was too kind of heart to want to hurt anything. When he cupped in his hands the bewildered moths that made their way into the house and released them out of doors, grandfather called Dyce a "softie," but always with approval.

Now the scrubland had been cleared and torn by Nordholm's plow. Dyce had noticed the bushy, stunted tops of soybeans planted there when he drove to the neighbor's cornfield where he hid his own car. For several hours he could faintly discern the sound of the tractor in the far distance, and when the wind turned and blew toward him, he could occasionally hear something of the music, a phrase or two of melody, or a few lines of the lyrics, not distinguishable as individual words but clearly a human voice. Twice he had started at the sound, thinking it was a real voice he heard, but there was no one there, not even a vehicle all morning on the long approach road that came through the fields to grandfather's house, then past it to outlying farms. From his vantage point Dyce could see not only the approach road but much of the valley and a long stretch of the county road that led to town. Anyone coming would come from there and he would be able to see them miles away.

At noon the tractor returned and stopped in front of the porch. Dyce could see him clearly as the driver descended and removed his cap, wiping his forehead with his sleeve. It was not Nordholm, but Nordholm's son, grown now to his mid-twenties and every inch the offshoot of his father. Dyce struggled with the sounds that wanted to come out of his throat, beckoned by the perfect look of the boy. He could have been Dyce's father himself, the way he kicked his boots against the stone steps, the way he hitched his pants before sitting with his back against the pillar, the way he stretched his legs and sighed as if they had been carrying a dreadful weight. The boy was thin like Dysen, and the sharp bones pressed against his skin so hard it looked as if it would be painful just to wear his face. The Adam's apple was prominent in his throat when he swallowed and even the hair was right, blond and short and straight as a freshly ironed crease. With the cap off, his ears stuck out from his head.

Dyce felt as if his father had somehow risen from the dead after all, summoned not by Dyce and grandfather's vigil of prayer, but by Dyce's inexplicable tears at the graveside the day before.

The cop lay still behind him, not moving, barely breathing, no longer a worrisome consideration. Dyce wanted young Nordholm, desired him so much, he could feel himself trembling. He had known it would build to this point again, the awful, irresistible yearning that had to be placated before it drove him crazy. He needed it and it had been presented to him in the form of perfection. In the dark, drained of color, still as death itself, the man would not just look like his father, this man would *be* Dysen as none of the others had ever quite been.

He would take this one, he would give himself this one, perfect man, and he would make it last longer than ever, days and days and days. And the cop could be a sort of side attraction. An appetizer or a dessert.

Dyce wiggled backward, still watching the farmer, until he reached the syringe. It was full and ready and all he needed was a way of getting down and appearing to the young man without scaring him off. Close enough to touch him, that's all he needed to be. Then he would handle him so gently.

Back at the edge, Dyce glanced up and saw three cars on the county road coming so fast that the first one was almost to the approach road before Dyce had noticed them. The farmer had pulled a bottle of bourbon from somewhere and was sipping from it while holding a sandwich in his other hand. He was oblivious to the cars, oblivious to Dyce stalking him.

All three cars were on the approach road now, sending up plumes of dust. The lead car was state patrol and its lights were flashing, but Dyce heard no siren. The lights went off abruptly as the patrol car approached the farm. In the distance another patrol car appeared on the county road, this time following a civilian auto. Lights were flashing on that patrol car, too, but it was not chasing the other car; it was following it.

The three lead autos tore into the drive and jerked to a halt as the Nordholm boy frantically sought to hide his liquor bottle.

As the men who poured from the cars spun and braced him against the porch pillar, the bottle fell and clattered against the steps, but did not break.

"Nordholm," the boy sputtered in answer to the first in a volley of questions. "Daniel Nordholm. This is my farm, my dad's farm. I didn't do anything."

The second team of cars ripped into the drive. Dyce, now far out of sight, heard doors slam like volleys of gunfire. The other men were shouting questions and commands at the farmer, fear and urgency in their voices. Dyce did not know how the boy decided which questions to answer as he pleaded his innocence of everything and anything, his voice even more fearful than the other men's.

Finally one voice took over, asserting itself over the police and FBI.

"The property is registered in the name of Roger Dysen," said the voice.

"Well—sure, but it's ours."

"How is it yours?"

"He made a deal with my dad when his grandfather died."

"Who made the deal?"

"Mr. Dysen, Roger Dysen. His grandfather died and the house burned down and he was going to college to study math or something. That's what my dad says. I don't know, I was too young, but there's no way to make a living in math around here, so he knew he wasn't going to be staying, he sure wasn't a farmer . . ."

"What do you mean by that?"

"Have you seen him?"

There was a note of annoyance in the voice. "No."

"He's soft, he's very soft, he couldn't farm a garden. My dad offered to buy the land, but he didn't want to sell. He didn't want to work the place but he didn't want to give it up, either. Like he expected to come back and fix up the house someday, you know? So he worked out a deal with my dad; he gives us permission to farm the land and all we have to do is pay the taxes on the place."

"When did you last see him?"

"Mr. Dysen?"

"He calls himself Dyce now. Or Cohen."

"I haven't seen him in years."

"Have you seen anyone around here in the last

three days? Anyone at all?" The original voice was back in charge again.

"No. Nobody."

"Have you noticed any sign that anyone has been here? Anything out of the ordinary at all?"

"No."

"How often do you come here?"

"Here? To the house? Every day."

Someone snapped off the radio as if it had just been noticed.

"Why?"

"I eat my lunch here. I like it."

"What's to like?"

"I—I just like it."

Dyce heard the clink of glass against stone, then the voice of another man.

"You keep your hooch stashed here, son? Come here to drink where your parents don't know about it?"

"I'm twenty-five."

"Didn't say it was illegal. Is that why you come here?"

"I like a drink once in a while," Nordholm said defensively.

"You know the place well, do you? Would you know where someone might hide if he had to?"

"The old well house, maybe. Or the cellar. But I would know if anyone was around."

A fourth voice spoke. "You can see right through what's left of the floor into the cellar from here. There's no place to hide."

"There's an old root cellar down there, dug into the

ground. I don't think you'd want to hide there very long, but you could."

"Marquand, check out the root cellar. Mr. Nordholm, I want you to show me the old well house. Lieutenant, if you and your men would examine the barn, please?"

Dyce heard voices scattering, then calling to each other from the distance, moving around. They stayed for a long time, searching, until finally the doors of the cars slammed again, then the tractor engine roared to life.

I've lost him, Dyce thought. He was perfect and I lost him, the police took him away from me. Just thinking about the young man made him terribly excited again. It was safe now; the FBI visit had just proven that. It was safe, but they had taken the young man away from him.

Dyce turned his head and studied the cop. The man's eyelids were beginning to flutter. He needed another dose . . . and while he had his sleeve pushed up and access to the vein . . . The cop was a poor substitute, but Dyce was so excited.

BECKER caught her as she walked in the door and lifted her off her feet, kissing her deeply, then standing her against the wall. He held her up with his body as he peeled off her clothes, then entered her while she was still off the floor, lowering her slowly as she wrapped her legs around his waist. His passion was overwhelming and contagious and Cindi was ready when he entered her, then ready when he was and they both cried out in completion as he was carrying her toward the bedroom. Becker stood on the stairway, shuddering like a man freezing while Cindi clung to the banister to support them.

After he laid her on the bed he kissed her lips and face with a tender urgency for several minutes. When he embraced her it was so firmly she gasped involuntarily and only then did the intensity of his passion subside.

"Not that I'm complaining," Cindi said after a few moments, "but what was that all about?"

"Lust?" said Becker.

"No," she said. "I mean, maybe partly. But it felt more like—need."

Becker was quiet.

"You felt wide open, John. I thought I could have reached right inside you and touched your heart—if I hadn't been so preoccupied."

Becker murmured something against her neck.

"What?"

"You already have," he said.

"Have what?" She pulled away from him far enough to look him in the eye. "If you're going to break down and say something good, I want to be sure I hear it right."

"You've already touched my heart," Becker said.

"Really?" She shook her head vigorously. "I'm sorry. That's all I can think of to say. You haven't whispered many sweet-nothings, you know."

"I know," said Becker. "I was afraid to start, didn't think I could stop."

"You don't have to stop now."

"I'm a frightened man, Cindi."

"You, John?"

"A frightened man."

She realized the seriousness of his tone. "I know you are," she said. "I've just never been sure of what."

"That's some of what Gold and I have been looking at," he said.

"You don't have to tell me if you don't want to," she said, hoping very hard that he would. "I know that's private."

"Part of the cure is making it unprivate. Admitting it. Aloud. To myself. To my loved ones."

He faced away from her, pulling his knees to his chest.

Cindi could see she would have to help him with this.

"And I'm a loved one?"

Becker nodded. She put her hand on his back and felt him trembling. For a moment she thought he was truly frightened—or crying, but when he turned to her again, he was grinning ear to ear.

"Isn't that stupid? I don't mean loving you; I mean that it's so damned hard to say. It's stupid, it's stupid."

"So is that what you're actually saying, John? You love me?"

"Yes."

"Would you care to say it directly? I hate to be a stickler about this, but everything is sounding rather oblique."

"I love you," he said.

She touched his cheek. "I'm glad you told me," she said. "I've been reading so many tea leaves, trying to figure it out . . . I'm sorry. I'm not really taking it lightly. Maybe it isn't that much easier for me to say."

"You don't have to say anything," Becker said. "I'm not asking for a response. It's just something I had to face up to and deal with."

"Why now?"

Becker eased back down on the bed. "That's the other thing that frightens me," he said and the joy was gone from his voice.

"What?" She rose up on one elbow to look down at him. He was staring at the ceiling.

"What else frightens you, John?"

"Me," he said. "I scare the shit out of myself."

The room fell silent as Cindi sank back to the bed. A neighbor slammed a car door and yelled at a child.

"Can you tell me why?" she said finally.

"When I come back," he said. "I'll try then."

"Come back from where?"

Becker paused a long time. "I'm not quite sure. Wherever I need to go." He rolled over and put his hand on her hip and ran it slowly along her thigh.

"And I'm not quite sure who I'll be when I come back," he said.

"What does that mean?"

He didn't answer but ran his fingers the length of her leg, then feathered them across the skin on the back of her knee.

He's the sexiest man in the world, she thought. I have no idea what's in his mind—I'm not sure he does—but I want him so.

"Can you promise at least that you will come back?"

"Yes. That much I can promise. I don't want to go, I don't want to leave you . . . I don't want to find out what's going to happen—but I seem to have a talent for coming back."

That will have to do for now, Cindi thought. He moved his hand to the very top of her inner thigh and just held it there where it burned a hole in her skin.

"You have a lot of talents," she said as she leaned forward to kiss him.

As they made love she thought of saying, "Thank you, Mr. Gold," but didn't for fear she would be misinterpreted under the circumstances.

CHAPTER 15

Becker found Nate Cohen's grave and stood before it like a mendicant before a shrine, his hands folded at his waist. Agent Reynolds, watching Becker through binoculars, wondered if he was praying. His head was bowed and he had the look of a man who had come to stay for a while.

Hatcher had told Reynolds that Becker would be there, if not today then the next, and the Duck had been right. "Donald" was usually right, Reynolds had to admit that. It was not a job in which a man could make decisions and hope to do better than be right most of the time. The problem with Hatcher was that when he was wrong he could never admit it; there was always someone else to blame. That someone else was invariably one of the agents under his command. What Hatcher didn't seem to grasp was that his men would hold his mistakes against him far less if he didn't shirk the responsibility for them. Apparently, Hatcher's superiors viewed things differently because the man held on to his job while the agents under him got transferred or held back from promotion. Hatcher was not a hard leader to follow; he made no extraordinary demands—but he was impossible to forgive. That was one of the things Reynolds most admired about Becker. He had never forgiven the Duck and was as vocal about it as Pavarotti with a paying audience. The man told Hatcher to his face what he thought of him while the other agents could only choke back their laughter and sit on their hands to keep from applauding.

Which made Reynolds feel a bit dishonest about what he had to do next, but then Becker wasn't really even a member of the Bureau now, just some sort of quasi for-the-case temporary agent, and Hatcher was still the man who made out the performance evaluations. Reynolds glanced at his watch and started walking briskly down the hill toward Becker's car. It had taken Becker three minutes to walk from his car to Nate Cohen's grave, which meant that Reynolds had at least that much time and probably considerably more, judging by Becker's leisurely demeanor.

The beeper attached itself by magnet so all Reynolds had to do was make sure the device was turned on, then kneel beside Becker's car as if he were tying his shoelace in case any of the locals were watching, slap the device under the inside of the frame of the wheel housing, straighten up, and walk back to his own car atop the hill. The entire procedure took one minute and forty-five seconds.

Becker was still at the grave, praying or meditating or thinking, whatever. He was a strange man, Reynolds thought. Good enough company, a regular guy most of the time, but moody. And his thought processes never seemed to be the same as everyone else's. Not weird, exactly, but as if he jumped steps in logic. Maybe his mind was just faster, Reynolds thought. Or it was always working on things from an angle instead of straight on. Whatever it was, if even half the stories they told about him were true, Becker would be the last man on earth Reynolds would want to have chasing *him*.

Reynolds radioed to the communications van and confirmed that the beeper's signal was being received loud and clear, then settled back to work on the day's crossword puzzle. He wished he had the Sunday *Times* puzzle; local papers published things for beginners. Reynolds did them in minutes, contemptuously using a pen and never once having to resort to the crossword dictionary in the glove compartment.

When he checked again, Becker was still there. What the hell was he doing, grieving or something? Nate Cohen wasn't *his* grandfather, was he?

BECKER lifted the piece of gravel from atop Cohen's headstone and tossed it in his palm. Dyce had been to visit, he was certain of that. There was no way to know just when, but Becker didn't need evidence. It was recently, since he'd been in Waverly, sometime within the last two weeks.

A spider lowered itself from the plastic flowers in the funerary urn, laying down the second strand of a brand new web. Becker lifted the flowers and saw the empty space in the bottom of the urn where something had once sat amid a circle of moss and dirt.

Raised letters on the bottom of the receptacle had

left slight impressions in the dust. Glass bottles were stamped on the base with the manufacturer's name; the size of the circle would yield the volume of the container. Becker would leave the details for the technicians; they were no longer vital to him. He replaced the flowers and looked up for the first time since finding the grave. The sky was dark and lowering and ever more massive banks of gray clouds were piling up and roiling overhead. It was thunderstorm weather; the electricity in the air could almost be smelled. Whether the storm broke or not, it would be very dark tonight.

Becker glanced up the hill toward the car parked at the top, facing the graveyard. It had been there when Becker arrived and sat there still, although Becker could make out a figure sitting behind the wheel. Hatcher's idea of inconspicuous, he thought. Not that it mattered now; they had already missed their shot at Dyce in the cemetery.

He had started to leave the cemetery before he realized he still carried Dyce's marker in his hand. He returned to the grave and replaced the gravel gently atop Nate Cohen's grave, then picked up another stone from the walk and placed it next to the first. One for himself.

Reynolds saw Becker's car make a U-turn and head up the hill. For a second he thought of ducking below the seat, but realized it was already too late. Becker pulled up alongside Reynolds and the agent leaned across the seat and rolled down the passenger window.

"How's it going?" asked Reynolds. "You get some communing done down there?"

"You might want to get some of the snails to look inside the urn at Cohen's grave," Becker said.

"I'll get right on it."

"Where do I find Hatcher?"

"Does he know you're in town?"

"Only if your radio works," said Becker. "Tell him I'm on my way."

HATCHER preferred to brief Becker while sitting in his car so that the other agents would not overhear the insubordination in Becker's tone—or the promises Hatcher would have to make. At times like this he wished he smoked so he would have something to cover the nervousness of his hands.

"We searched the house and barn thoroughly," said Hatcher. "We went into the root cellar, we checked the well house. I'm not saying he's not lying in the cornfield somewhere, but he's nowhere in the house or the outbuildings, unless he's a spider hanging in a corner. There's enough cobwebs around to . . ."

"Did you look everywhere?" Becker asked. His tone was flat, almost bored.

"I just said . . ."

"Did you look in the chimney?"

"The chimney? Did we look in the chimney? . . . I'd have to ask. Someone probably . . . The chimney, Becker? Come on."

"You told me it was a stone house over a hundred years old. It must have a big chimney. Where else didn't you look?"

"We looked everywhere . . . except maybe the chimney."

"In the basement? You checked the foundation there; there aren't any hidden rooms?"

"We checked. I know you don't mean to sound insulting, but . . ."

"The attic?"

"There isn't an attic, just a few rafters with some boards that didn't burn completely—you don't understand, the place looks like it was bombed."

"So you checked the attic or you didn't?"

"It's thirty feet in the air, there is no second floor at all, there is no stairway leading up. There is no attic. What makes you so sure he's at the farm?"

"I'm not sure, I'm just making sure you checked. He's still around here, I feel certain of that. The farm is the logical place for him to go. He knows it, he knows where to hide."

"We saw no sign of him. None. He's not there."

"Unless he's in the chimney."

"Or maybe he buried himself underground and is breathing through a straw."

Becker shrugged. "You're probably right."

"We've already started the house to house; it should take two more days . . ." Becker was no longer listening. He thinks he knows better than I do, Hatcher thought angrily. He's convinced I've made some mistake but he's not going to tell me. He's just going to do things by himself. As usual.

"Can you get a chopper in here in the morning?" Becker asked, gazing straight ahead.

"Do you know how expensive that is?"

"No. How expensive is it?"

"What do you need it for?"

"Where did he put the cars? He's ditched two of them, his and Tee's."

"If he has Tee," Hatcher said. "We don't know . . ."

"There are acres and acres of corn around here; you'll never find the cars from the ground unless you stumble over them."

"I'll see if we can afford a chopper."

"And I want to be left alone, you understand that."

"This is my operation," said Hatcher.

"I won't interfere with your operation. Don't you get in the way of mine."

Hatcher noticed Becker's clothes for the first time. He was wearing black chinos and a navy blue turtle-neck. The sweater would be black by night, too, and the long neck would roll up to cover most of Becker's face. Hatcher remembered seeing it the day Becker went after the assassin, Bahoud, in New York. It was his killing outfit.

Hatcher crossed his arms over his chest, tucking his hands under his armpits.

"Have it your way, since you will anyway. I won't interfere."

Becker turned to face Hatcher. Hatcher felt he was uncomfortably close in the little car.

"You nearly killed me once," Becker said.

"That wasn't my fault," Hatcher said. "Some of the agents got overzealous . . ."

"Not again."

"There was a full report on the Bahoud thing, I was cleared . . ."

"Not again," Becker repeated. He turned away

from Hatcher and started the engine. Dismissed, Hatcher got out of the car.

BECKER drove down the county road and caught sight of the farmhouse from atop the hill. He could make out the general layout of the place before the road flattened and he lost sight of it over the corn. Driving at a normal speed, he took the approach road, his eyes taking in every detail as he drove past the Cohen farm and off into the distance. He had not seen much but it would be enough to orient himself when he returned by night.

Thunder rumbled ominously in the west. The cloud cover was now so thick that it was already prematurely dark, as if dusk had come two hours early. Whatever he was going to have to do, Becker reflected that he would have a good night to do it.

TEE woke from what had seemed an endless dream in which a beautiful woman had tied him to the bed and left him, subdued but eager for what was to follow. When she returned he arched to meet her, but she smiled at him with fangs and walked to the bed on six stalklike legs. His eyes fluttered open to see Dyce leaning over him.

"You're doing fine," Dyce said in a voice so soft Tee could scarcely hear it above the rush of wind outside.

Dyce's bearded face vanished for a moment, although Tee made out his form as a darker shape against a dark background. The lightning flashed again and Tee suddenly saw everything in a second, as if in a photograph.

He was lying down, close under a roof in an attic of a house that looked as if it had not survived an air attack. There were gaping holes in the roof, and rafters without crossboards gave way to emptiness below. Dyce was sitting astraddle a rafter, legs dangling into space, and just behind him, several feet away over the void, was a small island of intact flooring just large enough for a man in the fetal position to lie on. On the island was a brown grocery bag, a bottle of spring water, a small container that looked familiar but which Tee could not immediately identify, and a gallon jug.

What held Tee in the air he could not tell, nor could he be sure what Dyce was doing to his arm.

Tee tried to speak but couldn't, but felt no surprise. He had known somehow on waking that he could not speak and could not move. It didn't bother him too much; he was more curious than frightened.

Lightning flashed again and Tee could see Dyce massaging his upper arm with his thumb, although he could feel nothing. A dark liquid dripped from a needle in Tee's arm into an empty spring water bottle.

"We have to speed things up with you," Dyce said, as if sensing Tee's curiosity. "I'm sorry to rush things, but we probably don't have much time. We'll both just have to do the best we can in the situation."

Tee realized then that it was Tee's own blood that Dyce was massaging from Tee's arm and into the water bottle. The bottle was nearly full and Tee had no idea if it was the first. He felt his heart lurch violently in his chest and for the first time felt the panic of fear.

Dyce kept droning on in his soft, patient voice.

"You're not really right, of course. I mean, you just don't really look right. That's not your fault, of course. It's nobody's fault. You're here—and I can't tell you how hard it was to get you up the ladder—I nearly gave up, but I couldn't leave you in the cornfield, you can understand that. And you're here now, that's the important thing, and I can't very well get anyone else under the circumstances, but that young Nordholm was perfect, just perfect. Your friends took him away from me. You can blame them for that."

Dyce scuttled back across the rafter with surprising agility and put the full bottle of blood on the island. He returned with a fresh, empty bottle and began to massage Tee's arm once more, pressing his thumb into the vein and sliding it down to the needle.

Tee's heart lurched again and his eyes widened; he was certain it was about to give out. Dyce stopped and placed his ear on Tee's chest. His hair brushed against Tee's chin.

"You'll be all right, I think," Dyce said. "That happens sometimes when it goes too fast; that's why I like to take it slowly. We'll just stop right here. Now listen to me. Are you listening to me?"

Tee stared at Dyce. His features had become clearer as Tee's eyes adjusted to the darkness. Dyce put his hand lightly over Tee's nose.

"If you're listening, just hold your breath for a count of six . . . Good, all right, you can breathe normally now. Now listen very carefully. I would normally give you another shot now to keep you quiet, but considering your heart and everything, I think I'd better not, so you'll just have to cooperate.

All right? What you must do is lie very, very still. Even if you feel some sensation coming back to your arms and legs, you must not move a muscle. If you do, first of all you'll fall and hurt yourself—it's a very long way down—but also you'll destroy the illusion and then we'll just have to start over. Do you understand? Hold your breath if you understand . . . Good. Keep your breathing as light as you possibly can. I don't want to see your chest heaving up and down; that makes everything silly. And your eyes have to stay closed the whole time. All right? Now that you're conscious you'll be tempted to want to see, but you must avoid that, all right? Hold your breath if you understand . . . Very good."

Lightning flashed and thunder followed it so quickly from so nearby that the house seemed to shake. Tee saw the ladder tucked into the space where the roof met the walls. If I could move at all, he thought desperately, if I could nudge the ladder with my foot so it would fall, do something, anything. But he felt so weak and tired, horribly tired.

"It will take me a minute or two to get ready," Dyce said, propelling himself across the rafter with his hands. "You can keep your eyes open until I tell you."

Straining his eyes to the side, Tee could see Dyce on his midair island begin to undress.

Becker turned off his headlights before he was halfway up to the crest of the county road. He drove in darkness, his eyes fixed not on the road invisible in front of him, but on the silhouette of the farmhouse that stood against the dark sky.

Coasting with his foot off the gas, he counted seconds from the moment the car started downhill. It had taken a count of twelve when he did it in the daylight. At eleven he geared down into second, using his handbrake to slow the car so that the flash of red brake lights would not betray him. His right front tire slipped over the edge of the roadside ditch, and Becker compensated accordingly with the wheel, pulling the car onto the access road. He was moving beneath the shelter of the corn now and was hidden from the view of the house, but still he drove with his lights out. If he turned them on, they would splash off the corn and into the air like a warning beacon for Dyce. If Dyce was there.

Becker waited for a flash of lightning, fixed the path in his mind, and drove straight ahead until the image faded from his retina. Then he stopped and waited for the next flash. When he was within a few yards of the entrance to the farmyard, he stopped. Timing his move with a clash of thunder, Becker opened the car door and stepped into the corn.

Gold's voice had been running through his mind like a tape since he got into the car and started toward the farm.

"IT's a function of will," Gold had said. "We all have fantasies. It's whether we act on them that matters. Most of us don't. You don't, Becker."

"Don't I?" thought Becker.

"What you do, what you have done—the experience with Bahoud in New York, the incident in Washington, the other times—they *cause* the fantasies. It is not the fantasies that cause the incidents."

"Incidents. You mean the killings."

"All right, the killings," Gold said.

BECKER bent between the corn rows and rubbed dirt on his forehead and under his eyes. The turtleneck rolled up to just under his mouth. Lightning flashed and thunder roared so close it seemed to be over the cornfield itself. Becker could smell the electricity in the air. Strangely, there was still no rain.

The wind was beating against the corn stalks so fiercely they sounded like acres of crackling cellophane. The earth itself was so noisy there was no need for caution, but Becker moved silently, anyway, from long habit.

Cutting diagonally through the field, Becker came to the edge of the cultivated ground where the corn stopped and the farmyard began. Kneeling, he studied the house and the barn.

His heart seemed to have ascended in his chest and was beating rapidly just beneath his collarbone. Becker recognized the excitement for what it was—an eagerness for action and a tingling of anticipation. There was no fear involved in it. Caution, prudence, but no fear.

"THEY were all justified," Gold said. "You were in danger every time. You did what you had to do to save yourself."

"Justified?"

"Justified. Absolutely."

"But were they necessary?"

•   •   •

BECKER approached the barn from the rear where there was nothing but blank wall to watch him. He did not expect to find anything in it, but this was not the time to go on assumptions alone. That was Hatcher's way, not Becker's.

"Why are you so sure he's at the farm?" Hatcher had asked.

Becker said, "I'm not sure of anything," but he was. He could not say that he was sure because he had come to understand Dyce on a level that Hatcher could not begin to comprehend. The man's life had fallen apart on him and he had fled to the place where it had all begun, the cruel, twisted injury that had made him what he was. He could not tell Hatcher that he understood the man's thoughts and needs and darkly contorted emotions just as he had understood Bahoud's and all of those since then.

He could not tell Hatcher, but he had told Gold.

"DON'T be so damned hard on yourself, man," Gold repeated now in his mind. "You don't want to do it; it happens because of circumstances. These are not pussycats the Bureau sends you after. These are multiple murderers, hardened killers who would have killed you in an instant."

"How do you know I don't want to do it?"

"How do I know? Because you don't do it any other time, that's how I know. What you experience isn't joy; it's a final release of adrenaline. You are in great danger, under terrible stress—you are feeling the sense of release, not pleasure. You were brought into this by accident. It turns out you've got great skills, but having empathy or understanding for these people does not mean you *are* these people, understand? You have the empathy to be a great shrink. I understand my patients, most of them. That doesn't mean I am them, doesn't mean I share their problems—but I understand them."

THE farmhouse had two stone chimneys, one at either end of the house on the exterior. The stone walls had been breached as if a tank had driven through them, but those sections that still stood were enough to hold up the roof beam and the unburned portions of the roof.

There was no blind side from which to approach. Becker counted on the darkness and moved swiftly across the yard. When the lightning struck, he dove for the ground and lay there motionless, hoping that if Dyce had seen his movement he would attribute it to a trick of the night.

He lay still until his heart stopped racing. It was a job he had to do, he told himself. Nothing more. A job. There was a maniac to find, possibly a friend to save if he wasn't already too late for that.

Becker tried to turn off the tape in his head, but Gold's voice insisted on being heard.

"I CAN'T give you absolution, I'm not a priest. I can forgive you, I can understand you."

"I don't want that."

"What do you want?"

"I want to *stop* it."

"You have stopped. Just keep stopping."

"And if I go after Dyce? . . . I do have to go after him now."

"Good. Find the bastard."

"And then?"

"He's killed at least eight men. He may have killed your friend . . . Find the bastard."

"And then?"

THE first rain hit him as he lay and it felt like the initial gush from a faucet. The clouds opened as if rent asunder by the last lightning bolt. By the time Becker got to his feet, he was already soaked to the skin.

DYCE was talking nonstop from his island in the air, but Tee was not listening. With every ounce of concentration he could muster he tried to move his foot toward the ladder. It was precariously balanced; it would only take a nudge to make it fall, but he could not move, he could not move. It seemed just a fraction away, as if a final effort could awaken his nerves and make them speak to his muscles, but it was a fraction he could not bridge. Tee did not think beyond the ladder. What would happen then, what he hoped to accomplish he could not say. It was an action, the only one available to him, or nearly available, and he had to do something before Dyce sucked him dry and left his husk in the deserted attic of an abandoned shell of a house. If only it didn't make him so terribly tired to even try to think.

Rain hit the roof over Tee's face as if a firehose had been trained on the house.

Dyce's voice rose, claiming Tee's attention over the noise of the rain. "I'm ready now," he said.

Tee turned his eyes to look at the maniac. Dyce was standing on his little space of floorboards, his arms spread as if to say, look at me. The container of talcum powder was still in his hand and sprinkles of the white powder drifted off his body. He was completely naked and white as snow. When lightning flashed it illuminated him as if he were lit from inside, but even in the dark he gave off an eerie glow.

The son of a bitch has an erection, Tee thought. He's mad as a hatter and hard as a rock.

"Remember now, try not to move when you breathe and keep your eyes closed."

Tee did not need to be told. His eyes were already squeezed shut. Whatever was going to happen, he didn't want to watch.

FROM the ground the chimney looked wide enough to hold a man. They had built them large in the last century. Not that Becker expected to find Dyce squirreled away in the chimney—although it was a possibility he did not reject. He had mentioned it to Hatcher just as an example of what he might have overlooked. Even if he had hidden there when the FBI came by, he would probably not be there now, not on a night when he could come out and move without much fear of detection.

The night is better for all of us, Becker thought.

A noise that didn't come from the storm teased Becker's hearing, something not wind nor rain but more familiar, chased by the tempest so quickly Becker was not sure if he had heard it or imagined it. He crouched by the side of the first chimney, his shoulder pressed against the stones, readying himself to look into the house itself. The porch was dangerous: too many charred boards that could break under his weight or groan to give away his presence—if any noise that weak could be heard now. He skirted the porch, crawling on his stomach to the edge of the wall where it had partially crumbled away.

Lightning like a row of flashbulbs crackled in the sky, giving Becker a full view of the house. He looked up at the space Hatcher had not investigated. Many of the rafters were still intact, but the flooring across them was scattered and broken, a board here, two or three there running only a few feet. It looked like a net with bits of flotsam stuck to the webbing in places. One section was severed by fire into the shape of the letter *C;* another section, three boards wide and tucked against the junction of roof and rafter, was a bit over six feet long. A man, lying perfectly still, could stretch out unseen on that platform. The C might hold a person on his side, but Becker could see why Hatcher had dismissed the attic, or what remained of it, as a hiding place—it could be a sanctuary only for the very imaginative and desperate. But then that was what made Hatcher the way he was. He never credited desperate men with being bold enough to take truly desperate measures. Hatcher judged the men he chased by himself, and assessed their hearts by what he found in his own. And I judge them by myself, Becker thought. Which is why I would have looked in the chimneys and Hatcher didn't. Hatcher is too sane to track the mad.

The light vanished, swallowed by the storm, but Becker had seen something in the last faint illumination, a movement of a ghost against the blackness of the night.

Crouched, he waited for the next flash, which

seemed to take forever in coming. Even without the
lightning, he thought he could almost discern the
movement under the roof on the C section of flooring,
something flapping, like the wing of a huge moth. But
he could not be sure if he really saw it or simply willed
it. Willed it because he wanted it to be there, he
thought. I want him, Becker thought. I want Dyce as
badly as I have wanted any of them. Running from it,
hiding away in Clamden had done no good. They are
all around me, the Dyces, in small towns and large.
Whether they are attracted to me or I am attracted to
them, we will find each other. The silent, secret killers
and the one who hunts them down. We are bonded
together, Becker thought. Opposite sides of the
coin—or perhaps the same side, he didn't know and
right now it didn't matter. He was here, where he
wanted to be, where he had yearned to be despite his
struggles against that desire ever since Tee told him of
the disappearance of the men. And Dyce was here,
where he, too, must have known he would end up,
waiting for the man who would put him out of the
misery of his madness.

Maybe Dyce was here above him, caught in the
web of roof and rafters, flailing like an insect. Be
there, Becker urged. He willed him to be there.

At last lightning struck again, followed by a roar so
loud and instantaneous it seemed to come from the
earth under his feet, and in the flash Becker saw it
clearly, a specter in white, thirty feet up, arms raised
and flecks of snow or dust wafting down. It was looking straight at Becker.

When the light faded, Becker moved, knowing he
had already been seen. The only way up was the walls

themselves. He removed his shoes whose soles would be as dangerous as if he had greased them. Although he hadn't paid any attention to the weather for several minutes, Becker realized now that the rain was still coming in torrents. Slender cascades of water rippled off the stones and into his face. He felt for his first handhold, pulled himself off the ground and began to climb.

DYCE had seen the headlights on the county road minutes earlier, had seen them disappear behind the screen of the corn, and had not seen them reappear. They're coming to try again, he thought, but still he had not been ready to see the man crouched beside the wall. He was there too soon—but then Dyce realized who he was. He did not recognize him, but he knew, remembering the sense of dread and respect from the hospital bed.

"He's here," Dyce said softly to Tee. "Your friend is here."

ONCE past the turnoff to the access road, Hatcher had the three vehicles shut off their lights. Agent Reynolds was sent to walk ahead with a focused flashlight to lead them on the dirt road, but even with a guide the road was treacherous with mud. The panel truck with the electronic equipment slid into the ditch and had to be pushed out, wasting valuable time.

DID they bring ladders this time? Dyce wondered. He was safe if they did not. The policeman would need another injection to insure his cooperation in any case. Dyce looked at himself and saw that his erection was still huge, despite the dangers. He giggled at himself as he sought his syringe.

IT would have been an easy climb without the rain, an ascent so simple that Cindi would not even deign to make it. Even now, with the stone face as slick as if it had been iced, Becker could imagine her lithe body shooting upwards as if each irregularity in the rock was a rung on a ladder. But for Becker, the climb was torturously slow and difficult. He felt horribly exposed, clinging by his inexpert fingertips to holds awash with pouring rain. If Dyce looked down the walls, if Dyce had a weapon of any kind—a loose board would do—Becker was finished. It was only the darkness that lent any safety and that could vanish in an instant if Dyce happened to be looking in the right direction when the lightning flashed.

He climbed looking upward toward the gaps in the roof, squinting against the rain in his face. There was no point in looking for handholds; he couldn't see them anyway. The climb had to be made solely by feel. He was looking for Dyce, hoping to see him peering down in the next flash of lightning to give Becker time enough to do something to save himself. There was little he could do but let go of the wall and fall to the ground below. He might break a leg in the fall, but at least it was an action, something better than clinging to the stones like a fly to be swatted.

Becker's hands reached a wide flat space and he pulled himself into a hole in the wall that had once encased a window. He sat there for a moment to rest, arms and legs dangling. His muscles were dancing from the strain.

He was halfway up.

THE technician from the panel truck was trying to explain, but Hatcher was no longer interested.

"It was that last bolt of lightning, the one that was so close. It screwed up all the electronics." The technician had his mouth close to Hatcher's ear to be heard over the storm.

"I've lost the signal," the technician said. "I don't know if it's the beeper that got hit or my equipment, but it's dead flat."

"I'm not concerned with your excuses," Hatcher said.

"It was the lightning."

"What you're saying is you've lost him," Hatcher said.

Reynolds had signaled a halt and vanished into the darkness in front of the convoy just as the technician ran forward to rap on Hatcher's car window. Hatcher felt the operation turning bad in his hands. Things involving Becker always seemed to turn bad; it had to do with the man himself. He would not submit to control.

"Christ," Hatcher thought, "if he gets Dyce here, if he gets him in a place I've already looked—if I'm not there when it happens . . ." He didn't want to think about it, but there would be plenty of necks on the chopping block in front of his if things did go rotten. This technician's, for one.

Reynolds reappeared, his thin beam of light pointed at the ground, approaching Hatcher's car.

"It's Becker's car," Reynolds said, leaning in through the window. Water dripped from his head and nose onto Hatcher's pant leg. "He left it about ten yards ahead and to the right. The driveway to the farm is just past that."

They all huddled around Hatcher's car now, awaiting instructions. Hatcher was the only one still dry as the others hunched their shoulders against the rain.

Hatcher grabbed the binoculars and slipped their battery pack around his neck.

"We don't need your beeper," Hatcher said to the technician dismissively, as if the faulty equipment had been the man's idea.

Lightning cracked close by and Hatcher winced, then recovered himself, wondering if the others had noticed.

"I've got a feeling Dyce is here," Hatcher said, getting out of the car. "Let's go find him."

TEE watched the white blur in the darkness that was Dyce move around the framework of rafters, looking for something or someone coming at him from the ground below. "Your friend is here," he had said. Did he mean Becker? Please, God, let it be Becker. The hope was almost enough to overcome the lethargy that gripped him, and Tee renewed his efforts to move his foot. It was so strange; he *felt* as if he could move, he could sense the movement within his limbs like an itch—but nothing moved. As if his nerves had been severed but not deadened. They wanted to move but could not relay the message.

Dyce moved close to Tee now and Tee could see the whites of his eyes standing out starkly within a small, dark circle Dyce had missed with the talcum powder. In a burst of lightning Tee could make out something in Dyce's hand, small and glistening. A hypodermic syringe. Tee remembered the needle in his own arm, but by the time he glanced down to see if the blood was still dripping from it, the light was gone.

Dyce had looked down within the cavern of the house when the lightning flashed, and Tee recognized the fear in his face. The snowy shape hovered close to Tee for a moment and Tee was certain that the hypodermic was intended for him, but then the shape moved off with surprising agility across the rafters and Tee understood that the needle was meant for Becker.

Tee prayed that the stories he had heard about Becker's prowess were true.

HATCHER scanned the area slowly with his night-vision binoculars, seeing the invisible yard come into view in shades of eerie green. Stored heat from the day made the barn glow slightly in the infrared sensing binoculars. Hatcher scanned toward the house, seeing only variations in emanated heat but no movement. And then, leaping out at him from the roof of the house like a flame from a sea of green, the shape of a man, arms upraised and gesticulating.

"Got him," Hatcher muttered triumphantly. "Bring up the vehicles and fan them out with their headlights pointing toward the farmhouse. We're going to need light, but none until I give the word. Not so much as a spark, you got it?"

"Got it," one of the agents replied.

"Do you see Becker?" Reynolds asked.

Hatcher returned to the binoculars but the man was gone. There was no movement to be seen anywhere at the farmhouse.

"Maybe he's lost in the corn," said Hatcher.

BECKER was heading toward a gap in the roofline that he had seen during the last flash. Moving laterally was even harder than going up. The wind screamed and slashed him with sheets of rain. Becker's foot settled on a small stone used as filler, and it tore at his flesh before pulling loose and tumbling to the ground twenty-five feet below. His other foot, yanked off balance, lost its hold, and Becker was slammed into the wall by his own weight. He clung to the stones with his fingers as his feet scrambled for a hold—then froze completely as a ghostly figure appeared in the gap in the roofline five feet above his head.

Dyce peered into the darkness, waiting for lightning to show him the world beyond an arm's length. Becker held his breath and willed himself not to move, even though his arms were trembling with the strain of supporting his own weight. Dyce had not seen him yet, he was certain of that, but the slightest move on Becker's part would give his presence away now; they were too close for the darkness to give any protection. He was alive simply because Dyce had not thought to study the stonewall itself.

His fingers screamed for relief, then his left hand went into spasm, the muscles jerking in protest against the strain.

"THE vehicles are in position." The agent's deep voice rumbled close to Hatcher's ear.

"Becker's here," said Hatcher, hoping the disappointment didn't sound in his voice.

Against the green field of the binocular's vision, Hatcher could see the glowing form that he knew was Becker, going straight up the side of the house. Like a goddamned spider. Christ, straight up a wall. The things they said about him must be true. Despite himself, Hatcher felt a sense of admiration for the man. Teamwork would have served better, of course. A little organization, a little planning, but still—the bastard had found him and was climbing a wall to get him.

Hatcher saw Becker pause, then stop abruptly as another form leaped suddenly into the binoculars' vision, almost atop Becker. Neither shape moved for long seconds, and Hatcher could not tell if they were looking at each other or staring into the darkness that surrounded everyone but Hatcher and his infrared vision.

BEAMS of light suddenly hit the house and Becker cursed under his breath, sensing immediately what had happened. I will kill Hatcher, he thought as a loudspeaker crackled against the storm.

He could see Dyce clearly now, the man's eyes wide and startled by the headlights, squinting momentarily as the beams struck him in the face, then looking down at Becker, seeing him for the first time. Dyce looked more pleased than surprised.

"I was wondering," Dyce said, looking straight at Becker. The rain caught Dyce as he stood in the gap in the roof, and the white of the powder seemed to explode off his body where the drops hit him.

Becker moved his feet at last, securing them in the stones and taking the weight off his fingers. He wondered whether to push off the wall and drop, but one of Dyce's hands was visible and it held no weapon. The other hand was out of sight, but his arm did not hang as if it held the weight of a revolver.

Hatcher was speaking over the loudspeaker now but his presence seemed irrelevant to the moment as Becker and Dyce looked at each other.

"I knew you'd come," said Dyce.

"I knew you'd be here."

Dyce nodded and smiled, a strangely kind, forgiving smile. It flashed through Becker's mind that Bahoud had done the same thing in the second before he had tried to kill Becker—which was the second before Becker had killed him. It seemed they had all smiled.

"You look just like him," Dyce said.

For a moment, a look of sweet understanding passed between them.

"You can sympathize with them, you can empathize until you're inside their skin—that doesn't mean you *are* them," Gold said in Becker's mind.

Dyce lifted his hidden hand and Becker saw the syringe.

Lightning seemed to explode inside Becker's left ear and the thunder boomed immediately after like a bomb in the yard. Even as Becker let go with everything but his right hand and swung free to avoid the sudden swoop of Dyce's needle, the headlights snapped off and he could hear the scream of human beings from the vehicles.

In the aftermath of so much light, everything seemed darker than ever.

Becker found another grip as Dyce's arm slashed the air again in the space where Becker had been. Becker could sense Dyce's hand probing for him, but for several seconds until his eyes adjusted he could not even see his own arms against the wall.

When vision came at last, it was with the flickering light of the burning panel truck set aflame by the lightning bolt. Panicked voices yelled instructions at each other, but both the light and the chaos were beside the point now as Becker moved lower and to his right, away from the stabbing arm.

He had not let go entirely when Dyce swung at him, he had not chosen to leap free. That's how badly I want you, Becker thought. Gold's voice started to sound in his head again, but this time Becker simply shut it off. He no longer had the luxury.

Crabbing sideways along the wall, he moved toward the next break in the roofline. Amazingly, neither fatigue nor danger affected him anymore. He felt fresh and agile, as if he were born for this kind of work.

IN the flicker of distant firelight, Tee saw Becker's shape slip into the attic behind Dyce's back. When lightning flared, Dyce turned and saw him, too, and fled across the rafters to the C-shaped island. Becker moved after him, balancing on the beams as deftly as a gymnast, and the two men stopped a few feet from each other, pausing like animals going through a ritual display that would determine if there was to be violence. Dyce stood on the floorboards of the island, which gave him a normal stance, but Becker was in a semicrouch, one foot in front of the other on a single rafter, arms out for balance like a tightrope walker.

"GRANDFATHER said you'd come," said Dyce. He held the syringe in front of him like a knife.

There are no options, Becker thought. If he steps to the edge of the boards, he can reach me with a jab. I am defenseless here, one step short of the platform.

"Grandfather prepared me," said Dyce. His tone was completely calm and rational. "He told me what to do."

Dyce stepped to the edge of the platform.

If he goes for my legs, he has me, Becker thought. I have a chance if he strikes for my body, but I can't move my legs without falling.

"What did he tell you?" Becker asked.

Dyce bent low. He was going for the legs.

"He said you would rise again," said Dyce. He leaned forward, judging the distance to Becker.

"Grandfather was an asshole," said Becker.

Dyce looked up abruptly, startled by the blasphemy, then lashed out angrily at the same time that Becker kicked with his lead leg and pushed forward with the back one. The kick caught Dyce in the chest and knocked him back onto the platform as the syringe fell from his hand and crashed to the floor below. Becker landed atop Dyce and heard the wind rush from the man's body.

Becker had Dyce's head in his hands, his neck twisted to the side. One snap, one final, violent twist was all it would take. He could feel his muscles shaking with the effort to stop and he heard a high, trembling murmur that he realized with surprise came not from Dyce but himself.

"IT's a question of will," Gold said. "We all feel urges of all kinds, we don't act on them."

BECKER felt the tension in Dyce's neck resisting his hands. It was turned as far as it could go without shattering the vertebrae. He could imagine the satisfying sound of the final snap.

"IT's what you ultimately do that counts," Gold said. "Not what you think. A killer doesn't just think about killing—he kills."

FOR the first time Becker noticed Dyce's moan. He didn't struggle; he lay beneath Becker like a lamb on the altar, bewildered but accepting.

Lightning flashed and Becker saw Tee's eyes watching him, wide and staring with anticipation. He read permission in Tee's eyes, approval.

"IT's what you *do*," Gold said. "Ultimately, you're in control of it. They're not. You are. That's the difference."

BECKER released Dyce's head and pulled him into a sitting position so that Dyce's back was against Becker's chest. Dyce sagged limply against Becker with a grateful sigh. Becker cradled him as the sound of Hatcher and the rediscovered loudspeaker moved closer in the darkness.

•   •   •

"You had no options," Gold said.

"I could have backed away."

"While balancing like that? You would have fallen and killed yourself. You had to go for him."

"I could have just waited. Hatcher was out there. He would have shown up eventually. There was nowhere for Dyce to go."

"That's pretty cool thinking under the circumstances. At the time, you felt that you had no option but to attack. You did the right thing. It worked, didn't it?"

"If I hadn't seen Tee looking at me, I might have killed him."

"You said Tee thought you should have done it."

"He told me that afterward. At the time I just wanted to think he approved."

"You don't know you would have killed him if it hadn't been for Tee watching."

"I don't know I wouldn't have," said Becker.

"You didn't do it. That's what counts. We'll just have to leave it at that."

"I guess we will," said Becker. He paused, prying the blinds apart with a finger and looking at the withering acacia tree on the street below.

"What will happen with Dyce?" Gold asked.

"He'll be declared innocent by reason of insanity and put away for a while until he proves himself sane. He probably will be able to do that eventually, won't he, Gold? Convince some people that he's sane?"

Gold sighed. "Possibly. Probably. If he's sane most of the time, he can get away with it."

Becker turned to look at Gold. "In other words, you admit you can't really tell."

"I admit we can't *always* tell . . . Can you, Becker? Can you always tell if they're sane or insane?"

Becker grinned broadly. "What's the difference?"

Becker turned back toward the window and watched the traffic for a moment before moving toward the door, rubbing his fingertips together.

"You should dust more often, Gold," he said. "The place is full of cobwebs."

CLOSE TO THE BONE

Terrorism, murder, and an ice pick-wielding assassin are the pieces of a deadly puzzle FBI agent John Becker must assemble before the killer strikes again in this harrowing prequel to *Prayer for the Dead*. In the end, Becker must battle against time and his own psychological demons to outwit and outstep the ruthless international terrorist.

DAVID WILTSE

Now available in hardcover at bookstores everywhere.

G. P. PUTNAM'S SONS
a member of
The Putnam Berkley Group, Inc.